THE FULLNESS OF EVERYTHING

ALSO BY PATRICIA POWELL

Fiction

A Small Gathering of Bones

Me Dying Trial

The Pagoda

THE FULLNESS OF EVERYTHING

PATRICIA POWELL

PEEPAL TREE

First published in Great Britain in 2009
Peepal Tree Press Ltd
17 King's Avenue
Leeds LS6 1QS
England

ISBN13: 9781845231132

Acknowledgements:

I'm indebted to AlLandra who started it all, and to Noel and
Mary, staunch supporters from the very beginning. Jonathan,
dear friend and mentor and reader extraordinaire, thank you;
Kathryn, Tanya, Teresa, and Prudence, my heart, thank you;
to my classmates and teachers and for the exquisite Miami
years, thank you; and dear Nora, dear Nora, as always, thank
you.

Peepal Tree gratefully acknowledges Arts Council support

CONTENTS

For Barrington and for Prudence

WINSTON

1.

It's way after midnight, way too late to be calling, but the telegram had come which meant either someone had died, someone was about to die and now he had to return home to bury them. He hadn't been home to Jamaica in twenty-five years, hadn't dropped his family a line, not even at card at Christmas with money, hadn't telephoned them either. How they had tracked him down he doesn't know, but there it is on the kitchen table downstairs, the telegram they sent. Five days ago it arrived, five days he's refused to open it and every night he goes to sleep there's his father dead and bloated and floating in the emerald current of the May Pen river towards him. Tonight it's no different; the dream starts out the same: he's bathing naked in the river, his brown skin covered with white suds, when the body, which starts out first as a swiftly sailing log, brushes against his legs and then the eyes pop open, big and red and streaked with iridescent veins, and it's the crumpled face of his father, not dead at all, but frightened as hell and flailing and howling and begging Winston to help me you brute, help me Jesus Christ, help me you piece of dog shit and Winston too stunned to cry bolts up in a harsh yellow sweat, tearing at his shirt and hair, and switches on the light. Around him he sees that all is well, the orchid on his dresser with its bouquet of purple flowers stares at him gentle and kind, the radiators rattle away quietly in their corners, the cat, stretched out on its back, is snoring peacefully at the foot of the bed, and out the window the snow comes down fast and furious and in great reverential silence. He moves the laptop and the book he'd been reading off the bed and onto the floor, he hauls on his slippers and downstairs in the kitchen he switches on the overhead and boils milk in a pan on the stove.

He calls Silas.

It's almost three, Jesus Christ, you all right, Silas cries.

Listen to this, he moans, tearing open the telegram that arrived five days ago and reading it to his friend. And then he tells him about the dreams.

That's a sign right there, Silas says wearily – Silas who's never believed in signs, but maybe all that's different now that both his parents are dead.

You must go at once, Silas says, go and see your people, fix up things with them. I wish I could come, he says, but I have Chris and Marcus all next month and the month after. Your people could die, he says, and then what, who'd you have to blame then, who but yourself.

He sighs into the night, nodding and shaking his head, thinking of a plane ticket now and a new black suit. Okay, he says to Silas, okay. He's been the best man at all four of Silas's weddings and the godfather to his two sons.

He drains his glass of warm milk, sets it down firmly on the counter and looks out into the night at the snow piling up a thick blanket on the hedge of evergreens, on the rosebush to the side and on the ground, which means tomorrow he'll be shovelling like hell to clear a path just to get to his car. Okay, he says again to his friend and hangs up.

He dials the number on the telegram, listens as the phone rings and rings undignified into the long and empty night. Finally his mother answers

Mother, he cries, it's me, it's Winston.

Winston, she moans out slowly, Winston, she moans out again, before her voice breaks down into a million small pieces.

And he sees his mother again as he'd last seen her when the car driving him to the airport pulled slowly away from the house. She was standing on the verandah in a pink crinoline dress and a white hat with the mesh shielding half her face from the sun that was already cocked in the sky and ravishing the morning. She did not wave and all around them was the swirling dust as drought had come and the ortanique trees were bare and the rickety cows lying out in the fields were parched and the fat black crows circling the scrawny brown cows cawed and cawed.

What's going on, he cries, wanting to sound gentle and kind, but instead everything reels out irritable and impatient. Everything all right?

You father is dying, his mother says, and we want you to come home.

She pauses and he hears his own breath catching.

First it was the useless heart and the valves they implanted to help it pump, she tells him. Then it was the stroke that froze the left side of his body, parked him in a wheelchair. Now it's the tumour in his brain killing him. The doctor gives him two months, his mother wails, two months. Then she is quiet.

And he thinks of how the cancer bloated and discoloured Marie Jose last year, how it peeled every strand of hair, drew her down to eighty pounds, and probably would've killed her if it weren't for the prayer circles, the chanting, the laying on of hands.

Sorry to hear it, Winston tells her finally, finding it impossible to imagine that great man cut down.

Yes, his mother says, doctor gives him two months, two months his mother says again, then she is quiet. Then she starts up again. What did I do, she barks harshly into his ear. What did we do to you, all these years, twenty-five of them, and not a word, not a line, to your own people. What did we do to you?

He sets the phone aside, impossible to deal with his mother and her anguish, and he pours himself another glass of milk. He picks up the black furry cat that has padded down into the kitchen. The cat is as big as a dog. The cat licks his face with a tongue like a grater and he can still hear his mother's voice from far away whining into the receiver. He puts down the cat, picks up the phone again. Mother, he cries, cutting through the bitter harangue, mother, and much to his own surprise he finds himself telling her he will come, just like that. Okay, mother, soon as I find time, okay. I will come home.

Somewhere he'd read that if he couldn't make peace with his first family, then there was no way in hell things were going to work with the second one, that over and over again he'd only be acting out the same damn foolishness. He didn't believe it at first until he started to look closely and then everywhere he turned it was his mother and his father, or the brother and the dead sister, and there he was like a blasted puppet, as if he had no mind at all of his own. Finally after eight sessions with Dr. Wolf at University Services, he bought a ticket for the Christmas break. He bought a gold watch too for his father, another one for his brother, and a necklace with pearl inlay for his mother. He bought shoes too and shirts, a few summer dresses. He bought tinned meats and boxes of detergent and rice and cakes of soap, all the things relatives from abroad used to take back in large carton boxes. And in the end, what was it that prevented him year after year: the flashflood that put his basement under water, the departmental chair who took ill and begged him to serve in the interim, the page proofs of his book that were due yesterday, the girl friend who'd had the miscarriage?

2.

It wasn't beneath him to pick up women at bus stops, at taxi stands, in the line at grocery stores, at a bar, singly or in a gaggle. It wasn't beneath him to pick one up on planes either, especially if she were reading *Waiting for the Barbarians*, a novel he uses in a history course he sometimes teaches called *Africa and its Fictions*. That, and the fact that her forehead was big and wide and strong, which told him right away she was smart. He liked bright women. She was not sexy in any conventional way. She was too tall and slim, looked too much like a boy with her hair cut so close to her head; and on her ears and fingers were a multitude of silver rings which he found excessive. Still, he was magnetized by her eyes, one of which had a tendency to wander aimlessly, while the other sparkled in at least four different colours.

When she laughed – which was with great abandon, her head flung back, the roar gushing from her throat, one foot jumping to tap the floor of its own accord – he was reminded of the women back home who sold cloth and hair pins and plastic combs in the open-air markets on Saturdays and who, when the sweetness took them, thundered into the heat, the sound seeming to come up from their bowels and trembling for minutes in the air afterwards. When they talked her head was full to the brim with all kinds of arcane knowledge, ranging from quantum physics to dream interpretation, to Akashic records, to astral travel, holography and crystalline technology; all this so puzzled and hypnotized him, he felt himself bristling with a strange and curious love. When he got scared though, which happened sometimes – because what did she really know of the destiny of souls, what did she know of karma – he focused on her moving heart-shaped lips as they

13

bunched around her teeth and he imagined himself battering them with kisses until they were bruised.

She worked not far from his office, as editor of an independent press started by Christian Scientists; they started fucking right away. For months it was like that, easy, uncomplicated. She didn't clutch, she didn't suffocate, she didn't even want commitment, in fact she wanted nothing at all, not even marriage when he proposed it to her after coming and going for a year. She'd just recovered her life after twelve years of marriage and two stepchildren, she cried, she was in no hurry now to tie it into knots again. She needed time to think, she said, time to find herself, time to figure out exactly what she wanted and how.

This did not put him off entirely, for he was not what you would call a rescuer. He was not a quote, unquote, white knight. He liked a woman who could stand on her own two feet, he liked her with the head settled and clear, he liked her in charge of her own life; he did not like them needy. Women like Marie Jose, women who needed to feel they were in complete control of their lives, as so much had already been taken away, with them a man had to be patient, he had to lie low; he even had to be sly. He had to show he wanted them but then again not come on too strong. He had to not be afraid to show his feelings. In fact it was a bonus if he liked to cry. All this he'd done with women before; all this he could do again. So he waited; after all he was in no particular hurry; there was no ticking clock. Still, in a year he would be forty-six, he already had tenure, even had a little nest egg put away; she was not yet forty, but approaching it swiftly; they could have a child, he was thinking, to replace the one he'd already lost in the miscarriage with Connie several years back.

But as luck would have it, all that talk of family and independence flitted away with one rotten Pap smear. All of a sudden he was driving her to hospital for tests, filling out form after form, sitting up with her under the harsh fluorescent, holding her hand as they waited nervously for results. Within a month they took the entire womb, and if that wasn't enough, a few weeks later they lopped off the left breast. Five, six times a week now he was at her house drawing baths filled with medical leaves and anointing the lesions that had broken out on her skin. Day after day he was

14

boiling rice and feeding her soup in bed and reading to her at night and holding her as the pain blazed through. Twice a week he was dropping her off at one therapist's office after another and picking her up again. What was she doing? This friend told her to try Jin Shin Jytysu, that friend told her Reiki, that other friend told her about healing with crystals and if that didn't work she should pick up shamanic journeying. Week after week, UPS dropped off packets of books on Ayurvedic Medicine, Vibrational Medicine, Auric healings, and chakras. Suddenly the house was full of crystals, huge ones of varied colours and striation, placed in auspicious locations that made him dizzy when he walked by them. A woman wearing a white turban drew strange symbols around the house, rearranged the furniture and put up extra mirrors. Friends with drums, with bells, with feathers and gems sat around her bed, chanted ceremonial hymns, banged their instruments, sprinkled the air with white powder and waved away entities they claimed were hovering around. She changed her diet. She started to hug trees whenever they stepped outside. She meditated four and five hours at a time, and sometimes walked around in a daze, her hands outstretched. There were times he did not recognize her, or she him.

Leave her, Silas said at once. He was a social scientist and had long since dismissed the non-rational.

But how could he leave when he'd slipped into some new and strange and complicated dance with her?

The breed of cancer was so vicious, doctors had her on chemo, on radiation, and an assortment of experimental drugs. She grew gaunt, her skin blistered, her joints swelled, she had boils in her mouth, her teeth went black, her breath smelled of crude oil. One day she got up from her meditation and announced she was no longer going to take the medicine. Just so! She wanted to heal herself, she said.

He looked at her as if she were crazy.

She waved him away like a gnat.

This is nuts, he cried. But he could tell her nothing. Nothing would change her mind. There was Carolyn Myss telling her she could heal herself, there was Deepak Chopra, Barbara Brennan and a whole host of others, including the healer she saw twice a week, who was blind in both eyes, had exceedingly long arms and a polyphonic laugh.

Within weeks though, the bloat and discoloration fell away. Within months, the rust returned to her cheeks, the emerald to her eyes, her appetite resumed full force, she filled out her frocks again as her hips widened, the house reverberated with her wild laughter and every drop of the cancer leaked out of her blood. Even the doctors were stunned. He was too. And all over again he began brimming with his mad and indiscriminate love; she had so much heart he decided. This was true courage. She could stand up to death, meet it face to face and then beat it back. What could he do? Not anything remotely close to that. He was not a brave man. He had run away from the Caribbean, he had run away from his people, he had buried himself like an ostrich in work, as if that would save him forever. They could adopt a child or two, he told himself, his eyes possessed by the possibilities he saw blossoming everywhere again; she could move in with him, they could buy a house together in Spain where she was born; they could marry.

He drives to the Asmara Yoga Studio after office hours to pick up Marie Jose for dinner. He's not seen her in a week; she's been travelling to book fairs and conferences for work. But finally she is in the car next to him and he is relieved to have her in his arms again, relieved to have her there solid and strong, and he holds on to her for a long, long time.

Everything is alright? she asks him in that quiet way, her eyes on his face, her eyes slowly reading, what's new, what's been going on?

He laughs nervously and begins twisting the knobs on the radio. Same old, same old, he cries. You work too hard. I miss you. He moves quickly over the flushed cheeks, the hair damp and flat on her head, the nose dappled with sweat, anywhere, anywhere but at the offending eye.

Outside the world is the colour of ash; the sky hangs heavy and low above them, and periodically the wind sweeping off the frozen river rocks the car from side to side.

At the restaurant, the waitress waves them to a booth against the back wall near the window that looks out over the dimly lit parking lot and at people hurrying to their cars, shoulders braced against the wind. They order and as they wait, he squeezes her knees underneath the table.

Wouldn't you like to escape this nasty cold and go somewhere nice and sunny and warm for a change, he says, somewhere where there's a beach and where you can stretch out under an umbrella and sip some good rum and enjoy the sunset? The truth is he cannot face his father's rage on his own, he cannot face his brother's accusations, or his mother's sadness, and yet he doesn't want to appear like a tub that can't sit on its own bottom. She hates nothing more than a weak man, and right now he has to collect himself.

She looks at him with suspicious eyes. What's this now, she says.

My father is dying, he says, a telegram came. I have to go home.

Really, she says softly, a frown starting to crowd her forehead. When did this happen?

Oh, he says, running his hand through his hair, which has started to thin significantly in the front and middle. He keeps it low, but he might have to do as Silas does, shave the whole head completely. Yesterday, I mean Saturday, I don't know, he says growing weary again, last week.

The waitress brings bowls of miso soup, warm and slightly salted edamame beans, and a plate of seaweed salad. They unfold their napkins, spread them out on their laps, begin the business of eating.

I know it's kind of sudden, he says, I don't even know how they found me. He is growing more and more disgruntled now. But I want to show you my home, he says trying to bring back the grin, the word home sounding suddenly menacing in his mouth.

It's weird, she says, all this has been going on, and you didn't even tell me. We talk everyday, she says, and you said nothing.

Well, he says, unable to meet her eyes, his gaze lingering instead at her nose, which is large and sharp.

I mean half the time I don't know what goes on with you, inside you, I mean half the time you're so damn closed off. I mean a telegram for Christ's sake and you're just telling me now. And we've talked everyday for the last week.

Okay, he says, pushing away his food, here we go with the character assassination. Here we go with the fault-finding. He's been called frozen so many times already and by so many women.

The waitress arrives with the barbecued eel, but no one has an appetite.

I bet Silas knows, she says.

He looks at her and at the concrete set of her jaw and he sees the miserable evening laid out ahead.

Silas knows nothing, he says quietly. This isn't something you can just blurt out to any and everybody. Silas knows nothing. He nibbles at his eel, clamps his eyes shut as the wasabi bolts through his face. Anyway, he says, I'm sorry I didn't say anything earlier, the truth is, I couldn't face any of it, he says, but I hope you'll come with me, he says, so much water under the bridge.

3.

In the boiling heat, at the overcrowded airport in Kingston, he plucks his brother at once from among the multitudes wielding boxes and suitcases, and throwing up in the air long-time-no-see children, and hugging onto old sweethearts and best friends and wailing out into the simmering afternoon and squabbling and laughing. His brother wears a long thin spade of a goatee, speckled now with white. He wears a black three-piece suit way too tight – he looks almost swollen inside it – and a black felt hat with a blue grouse feather.

What to say to his brother after all these years? He does not know, his brother was a boy still when he left, a boy of fifteen. He pumps his brother's hand long and hard and then he looks past his brother's shoulders at the long black hearse parked at the curb with the motor still running and a boy, who has his brother's face, waiting for them in the front. He's brought shirts for his brother, trousers and shoes, but he doesn't think anything will fit.

He introduces Marie Jose, and his brother, in a burst of enthusiasm completely uncalled for, sweeps her up in his big arms, spins her as if she is a child, and then sets her down again proud and grinning. There's nothing on the surface of his face that tells Winston his brother is surprised to see that his girlfriend is white. Perhaps all along he knew it would be so, knew this was to be expected. Winston swallows.

You'd a good flight, his brother asks, heaving their bags into the trunk while the boy, the nephew, who has not stepped out to greet them, waits inside the air-conditioned hearse.

Very good, Winston cries, very well. And then they lapse into an unbearable silence as the car pulls away from the curb and heads into the hushed and mazy afternoon.

He'd asked a graduate student to finish up the fall semester, teach the last few weeks of his classes, and administer and grade the final exams. The departmental secretary he told he'd be gone eight weeks total, until the start of Spring semester, he said, February. He figured he could teach something he'd taught a hundred times already so there wouldn't be the stress of a new course. He'd cancelled all his appointments and talks, and brought the cat, which was really Connie's, and the three orchids over to Silas's house. This was late November.

So, how is he, Winston calls from the back of the hearse, which smells like embalming fluid and sacramental oils, how is he holding up?

Who, the old Lion? his brother cries, watching him from the rear-view mirror and pealing with laughter. Pa's going to outlive us all, man, mark my words. Outlive us all.

But I thought it was urgent. He hears his voice failing him already. Mother said he only had the few months, I thought.

How else could we have gotten you to come? You didn't answer the letters, you didn't write us, what would you have done? His brother is glaring at him now.

Out of the tinted windows, everything is coated in fine yellow dust: the spindly palms lining the roadway and forming an arch, the dilapidated cars racing dangerously on the destroyed roads, the extravagant houses ringed with burglar bars and sheltered behind concrete structures, the faces they pass later on, drawn and malnourished and gaping at the long black hearse barrelling through the rotten streets. Only the glittering sea, running alongside the car on the left, remains blue and unwrinkled.

As if to fill the air with jubilation, his brother slides in a tape and a religious hymn comes hurling out the speakers and immediately his lunch comes rushing up into the back of his throat, almost in his mouth, and he clutches Marie Jose's clammy hand. I have to be alone, he announces, his face drenched in a malodorous sweat, and a mile from the house he has not seen in over twenty years, his brother pulls over to the shoulder.

The nephew, as if now just noticing him, turns to study him. Winston ignores the boy and opens the car door. Marie Jose's face is already sewn up and glued to the window. If she's pissed, she doesn't say it. How many days he begged and coerced and made promises, but now that she's here, everything feels harder already.

The hearse lurches away on the newly tarred road and he lopes into the evening, relieved to be on solid ground again. All around him, mockingbirds whistle their jaunty tunes. All around him, fireflies step out early to blink. And he breaks out into a harsh dry bark of a laugh at the way they'd tricked him.

A fork and the road empties into the village square. Music roars out of a shop window. Three men sitting on the bench outside the piazza stares openly at him, with raw, rum-soaked eyes; and he stares back at them sullenly.

All over the world, there is the smell of breadfruit boiling, green bananas boiling, cocoa and St. Vincent yam boiling. Bats shoot through the cyanic blue of the sky. Chickens setting up to roost for the night complain in their foul-smelling coops. And the craven dogs bark and bark all over the valley and into the grey hills surrounding the district.

An old woman in a white frock waits for him at the gate. How long has his mother been waiting there at the gate? Night has fallen. The cicadas have sharpened their song; a mild breeze brings a wave of eucalyptus. His mother's hands are big and cold. Dew is already falling on her head, and on her breath there is the smell of the broom weed tea for high blood pressure. His mother moans. A deep gash tears at the pit of his stomach and in his arms, his mother now, a frame of bones.

Go and tell your father good evening, she cries, the eyes round like marbles, as the hot, white moon appears from out of hiding.

Go, now. She's suddenly tight and hard and edging out of his arms and marching ahead of him into the house.

To this day, he still doesn't remember what he'd said to his father. He doesn't remember what had ignited it. But he must've back-answered him; he must've said something nasty. Immediately a shriek tore across his father's face and his father's fist shot out knocking him across the room. Windows whizzed by, and outside the windows, his mother's prized bougainvillea, the clothes-line full of his father's white Arrow shirts, his father's blue van parked in the carport, and the rope swing in the almond tree where he pushed his sister on Sunday afternoons. Finally he crumpled into the wall. He did not move. His mother was wailing and clawing at her hair. Yes, she said, yes, you kill him now. You kill him with your anger and your violence. And who will it be next? Who?

He did not move. He was exhausted; he wanted badly to sleep. He wanted his bed but his bed felt far away and he wasn't sure his legs could carry him there. If only the bed could come. The seat of his trousers was warm and he was comforted by this, and perhaps he nodded off, because when he woke again, it was night, and his bed had come and his face and shoulder clamoured with pain and Dr. Anglin was there, and his mother too was there, and he remembered thinking that the minute he got better, the minute he was well again, he was going to leave. And he was never ever coming back. He was going to make them suffer. Suffer. It was a very clear and precise thought and perhaps he said it out loud, because his mother's beautiful grey eyes filled at once.

She did not speak to their father for two full weeks. Two full weeks she slept on a cot near Winston's bed. She took time off from the bank and stayed home with him. She bathed and dressed him and wept over the bruised and broken parts of his body. She did not let the housekeeper touch him. She cooked again and again all the dishes he requested, and she fed him off her plate and from the same spoon she fed herself. It was not the first time his father had hurt him, but this was different. Two full weeks she was devoted to him and he loved her back in return, he loved her desperately, and he surrendered himself to this love. Then after two weeks she went back to her husband. Just so! She fussed over her husband at the dinner table, serving him the choicest pieces of meat, filling up his water glass, running to the fridge to get him his stout, looking in his eyes over and over again to check for pieces of herself. After two weeks, her son had become again what he'd always been, her son. But her husband, her husband was again the kingpin. He was her eye and her beating heart, and without him, she was nothing at all. Better to turn a blind eye, better to keep pursed lips while he beat her children. Ten times worse to have that man walk out and have the whole damn world looking on at her empty arms.

He was fourteen years old, but he saw it clear as day, this great betrayal, and it was not just in his family alone, he saw it everywhere he looked now in the village; he saw it every day that there was light. He saw parents turning their backs, parents drawing a mask over their faces so as not to see, parents breaking their word, violating their own laws, perpetrating violence again and again against their own flesh and blood. Those weeks he was laid up, he got a brand new bicycle, an Encyclopedia Britannica set and his own battery-operated record changer and a slew of forty-fives. But what was the point? His father had thrown him into a wall crushing his arm. He couldn't go anywhere; he couldn't spend the money he'd also got, or wear the new clothes. He could only stare at the bicycle and at the pictures in his books. His mother, who all along he thought was his friend, had deceived him; she showed solidarity for two good weeks, two good weeks she was vexed with her husband, she didn't speak to him, but in no time at all she had picked up again with the culprit. Where was the love in all of that? Destroying him one day and loving him the next! Where was the justice?

The cover of the pump organ is lifted and the hymn book, held together with duct tape, is wide open and turned to page sixty-seven, *Do You Remember When They Crucified My Lord?* The coffee table with his initials knifed into the mahogany, the Morris chairs, the red sofa with the narrow silver legs, the grandfather clock that chimes on the half-hour, the rocker with the embroidered antimacassar thrown over the back, everything the same, as if life had not carried on. The portraits are still on the walls. Oil and watercolour reproductions of his mother's near white family, and of him and his brother and the dead sister, Althea. The same sculptures by Edna Manley and Colin Garland and Woody Joseph sit out on small narrow tables with spindle legs.

He smells his father before he even sees him and it's the smell of a man gone completely to rot.

Papa, he says, turning slowly, it's me, it's Winston.

He sees nothing in the shadowy darkness, hears nothing, until he backs into the handle of the wheelchair, and then he stops, afraid to turn around, afraid to see the face, half of it frozen now, one of the eyes covered up in white gauze, and the teeth, all of them black with decay. Where is Marie Jose, he wonders, poor Marie Jose whom he abandoned earlier, left her in Septimus' care.

A little girl appears from one of the rooms wearing a long white shirt, her arms swallowed by the tall sleeves. She has his father's ears, like bellows, the high dome of a forehead. She slips past him, hoists herself into his father's lap, wraps her arms around his neck and peers out at Winston with dark almond-shaped eyes that remind him immediately of the dead sister, Althea, and he hears the yap, yap of Althea's laugh, feels the breeze blowing off the river where he's teaching her to dog-paddle and breaststroke and to straddle water.

Papa, he says again, taking a long, slow breath, I'm home.

And the room, reeking with the smell of mould and damp and dust and decay, utters no sound at all, only settles itself more deeply into the belly of the earth.

In the kitchen, they have started dinner without him. His girlfriend is there, sipping a mug of bitter bush tea – her stomach probably upset from all the commotion – and wearing a face that says nothing at all and everything. He wishes she hadn't come. Everything is too raw and gritty here; how is he to protect himself and protect her at the same time? No one pays him any mind; they are absorbed in the slicing of meat, at blowing steam off the hot soup spoon, at sucking the marrow from a bone. He can't decide if he should sit near his mother or near his girlfriend; either way feels dangerous, as if he's taking sides. His eyes finally come to rest on his mother's face, which he can see clearly now in the light. Grey matter has taken over the eyes. Now you have to strain to hear as her voice-box has gone hoarse. The big hands with the long, shapely fingers tremble from nerves – his mother who, on the side, used to take in orders for wedding dresses from as far away as Cuba and Costa Rica. Now she can barely hold her spoon steady, hold the mug she is trying to bring to her lips. He turns away from her eyes, dark inside that face like a cave; he remembers Althea.

Who is the little girl? he asks, still hovering in the doorway, his shadow long and lean and uncertain, and inside his chest tightness fills the entire cavity.

No one utters a word, and he thinks perhaps they've not heard him. Septy, he calls to his brother, whose flat, smooth face sweating over his bowl of oxtail soup resembles their father's so much he has to turn away – the eyes sunken deep into his head, the nose like a fist on his face, the shoulders hunched into his chest. He turns to his mother, whose face has suddenly turned to stone, and then to the nephew who looks like a girl from this angle and in this light. Who is the little girl? he asks the boy, his nephew. Still no one says a word and he thinks, what is this, what is this? Didn't he see a little girl out there perched on his father's lap, and he takes off his wire rimmed glasses and wipes them carefully with the tail of his white shirt and sets them on again and fixes his eyes on the girlish looking nephew, who must be part Indian, the gleaming black hair ribboned with so many large curls.

My auntie, the nephew says, looking at him with what looks like a grin beating around his mouth and he finds himself wanting to slap the nasty little grin off the boy's face.

Your auntie, he says slowly and the boy nods and he's confused. Auntie, he's thinking to himself, how the hell, Auntie, and he's unable to put all the pieces together with this Auntie.

Your new sister, the boy says, Grandpa's outside child.

Aahh, he says long and loud, as if all has been made clear, and he starts to nod, and at the same time he tries to figure out where to sit now, where to sit and digest this piece of news. So much shame in that green kitchen with the candles hissing and smoking as they steadily burn down into pools of grease and harden on the plates. He turns to find his mother scrunched up inside that tall narrow white dress, looking as if she's been mourning forever.

He must sit, he thinks, he must sit and relax and digest all of this slowly, except he cannot sit, he cannot relax, he cannot do anything at all, but look at his brother. What you mean sister? he says to his brother, but he's turning to his mother as well, turning to the boy, his nephew, what you mean his outside child, his outside daughter? His lips are moving, he might even be shouting, but is he even saying anything at all? Nobody is answering, nobody is looking at him; and there is his brother who has spent his entire life underneath their father's thumb, there is his brother who has never stood up to him, never stood up for their mother, never stood up for anything, all his fucking life, a lackey.

Suddenly he is leaping way across the room and collaring his brother, knocking over his food and upsetting the table. You let him carry on with this shit, same way you let him bring in whoever, mistreat her whenever he likes, you let him. He crashes into the side of his brother's head with his fists, the brother who has never protected their mother, never stood up for anything, he cracks him on the nose, on the right jaw, until the nephew sends him reeling into a corner, and he crumbles into a chair where he sits with his hands trembling, trying to find the damn breath to still them.

The house now has grown completely still. The boy brings cotton and iodine to Septy. The boy is gentle with Septy, he talks softly to Septy, he settles Septy into a comfortable chair so he can incline his head to stop the bleeding nose. Winston turns away from this picture of a boy and his father and wonders briefly about that other one, that other one nailed to death in his chair and stinking. His mother refuses to meet his eyes and just as well, he thinks, he cannot bear her suffering, has never been able to bear her shame. Wasn't that why he had kept away all these years – he could not stand to see the way he treated her, and the way she held up year after year, as if this very thing was her calling in life. At Marie Jose, he dares not look. He can only imagine that already she has left him; already she has one foot on the plane. His mother continues to eat, grinding her teeth with tremendous intent, her face unrecognizable to him now, the face like granite.

We should leave, he says, tomorrow first thing, we should go.

They're in bed now, in the room at the side of the house facing the tank and the tiny cemetery where Althea is buried and beyond that the little Presbyterian stone church he attended as a boy and prepared the sacrament for first communion.

She says nothing, but she doesn't have to, what's there to say.

Worst of all was the look on his brother's face, the look that said to him, you fool, you stupid, blasted, ignorant fool.

Please talk to me, he says, this is not the time for the cold shoulder. There's all this rumbling near his heart and it feels unbearable, and it's moving now and sitting on his chest like a great wave, pressing into his sternum.

She chuckles.

And he is so relieved to hear her chuckle, he heaves a great sigh, but immediately grows worried again.

It's too warm to sleep, and the old rusty fan only makes the air warmer and they're stretched out side by side, still as boards, and naked underneath the thin cotton sheets that smell of camphor.

He fits his face in his hands, and for a long time they are quiet. Around them the house creaks and moans, and outside the strange singing of an animal. He wanted his brother to fight back, he wanted to be wrong and to have had to buckle under his brother's fists, but his brother did not fight back, punch for punch, his brother swallowed them down, as if he deserved every single last one of them.

Would you like to open a coning, Winston?

Suddenly he's irritated as hell with her. Look, he says, harshly, this is not the time. I respect all these spiritual and healing things you do for yourself, he says, but right now is not the time.

That's fine, she says, that's perfectly fine. Then she is quiet.

But it's not fine, he knows that tone, and the last thing he needs now is this punishing silence when he has his mother's face on his hands.

Look, he says wearily, I didn't mean...

It's fine, Winston. I just wanted to help. You're up over your head, drowning in this family shit. Just wanted to help.

Can you help me some other way, he says, just not this energy stuff right now. He can just see the whole damn thing unfolding, the two of them stretched out there, Marie Jose calling in the entities, and within minutes the heat filling his limbs, one by one, the chatter in his mind coming to a halt, images coming in and stopping by and going on again, images, sounds, his breath, his blood, his body falling down with the weight of inertia.

Can you help me some other way? He begins again. He does not know what to do with this pressure bearing down on his chest, on his heart.

27

Against the windows, the elaborately decorated sphinx moths beat themselves to death.

You want a massage, she asks, turning to him.

No, he does not want a fucking massage; he just wants this fucking thing to dissolve. No, he says, tightly.

What can I do then, she says, you're full of rage, you're acting crazy. I don't know you. I don't feel safe around you. What do you want me to do?

Oh Christ, he cries, leaping out of bed and fumbling around in the dark until he finds shorts in his suitcase, hauls them on and yanks open the door with a loud scraping noise. The night rushes into the room along with hordes of singing mosquitoes and flying ants and bats of assorted types and there's the echo of dogs barking and barking way down deep in the valley and the insects feeding on them and on each other and shrieking. Jesus Christ, he cries, jumping away from the night and slapping at the mosquitoes flying around his head and building nests in his hair. He slams the door. He sits down on the side of the bed trembling. Murky moonlight slopes in on them. Way out deep into the night, an owl calls. His knuckles pound like hell.

I came so I could help, she says. You asked me to come and help you. You have all this rage at your father you're just lashing out at everyone. Tonight wasn't a mistake, she says, it's going to get worse before it gets better. That's how these things work.

He says nothing. More than all this energy and this spirit, he hates all this psychology. But perhaps she is right. Perhaps Marie Jose is right as always. It's impossible to think, his mind, his heart; everything inside him ablaze.

I thought things would be different, I thought none of this would matter, I thought, I don't know, he says, everything is the same.

You haven't changed?

No, he says. Otherwise none of this would bother me. None of this would matter.

Well, it can still bother you, she says, many things in life will bother you, even after you change, but you can't just knock down everybody in your way, beat down everybody. How is that different from your father?

So I'm like my father, now, he cries. I take up for my mother and I'm like my father now. This is just going from bad to worst, he thinks. This is just fucking awful.

Well, when he used to beat you because he couldn't control you, couldn't bend you to suit him, how is that different from what you're doing now, striking out at things you can't control?

That is not what I'm doing, he says. There's all this iron in his voice now, all this hurt in his eyes now.

Okay, she says. Okay, and then she is quiet.

At the window, the moon moves slowly among the trees and there is the one lone star singing out there in the heavens. He wishes he could have a drink, nothing fancy, even the rot-gut white rum would work, just something to soothe him right now and help his mind quiet so he can sleep and forget, numb out the world.

Maybe the coning wouldn't be so bad after all – something to soften him, to drain this bile roiling inside him. It's just that she does all this healing stuff now on a regular basis, and if he's not doing it as well, if he's not following behind her pee-pee, cluck-cluck, then he's not growing, they're not growing together and the relationship is just going downhill. That is her new discourse. Isn't that a form of control too? She's not interested in him, his individuality; she just wants to change him. He should never have come. What was he expecting, a fucking celebration? He came to see them, to see his brother, and what does he do, feed him blow after blow. And there was his brother refusing to stand up like a man, refusing to stand up for himself as his mother has done all her life with this man, refused to stand up for herself.

I missed them, he finds himself blurting out into the dark.

Of course you miss them, it's been twenty-five years.

I had no idea, he says, moaning, I had no idea. And from somewhere inside the crevices of his abdomen, he feels things shifting and breaking. Oh God, he cries, and she pulls him into her arms, rocking him, and he wheezes into the night, the sound rushing from his lungs rusty and broken and scraping like metal. And he does not know what to do with this sensation; it is like nothing he has felt before. He should never have come, he tells himself over and over again, willing the trembling to subside, to disappear altogether.

From there in her arms, he must have dozed off, the smell of ginger and basil from her hair and skin lulling him. And he dreams he's alone on a boat with the wide open river ahead of him, and there he is on the boat, rocking and rocking with the currents taking him and turning him, he has no idea of the destination unfolding, he just knows he has to stay awake and observe the twisted trees collected at the side of the river like sentinels, and the passing rocks crowded into heaps in the middle of the channel that now and again obstruct the boat, but the boat has a mind of its own, and he knows that there are messages in the clouds, but he's not learned yet how to decipher them, there are writings on the trunks of trees, coded in the harsh red bark and on his way he will learn them.

4.

The next morning, early, he calls his brother at the funeral home.

The phone picks up at once. Rowe's Funeral Home, his brother cries.

It's me, Winston says.

His brother grows quiet on the line. Just a minute, he says, hold just a minute.

He imagines his brother setting aside syringes, bottles of embalming fluid, wads of cotton, a pair of scissors, a length of cord he uses to tie the big toe. He takes off his gloves and overcoat, the mask he wears over his face, he throws a white cloth over the cold black body and closes the door gently then takes the phone with him into the tiny bathroom where he washes his hands slowly at the sink, dries them with a piece of paper towel. His brother does not look at the face, puffy and bruised, the right eye half closed. He blows his nose into his handkerchief, which has his initials embroidered in the right corner. Outside in the harsh morning light under a banyan tree, he lights a cigarette and sucks down deeply on it before he lifts the phone to his face again.

You there. His voice is phlegmy.

Sorry about last night, Winston says, I lost my head. I lost my frigging head. He can see now that his estimation of his brother isn't exactly correct. His brother did not take over their father's two bakeries as to be expected, he did not build a house hitched up underneath their father's backside, he moved away to the farthest edge of the island, he took up with a woman not of his clan, he carved out his own way, morbid as it may seem, he turned his life into a burial man.

I just didn't expect that at this late stage he'd still be carrying on like this, bringing in whoever he pleases, Winston says. I thought you'd talk to him, council him, stop him if needs be. After all, you were the one he liked.

Pa is a grey toned man, his brother says. Unless you haven't noticed, Pa listens to his own self.

Yes, Winston says, but you could've stopped him, you could've done something. The child he made elsewhere, he can't just bring it in, rubbing it in our faces, over and over again disrespecting our mother.

You're talking as if our mother is a child. Can't stand up for herself, can't do for herself.

When has he ever listened to her, Winston says, when has what she has to say ever counted for anything? You're a man at least, you he will listen to, you can stand up to him.

I didn't see you standing up, Winston. You left like quashee, ran away to America. Years pass, nobody hear a word from you. How many letters we wrote, you didn't even answer one. I didn't see you standing up.

Winston grows quiet on the phone. Indeed he had run, but what else could he have done. At first the letters came directly to the college where he was enrolled, and then he'd get the notices that they'd telephoned, which meant his mother must've travelled the sixty miles to her cousin's house in town, for in those days there were no phone lines in the district. He did not know the hardening would've come to this, this long estrangement. By the time he actually left them early that Tuesday morning for college in North America, his mother fussing with his hair, brushing specks off his suit, wetting her thumb with her tongue and pressing his jumbled brows, he was already gone. Just a shell she was talking to, a dry cornhusk. You have your passport? Her eyes were jumping up and down in her face, white with powder. You have the envelope with your money? Both were attached to the inside of his jacket with a safety pin. Don't bother to start up the wailing, she was saying to him, but actually she was only consoling herself. And write once a month, she moaned. Write!

Well, I've come back, Winston says. I've come home.

To do what? Septimus cries. To criticize us, to act like you better than us, like you know what's best?

The problem is we've never asked anything of him, Winston says, slightly calmer now, but for how long. We've never asked him to respect us. We've never said this way you treat us, this way you treat our mother, this is not acceptable. We've never set limits with him, kept him in check. We've been too in awe of him – or too afraid of him. Now he's dying and here we are tumbling over ourselves to take care of him. Now he's dying and he doesn't have to repair any of the damage he's done. He has gotten away with every fucking thing, Winston says. Everything!

His brother is quiet on the line; his brother doesn't have one word to say to that. He hears his brother strike a match, hears the sound of him inhaling, sucking on another cigarette. His brother is still silent; then he hears him spit, clear his throat and say, I have to get back to these dead people, you hear, they have family coming later to see them and such. I have to go now.

Okay, Winston says, but I just want you to know, okay, I just want you to know that I came back because it's my home too, and because I missed you, you hear that, I missed you.

Days later in the boiling sun, he shambles all over the village with Marie Jose in tow, pointing and jabbering and reminiscing and recollecting. He shows her the brown mouth of the river where he used to swim naked with his best friend, Bone; the flamboyant tree where a boy named Knuckle Post used to suck him off every Tuesday after Spelling Bee practice. The salmon-coloured house where his god-mother once lived is in ruins now among dead fruit trees, the eyes of windows stuffed with newspaper or boarded up. She was in a coma for forty days and he went every evening after school to hold her hand, which reminded him of a mackerel, and to recite the Lord's Prayer. A drunk stumbling down the road belts out an ancient calypso. A flock of school children shuffles behind them for a good mile before disappearing. And everywhere he turns: voluptuous vegetation, small falling-down houses, brightly painted stuccos with great gangly rosebushes in the yards, paint-flaked buildings with crumbling walls, animals parched and bloated in the fields, dusty, brown trees leaning away from the sun and parakeets bobbing and preening and shitting from their high branches. He takes her to the infant school up the hill overlooking the cemetery, where he practised his letters on a slate; the little stone church next to it, where Mr. Lewis was rumoured to practice his sorcery: the blind were known to walk away blinking the next morning, the maimed and crippled to jump up again and sing.

They pass the workers, men and women alike stooped over the land, swinging machetes and yammering to themselves in the blazing heat. They raise up to study him and the meagre white woman at his side with eyes reddened from the sun, and they show no signs at all of recognition though they know it's he, Mass Sam's son, the worthless one that left for foreign and never turned the black of his eyes again to say, hey dog, how you keeping.

On and on they walk, the sun dipping momentarily to cool down the world, then firing up again. Tired and thirsty, they step inside a bar and he orders two cold aerated water, champagne flavoured, and they sit down on the bench facing the roadway, fanning with their hats as the cars race back and forth stirring the red dust on the unpaved road. There is no one else in the shop, just the proprietor, an East Indian named Eustace whose right eye winks with a mind of its own. The whole long walk, he recognized no one and no one recognized him. It's as if he belongs nowhere at all, nowhere in the world and the whole damn thing leaves a bad ugly taste in his mouth that he wants to spit out but doesn't know how. He pays, what else is there to do, Mass Eustace winks at the two of them, they stumble into the heat, nothing else to point out now, nothing else to show. He breathes into the burning dust that has laid down an extra skin on their clothes. He breathes into the afternoon, the murderous afternoon, as he shambles slowly behind her down the endless road of his youth.

5.

He finds his father's daughter at the bottom of the garden lying on her back on a bed of yellow poppies and staring at the sky, which is pregnant with the look of rain. He wanders over slowly, studying the face, which has their father's sharp cheekbones and his arched brows; still it is the dead sister Althea that comes to mind, her hair plaited into neat rows, the ends tied with the red and blue ribbons she wore that morning to church, stars of gold at her ears. She knows he's standing there, but she doesn't look up and he does not say a word. A breeze passes through the leaves and the willow trees moan and sway and dip their branches toward them, and the squawking birds skip from perch to perch, watching them and nodding.

This used to be my favourite place when I was a boy, he tells her, remembering he used to study his timetables and play jacks with Althea and read his L'Amour westerns when the house gave him no peace whatsoever.

Finally she turns to observe him, which she does for a long time and then, as if she's gleaned all the information she needs, she breaks off a Spanish needle, sticks it in her mouth and begins to chew. She says nothing. He takes that to mean he can sit or he can go, suit himself, and he sits down near her head on the grass.

I used to read with my back up against this stump, he says, pointing to a tree that'd been struck by lightning, just a rotting log now, full of carpenter ants and ground mice.

She is not interested. Her eyes are not trained on him but up into the trees where the birds babble at their nests and the light splinters through the leaves which, when troubled by the wind, make a great rustling sound, a sound like a great many bushels of peas falling out of a crocus bag onto a concrete floor. Marie Jose has been gone all afternoon; she went with Septimus and their father to the sea. Just like that she got up and said she was tired of the house and next thing he knew she was gone; there was Septimus and the driver stuffing his father's wooden legs into the car, and there was the car moving slowly down the hill blanketed in a cloud of red dust.

They didn't think you were going to come, the little girl says, nodding toward the big white house with red doors. But I knew you'd come.

How'd you know, he says, watching the eyes, lazy and brown, the mouth pulled up at the corners like Septy's, same widow's peak and dimples as Septy's.

I saw you in the dreams, sometimes every night for a whole week. I told Grandma, she says I was making story.

Grandma? he says, wondering if this is his mother she's referring to.

She nods. She says I was making story.

Were you? He is amused.

No, she says, I don't need to. I know a lot of things.

He wonders how is he to read that.

Who is Silas, she says.

This time he feels slightly queasy. You saw him too? he asks, wondering if she's been eavesdropping on his conversations with Marie Jose.

No, she says, just now his name came to me, and Chris and Marcus too.

He swallows.

In the distance someone is calling Darleen to come right away and pick up the white clothes from off the line before night comes. Dar-Leen, the voice wails out again from way down deep in the valley. He can barely make out the moving bodies in the distance, only the smoke from the outside cook fires pouring out against the slate-coloured evening.

He will help you, she says.

What? he says, irritable and a little put off now.

Silas will help you.

With what, he cries, what exactly does Silas need to help me with?

When the time comes, she says.

He laughs harshly. I see you like to play with people, he says.

This isn't play, she says, drawing a frown across her forehead and glaring at him.

He remembers the string of women who used to come up to the house on a Sunday evening and dawdle about the gate, waiting for signs from his father who was inside resting. They talked in loud voices and gave out lascivious laughs and sang rude songs with suggestive meanings until Constable Roache drove them away with his baton. Then there were the ones who were always stopping him and Septimus on the road and giving them packages to deliver to his father. At night he'd hear them quarrelling in the bedroom, his mother's high-pitched shrieks, his father slamming out of the house in the middle of the night, the tires of his truck screaming down the road, not to be seen again for days. Soon they stopped quarrelling altogether.

Which one is your mother, he asks her.

She shrugs. Don't know, she says. Everyday they say something else. Her eyes are narrow and dry and burning. First they say she was sick, couldn't take care of me. Then they say she was young. Then they say the father was worthless. I don't believe them, she says, the old woman would've told me.

His head is reeling. Which old woman? he says.

She comes all the time.

She comes here to visit? he says, wondering which woman this is now.

Doesn't matter, she says, impatient with him now. Grandpa and Grandma love me, and I have a nice home and the parrot is mine. Did you see the parrot? I'm teaching her to talk. It can say *school starts at eight o' clock* and *later alligator*. It even knows some bad words. It can say *kiss my ass*, and she breaks into a loud, mischievous giggle.

He tries to imagine the moment at which his mother began to love her. His mother closing her eyes to things and pretending, the story she spun for her sisters at church to ease her shame, the stories she told herself at night so she could sleep. He tries to imagine his mother putting down her weapons, putting away her fight; his mother thinking all this will change and the meek will inherit the earth after all; his mother swallowing the spit of her hate and carrying on nonetheless.

6.

Does my father say anything to you about me? he asks Marie Jose.

A whole week now his father hasn't said a word to him, an entire week he has sought out his father, asked after his health, and not a word out of his father's mouth and then just yesterday morning he awoke to find the bed beside him empty and when he hobbled outside there was just the tail of her shirt bending the corner. There she was wheeling his father down the marl road, his head bandaged in white cloth, his father who was supposed to be sick onto death with just weeks left to his name. There she was pushing him through the Village Square. He saw the people opening doors and stepping out to greet them, as if the hero had come home, the hero who had brought his outside child into the house, and who had her there posing as his granddaughter. He saw the gaggle of children peering at Marie Jose from behind their mother's skirts and giggling, their hands holding up their mouths. He saw the hungry, three-legged dogs twitching their tails and shoving their nuzzles into her red skirt. For hours after that, he couldn't speak two words to her, couldn't even meet her eyes. Was she also turning into a snake? Yet wasn't this what he loved, that whenever she walked into a room full of people, everybody wanted to be her friend.

I make an effort with your father, she cries. If you want results, you make an effort. You put yourself aside. Stop thinking of you all the damn time, she hisses, and then she turns away, drowning her tea with steamed milk.

When he was a boy walking home from school, he'd glimpse his father through the windows of his bakery wrapping up loaves of bread in brown paper, making change for his customers, haggling with the man over the price of wheat flour, shoving a handful of sweets into a child's mouth, and his father's face glowed, his laughter, speckled with gold, rang out into the zinc roof of his shop, rang out into the yellow hills to the west beaten down by drought. When a man whispered in his ears a piece of tragedy, his father's eyes grew wet immediately, but just as suddenly he was holding up the man in his arms and soothing him down and cutting him a slice of Christmas bun with the New Zealand cheddar; just as suddenly he had the man in stitches again, and they were holding their bellies and stooping down, showing only teeth and their great gullets. But the moment he put up the shop windows, switched off the electricity, turned the deadbolt on the door and headed up the hill to the house where he lived with his family, the glimmer fell out of his face altogether. His gait was no longer steady. He turned the corner at the cedar tree; the garden full of Lent lilies opened up before him and maybe he saw all his failures laid out plain as day, because suddenly his face was like a barred door. Was it that here at his house, in front of his wife and children, his jokes, his flamboyant talk, his big laugh, his stature in the community meant nothing at all? Did he feel that here at the dining table, the gallon of fresh milk from Elders' heifers, the crisp, clean bills he laid out, the leanest cut of mutton he got from Mass Enos, meant nothing at all? That something else was required of him, and everyday he disappointed us, because he could not give us this thing, he did not know in which part of his gut to call up this thing we needed, and he needed as well, to bring radiance.

So what if he doesn't respond when you talk. So what, Marie Jose is saying, sitting on the steps at the bottom of the verandah nibbling on a slice of cornmeal pone. You could just sit with him, half-hour each time, you don't even have to speak. Just sit and breathe with him. Or if you want to talk, tell him about your life, tell him about your work, your travels to Africa. Set the tone. And grow up, for Christ's sake. He's dying.

In a few days she will go; nothing he can say will stop her. And just as well, he tells himself, sipping on a glass of hot milk laced with nutmeg and molasses and ginger, just as well. He gets the feeling they're simply biding time, waiting for her to go, so they can have him alone to themselves. And what will they do to him? Nights, the same dream haunts him over and over, a nine-night celebration, a pig still alive roasting on a spit, that same pig squealing and squealing as the great jumping flames below lick him at every turn, and the squeals only seem to agitate the crowd of mourners as their dance grows more frenzied, their wails more fervent. Always he wakes with the smell of burning hair in his teeth; always he wakes in a sweat that dries immediately, leaving a sticky yellow film on his skin.

7.

Don't wait til it gets really bad, she says at the airport, open a coning. I've taught you how. Take long walks, she says. Pray.

She looks him over, kisses him lightly on the lips and on the lobes of his ringed ears, and he knows that when he sees her again in a few weeks, everything will have changed. He doesn't know how he knows this, but it is a certainty he can feel.

You remember how to open one?

Don't worry so much, he says, kissing her on the forehead. He wishes she would just stop with this healy-feely stuff.

You remember, Win? She is insistent.

I remember, he says. How could he not remember?

They'd been fighting. This was not new. He wanted them to adopt a child they could raise together. She wanted none of that. Hadn't she just been cleared of cancer? Hadn't she just gotten her sweet life back? Well, then! She wanted now only to sit and catch her breath and figure out things slowly. He had threatened to leave. I mean, how long was he supposed to wait. At first it was the divorce, then it was the cancer. What will it be next, he'd asked her. How long was everything going to take. Was she just leading him on, was that it?

Let's try a coning, she had said.

He had said, what the hell is that going to fix? He wanted action. He wanted a child. He wanted her to marry him; he wanted a decision made. How the hell can a coning do that?

It'll calm us so we can talk through it more clearly, she said.

I don't need clarity, he had cried, I know what I want, and I see I cannot get it here.

In the end he took off his shoes. In the end he stretched out beside her on the bed, on his back, his eyes closed. Okay, he said in the end, sighing heavily, open the coning. What did he have to lose? Maybe nothing would happen. Maybe everything would happen. It had worked for her, who knows, maybe he would get this kid; get her to see reason, maybe, maybe not. He was curious. But he wouldn't put any stock in it. He'd just see.

Relax, she said.

And without even realizing he'd been holding his breath, he exhaled and his eyes turned wet.

The coning was basically prayer, though not in the conventional way. It wasn't just between you and God or Jehovah or Yahweh or Mohammed or whomever. It was between you, your higher self and an entire council of beings, guardian angels she called them. And where was God, he wanted to know, too busy? One by one she invited them to come: the over-lighting deva who was supposed to be the head angel in charge of healing, the nature spirit pan, some kind of mediator it seemed, the white brotherhood who are evolved souls and not Klan members she had pointed out when she saw the expression on his face, her higher self, his higher self. Then they waited.

If Silas could see him now, he was thinking, or any of his colleagues in the history department, what would they say to him, and out of which corner of their mouths would they say it? He loved her, that was why he was doing it. But then what if it actually worked?

When the council arrived, it was a sensation like heat filling all his limbs slowly, and he started to sob; at first from the pressure that had been swelling up his chest all morning, the pure raw rage he'd been feeling toward her, the disappointment, and then the fright, for he had no words to attach to the sensation, no memory, and then again he felt so relaxed, like right before sleep, and yet he was strangely alert. It felt like the breathing meditation he sometimes did in yoga where, after a while, the whole body fills with a tingling so delicious it makes you want to sit and sit for hours in this tingling, just savouring it as it courses through all the bones and ligaments and tendons and cells. In this coning though, the tingling was amplified twenty times. He laughed to himself; he imagined trying to explain all this to Silas and he could see how vocabulary was failing him big time. Beside her in bed against the pillows, his entire body felt nailed to the sheets in a state of relaxation that felt both expanded and beyond death.

He began to talk, as that was all that was required of him, just to say what was on his heart. He wanted a family, he said. He has wanted it for the last twenty years, ever since he left his country and came to America. He'd been no good at love, had no idea how to hold on to a woman, but then Marie Jose had come and he'd started to hope again. Okay, so maybe they didn't need marriage, but what was so damn wrong with a child; he'd pamper and love it, he'd take full responsibility for it, showering it with everything positive. Why couldn't she share that with him? So, okay, she'd had her wounds, she'd had her disappointments, everybody has those. But here he was ready to move forward; here he was ready to help her resolve some of them. Isn't that what love was, someone who would meet him half way, give of herself in a way she didn't know was possible and look, see, the gifts that would come to her in return, look, see, all the surprises waiting.

Three years they'd been engaged before Ruth called it off and moved back to Australia. Then there was Cheryl and Rose and finally Connie, but after the miscarriage, she left as well. He wanted the real thing now with Marie Jose, he wanted finally now to settle down, not to search any more, but to come home.

He talked and dense tight things inside his throat shifted. He talked and dense tight things that had been swelling up his throat rolled away, dissipated, shifted out to sea. He tried to stay awake to hear what she too was saying to the council, but he was so, so exhausted. It was like his sessions with Dr. Wolfe he remembered thinking as he drifted off to sleep, and then again it was completely different. There was no one there he could see, though he could definitely feel them, but what exactly they were doing, he could not find the precise words.

Days afterward, he waited for miracles to occur, though he was not exactly sure what to look for. He waited for her to change her mind about the child. She did not. He waited for his frustration with her stubbornness to subside; it did not. One thing he did notice, though, was that in the days immediately following the coning, he felt closer to her than ever, and for a while he thought maybe he didn't need a child, maybe she was enough, she was all the family he needed, but that too soon passed. He grew irritable and impatient with her again. They did the sessions twice a week for a month. It was exhausting. Finally he stopped. He didn't see the point. For one thing, they weren't asking for the same things, he was asking for a kid and she was asking for better communication, better connection, more intimacy and sharing. Furthermore the whole damn thing was making him claustrophobic. He couldn't tell anybody about it; who would believe him? Sometimes he worried that if the council could do good things, heal her and such, bring good tidings to bear, couldn't they also do evil?

Still, he did not think he was asking for a bad thing. He was asking for family. A man needs a family to feel at home in the world, to feel as if he belonged.

Did Marie Jose need it?

Well, no, not exactly. She had her people there in Spain, old and lame now, her parents, but that did not stop them from calling almost every day during her illness, and sending letters and gifts once a month. She'd not left in the same way he had. She'd not cut them off in anger, and then punished them every day thereafter.

Was he forcing this family business on her, was he projecting onto her something that he needed to fill his hunger?

Well, perhaps that is so.

There is no forcing current in love.

Okay, he cried – he was having these conversations with himself almost every day now. Your only purpose is to give love, not to expect it from others, not to force others to give it, but only to learn how to love and then to turnaround and give it.

If he had to describe it, he would say the coning was both meditation and prayer. That like prayer you needed faith to believe that someone, something, some entity was actually there listening and looking out for you each time you asked, and that like meditation, you quieted yourself, pried your heart open and listened to what is being said to you in return.

Okay, Marie Jose cries, tugging at his shirt and kissing him one last time. I've to go.

Her eyes have grown wet suddenly. And her skin, he notices, is unusually blotchy and red. Too much sun, he thinks, kissing her. I'll be home soon, he says, the minute he croaks, I'll be on the next flight.

She chuckles. Okay, she says, walking toward the security gate.

He blows her a juicy, orange kiss, watches her open to receive it, chew it slowly and then swallow. He loves her. One day in his life, he'd like to be brave so she can respect him. She has suffered. She's been dealt life's cruel blows, and still she is the one who is standing and who is steady as a rock and she's held him, held the two of them steady together. But now she will go.

Through the windows that look out on the Tarmac, there are still traces of sunset on the horizon. There is the look, too, of rain in the clouds and a crow with iridescent wings watches from the roof of a hanger. He sees her out there on the Tarmac as she swings up the steps with purse slung over shoulder, a red purse he bought her three birthdays ago, long before the cancer and the hands-on healing and the telegram. The purse is fiery against her brown hair and the suede coat, the bitter winter that awaits her.

The plane taxies slowly out onto the runway and the crowd gathered about him holds a collective breath. What is to be done now, but to wait? A spark of lightning lights up the evening sky as the plane speeds up in a burst of pinkish smoke, and then lifts, leaving just a white tail trailing. At first there's just a long, slim glittering star in the orange sky strewn with other stars. After that there's only a speck of light and within seconds, there's absolutely nothing at all, just the flat, blue face of the moon trundling happily across.

8.

I don't know how she and the baby got past the dogs that night. But there it was on the verandah in a little carton box at the doorway, naked as the day it was born. There it was, with just a little red scarf thrown cross way to stave off chill. It was the wailing so close to my head that pulled me out of bed. One look and I knew right away it was his: the tall forehead, the eyes long at the sides, the button nose and Althea's spirit whirling round her.

I gathered up the screaming baby. What else was there to do? It was wet, probably even starving to death, how long it had been lying out there, I did not know. Outside in the sky the moon was just about to dissolve. What was I doing raising his outside child at this stage in my life? I was ready now just to watch television with him in the evenings, listen to a radio play, go to my book club, drive to town every other month or so to see Septimus and Fiona, catch a performance at Little Theatre. What would I be doing now with this disgrace on my hands, at this time in my life?

With this last piece of news, his mother's hands finally come to rest in her lap, the rimpled mouth no longer moving and something like a curtain lifted from her face so she seems lighter to Winston who is sitting with her on the verandah taking the bitter cerosee tea that is supposed to be good for the heart.

It is early, around them the hills are still shrouded in mist and white light peers half-heartedly through the trees from the overcast sky. The hummingbirds are busy already at the banana trees, and the croaking lizards, who'd been asleep underneath leaves, scuttle out now to greet the morning, leaning up on their elbows and nodding at the blades of white light, and from the slit in their throats they stick out an orange-tongued hello.

He has been coming every morning now, since Marie Jose left, to take tea with his mother and to talk. She tells the same stories over and over again, about her red people in St. Ann, the ones in alms house, and those in lockup, those who left for America and those passed on from cancer and sugar diabetes and heart. This is the first time she's brought up Rosa and their father, and he can tell that it's been heavy on her chest, that she's told no one at all, that perhaps all this time she's been waiting for him to come so she could unburden herself. It is like the old days when he was a boy and she'd come to his room in tears and sit on the crumpled bedspread and he'd take her in his arms and rub circles on her back, and advise her how to handle his hardback father, which was preposterous of course, but there he was, eleven years old or was it fourteen, and there was his mother, like a little girl still, afraid to talk back to her husband, afraid to speak up for herself and her children, unable to control his comings and his goings, cowering before him still.

As long as he has known her, his mother has stumbled blindly though her life, and her decisions, as far as he could see, were led by her intense anger at her own mother, the disappointments meted out by her marriage, her unending quarrels with her red people over money and land, her unfulfilled longings which erupted now and again into fitful rages. She was not the kind of woman to look over at her life, to sit down and question her motives. When her intense emotions flung her into depression, she hurled herself into the sewing room at the back of the house and did not emerge again until the white, lace-wedding frock that had two yards of train running behind it was complete. During that time, she spoke to no one, ate in complete silence at the table, and walked distractedly around the house with the pins and the buttons propped between her lips. Nothing at all pondered or processed, everything stuffed away inside the frock she sewed. That was his mother when he left her and that is his mother in front of him now. He doesn't know what to think, what to feel towards his mother. But after all these years, he is glad to see her again though time has wrinkled and stooped her, and she is frail now, doing poorly in health and yet, it is still his mother, same person he left, same person he's come back to find, as if nothing at all happened, and perhaps he is the only one carrying around all this rancour, as nobody else seems to remember, nobody else seems to care, just him, and his hurt and his betrayal.

I knew that this was another test from The Almighty. His mother has started up again. You well know your father. He wasn't always a good man. How many times I had to borrow money from my people to bail out the bakery, to pay off people who threatened to cut him? How many times he disrespected me with his whoring and his gambling?

But God is not sleeping, you hear me, God ain't dead. Not long after the baby came, one day the stroke knocked him down and for weeks he could not move. One day the heart collapsed on him and he had to shut down the bakery. And then he turned, you hear me, he grew soft, he didn't always have to override you in everything. He wasn't busy or irritable or distant or exhausted or drunk or wild with the fight inside him, ready to beat down somebody. At night, when he lay down close to me, a fierce gentleness was charging out of him. He had stopped running. He was no longer frightened of my colour, or my money, or the hunger inside me. In the evenings now, he kept me company out there in the living room while I plunked out hymns on the organ. He sang in an off-key voice. He recited the psalms out loud to me. You don't know what it is to be waiting for a thing, to be waiting forty years for a thing, and then to finally have it.

She stops again, this time to look fiercely at Winston and then to stare with her face full of wonder at the hills beyond his head crowded with patches of sugarcane and the golden-eared corn and the broad-leaf cocoa. And then closer to his left ear, the pink cassia tree, her favourite, in flames.

Of course it makes him wonder. What does she think she finally has, a half-dead man rotting to death in a wheelchair, can barely walk, can barely talk, is that what she waited for, all these years, a half-dead man? He cannot bear to see his mother still making excuses for him, still protecting him at this late stage in her life. He has listened to this stupid song and dance too long.

But mother, he cries, who wouldn't be sweet to you if they brought in a baby for you to mind, who wouldn't be kind and gentle and loving. He is so tired of her apologies.

Could be, the mother says in a small voice, turning her head away slowly, as if she cannot bear to hear what he is saying to her. Could be.

But he was never a calculating man, she points out, her eyes beaming with a strange glitter. Your father was many things, but never calculating, she says. He was my first, she says proudly, and he rolls his eyes, so clear it is to him that she still isn't ready to hear, still doesn't want to know.

There I was, brown-skinned, university educated, and still with not a man to my name. I can't tell you the shame that brought my people in those days. There I was with my flesh turning tepid on me, untouched, she says to him. And the loneliness, she wails, like a shadow dogging me. It did not look good, a woman of my colour and station. All my sisters had already married, even Judith with the lame leg and frozen mouth, and all the cousins were coming round with babies. I fell for him the minute I laid eyes on him, for he had that kind of draw. He could dazzle you out of your last dollar, she smiles with glazed eyes, and out of every stitch of your clothes.

All these stories he knows by heart, all these stories she's told over and over, all these stories, he's come to see now, are there to justify to herself why she put up with it all, why year after year she stays. He imagines his mother in those days, tall and austere and proud in her brown skin and her degrees, and what a catch it must've have been for his father, who came with nothing at all, his mother has always said, not even good teeth in his head, could barely read and write. But he had a walk that had confidence written on it, and when he talked, people picked up their heads and listened.

Her parents weren't keen on the match, as he had neither name nor money, didn't even have a little colour, just the little scratch of rock in the country he called arable land, but they had to marry her off quick, for there she was sitting up in the house looking like priceless furniture, there she was turning ripe on them.

You've met the mother, Winston asks her finally.

His mother, jolted from wherever she has escaped to, fixes her eyes on him as if seeing him for the very first time that morning.

Which mother, she asks, touching her chest, the part where her heart is located, quickly, as if to soothe it.

Rosa's mother. The woman he picked up with. She doesn't come round to see Rosa?

Young, young girl you father picked up with, you hear me, thirteen years going on.

She stops to catch her breath and to sip from her mug and to swill the liquid in her mouth before swallowing.

Winston cannot meet his mother's face now, and he's not sure where exactly to put his eyes.

The girl was thirteen years, Mother?

His mother is quiet.

That means she wasn't much older than little Rosa inside there then.

His mother is still quiet.

That means he raped her then, Mother.

His mother looks at him with a start.

I mean, what can ever be consensual between a grey-assed man like that and a thirteen-year-old girl.

Your father is none of that, she barks at him; he is many things but none of that.

The girl was thirteen, Mother, same age as Althea when she died.

The girl was a whore, a prostitute.

Even so, he cries, even so. But how do you even know, he says. You don't even know where he goes, who he sees, you know absolutely nothing at all about his life. How do you stand it, he says, month after month, year after year. After everything he has done, he says through his teeth, where is your rage, he says, where is your moral code. Even the way he treated me as a boy, he says, all the lashes, all the blows, and you did nothing at all. Here he was destroying your first boy and you sat there, turning away your face, casting your eyes, so as not to see. I don't understand you, he says, shaking his head and muttering to himself. I don't understand you.

I sent you to the best schools, she said, you had the best teachers; how you think you passed exams to go to America? How you think you got to where you are now? I mortgaged the house,

I sold the land, and I went to my people for money to pay your fees at the private schools. I gave you everything, she says, you had food, you had clothes, you had money.

I didn't want school, he says, shouting at her now, I wanted protection, you hear me, I wanted to feel as if I mattered to you. I didn't want fucking school, he says, I wanted you to care.

Exactly like your father, she says, turning away from him with her entire body; full of rage just like him, just like him.

At that he backs down, and out there in the hills somewhere an owl calls with the voice of a woman and then he starts up again. I was your child, he says, much calmer now. Who else could I have turned to?

I did my best. She is fatigued suddenly and sweat springs out on her forehead. She fans with her hand and slurps noisily from the mug of cerosee tea. Christ knows, I did my best.

You used me as sacrifice, he says.

I loved you, she says stubbornly, and on her face it says, where did this dirty viper come from.

You have no idea what that is, he says. You only had eyes for him. Everything you did, you did it half-assed so you could get back to him.

You come back the very same way you left, his mother turns on him. Angry and bitter. America did not change you, she says. It froze you; it hardened you. Is a good thing you've come home, she says, to thaw.

And at that he says nothing else; what else is there to say? Perhaps she is right and Septimus too is right; he needs to relax into life, he is too uptight, too full of demands. What's gone is gone, can't change the past, can only make the best of what's in your hands. Right?

You have to understand life, his mother says, after the dust has settled and his heart too has settled back into its rightful place near his lungs, you have to understand love and sacrifice, she says, turning and sighing and laying her hands to rest in her lap and then picking them up again to study her nails. But time changes everything. Time is a good good friend, she tells Winston, her voice suddenly joyful again. Weeks pass, his mother says, months pass, she says, years, and now here it is, here we are, we can't imagine life without Rosa, we can't begin to imagine. For she is pure love, you see her there. Pure, pure love. Try as you might to harbour bad feelings, it is impossible, you hear me.

This silences him, for despite himself, despite what she is, he too has come to adore her. The rims of her eyes, the mouth still crusted with sleep, the long and skinny limbs; he can't pull himself away. On windy days they fly kites, and when it rains, they race paper boats in the gutters of running brown water. They dig up worms from the mud behind the house and use them as bait to catch fish in the river near the cemetery. He builds her a rope swing in an almond tree and pushes her into the sky; he shows her to hold the catapult, how to aim, let loose and shoot at the targets laying low on the highest branches of the Seville orange trees. Once, while putting her to nap one afternoon, while singing her a song in a soft voice, she began to cry for their father who is dying. He held her, unsure what to say, his own feelings for his father so troubled now. He'd come expecting it all to be quick so he could get back to his life, get back home, but there it is, everything stretching out longer, growing more complicated.

Sometimes the housekeeper wheels his father out into the kitchen to join him and his mother for breakfast. His mother, as if glad for the interruption, as if glad to be free of Winston, fusses over his father, as she does the little girl he made elsewhere with another woman and brought into their lives. Winston doesn't understand his mother. He doesn't know where she puts her rage, how she even sleeps through the night. His mother fixes all his father's favourite things and feeds him off her plate. She chews, then produces her offering. She wipes his leaking mouth. She kisses him often on his forehead. She whispers his name with her face glowing. Mass Sam, she says, over and over. Winston thinks she might even be in love with him all over again, this person who was once a man but has become a child now, dependent now, for this is what each illness has done, it has diminished him. It has brought the great man to a finish. Every morning he wakes, he does not know if this will be the end. The tumour is there, Dr. Anglin had confirmed, it is there and it is spreading. He might go to sleep and not see daybreak, it might be another stroke or the failed heart, but you father is a strong man, he has a will there that is unshakeable, unbreakable; never seen anything like that, Dr. Anglin says; he can will himself to step out of that wheel chair if he wants, and walk down the road, but all that said, it could still be quick.

Looks as if I wronged you, Winston. Looks as if I wronged you, didn't protect you. His mother is speaking again, she is not facing him, she is turning away, but she is speaking to him nonetheless, her voice low and clear, and the eyes behind her glasses big and red and dry. Looks as if I didn't protect you, she says, and I see how you could carry those feelings round with you, she says. I see how such a feeling could take set, take root and flourish. I see how those feelings could harden into hate. I sorry, she says, I sorry.

9.

At dawn, every morning now, he joins his mother on the verandah with only the smell of the coffee between them, coffee that
the housekeeper makes from scratch once a week – picking the
red berries from the low bush and laying them out on the
barbecue, so the sun can peel away the skin and the sticky meat,
then roasting the beans in the Dutch pot, turning them over and
over before beating them, grinding them, pouring hot water
through the cheesecloth full of pure coffee dust and sweetening
the brew with condensed milk. They sit in absolute silence,
Winston and his mother, in matching green chairs and they watch
the sun shimmy over the horizon, the changing hues of the sky.
Later on, when Rosa awakes, they will open the circle to receive
her, but for now it is simply the two, sitting in the dappled light,
listening to bird songs and identifying each call, watching the
bloated honeybees storm the centre of the yellow bells and
ostrich plumes in the garden. No matter how conflicted he feels,
he still can't stay away from his mother's voice, and the shape of
her lips stretched over her teeth and her hands moving quickly
over the tapestry in her mind, how she throws her head back and
the laughter gushes out her white throat and the gold in her
mouth glitters. He wakes every morning now to the kettle wailing
away in the kitchen and he leaps up at once, impossible now to
face the day without her. He, too, has been waiting all these years
for just this moment. He loves his mother. He adores her more
than he can even imagine and he spends these moments just
soaking up this bliss, basking in the pure glow of it, and turning
his face like a moth so he feels the full force of it, the great warmth
of it, on his chin, on his cheeks on his forehead and chest. As if he's

sipping from a deep well, it so satiates and calms him that by the time he calls Marie Jose later on for their daily check in, he's simply himself, solid and still.

1 0.

One morning he's sitting on the steps at the bottom of the verandah waiting for his mother to come when he feels a presence at his back. How long has his father been sitting there waiting, Winston has no idea, and his tongue comes out quickly to moisten his lips which have gone completely dry. He moves up the steps slowly toward his father, he moves up the steps one at a time. Three weeks now his father has not spoken a word to him, three weeks. He stares at the almond-shaped eye, muddy and dark and without light and then at the useless legs trapped in that chair.

Where to start now, the list of atrocities so long and wide, but he wants to put all that aside and meet his father. They have good doctors abroad, he hears himself saying, they have good ones near me there, maybe we could fly you up, so you get good treatment, maybe even cut out this cancer you have here.

From where inside this offer emerged, he has no idea. He clamps his mouth shut at once. His father blinks from the one good eye, his entire face twisted now into one of those smoothly carved and polished Benin masks. But elegant, nonetheless, in the crisp embroidered shirt the housekeeper dressed him in, the seams of his trousers jutting out over a pair of two-toned shoes. Winston has an exact pair of those two-toned shoes and on special occasions he wears them with a similar pair of silver suspenders his father has on now. To think all these years he did not come back because he was afraid of this man who only has weeks left of his entire life, who smells death everywhere he turns; every morning his eyes flutter open, there is death already descending.

When he first went to America, every night he dreamed of his father, no one else, just his father and him, a boy of four and five and six. Sometimes his father has him on his knee and he's teaching him a song, clap hand, clap hand, his father sings in a hoarse voice; or he's playing marbles with him, the two of them sprawled in the dirt, his father wearing a white cap; his father is teaching him to play dominos, reading the cards in his hand, play the six, Winston boy; his father is waiting at the bottom of a tree while he picks and throws down some jelly coconuts. But then he'd wake and he'd feel this hole, as there'd be no correlation at all between the dream and what he'd actually lived with his father. And for a while he thought well, maybe he just couldn't remember how it had been back then when he was a boy of three and four and five. For how could a man not love the very baby he had produced, not love his small toes, the brown gums in his mouth, the dimples on his bottom, how could a man take one look at his first born and hate everything about that child. Back then they lived with his grandparents still, and a horde of cousins, before his father opened the bakery and built the house they have now way out in the bush, not a neighbour to be seen for miles, adding on room after room as the bakery prospered. He didn't want any of his wife's people's money, or any of his wife's for that matter, even though she worked at a bank and drew good earnings, still he didn't want to hear behind his back that her red people had helped him to prosper, even though in truth they had put up the money for the bakery and up until now not a penny had been repaid.

He takes a low seat across from his father. No need to tower over him, he thinks. His father, after all, cannot beat him any more. To think all these years he couldn't come home because of this man sitting here, the moustache big still and arrogant. He sighs heavily. Around them the world has gone dead; he does not hear his mother shuffling through the house, he does not hear the housekeeper's mourning songs; there is no sound of the kettle's wild whistling. Did his mother arrange this, he wonders angrily?

He's offered his father all he can. He's given him a gift. It's up to his father now. But his father isn't saying a word, and he knows he can hear, he knows he hasn't gone deaf; he has a word for everybody except Winston. Sit and breathe, Winston. He hears Marie Jose in his head, as the panic starts to seep in and yet here is his father who has sought him out.

Before he left for America, prosperity had come and there had been the chain of his father's bakeries crisscrossing the island. They saw him mostly on weekends, definitely on Sundays for the big after-church dinner, when the table would be covered with stewed rabbit, curried goat, roasted pig, baked ham, black cake, cornmeal pone and the ginger bread his mother spent all morning with the cook, Mrs. Gladison, preparing. And there is his mother, fluttering around his father like a giant nightingale, her hands flying to her hair to touch the bun and back again to her dress, smoothing down the pleats, all the while pacing, and clucking, all the while trying to appease him, to calm him, as he is disgruntled again about the tough meat, the runny rice, this man who was supposed to do business with him, that man who was supposed to bring him a thing. Winston is sitting at the table across from Septimus and Althea, and he is watching the entire scene unfold as it unfolds every Sunday when his father comes home from his long week on the road. His father has not brought a gift for any of them, he does not have a smile ready for their mother, he is quarrelling with her, he is complaining, he is insulting her again in front of everyone, in front of Mrs. Gladison, the housekeeper, and his mother is swallowing her shame, and nodding like a lizard, the smile frozen on her mouth. Winston wants to put down his fist through his plate, and roar into the air. But the tongue in his mouth is like a dead log.

Life has truly humbled you, Winston says to him finally, quietly walking around the chair and inspecting his father inside it. Look at you, he cries, you can't walk, you can't talk, you can barely lift up your hand to strike. All these years you treated us as if we weren't precious, we weren't for you to love. And look at you now, if it weren't for the goodness of mother's heart you'd be sitting in your own shit, excuse my language, and eating it. Look at you.

Still, the old man is as solemn as a tree, and he shakes his head slowly, slides past his father's chair and slips away into his room, his fingers shaking at the latch.

Out the window is the tank which gathers all the water for drinking and bathing and washing and cooking, and beyond that the stretch of green where his sister is buried, and beyond that the

58

idly running river where he takes Rosa swimming late in the evening when the logy heat has dissolved. He makes out the headstone from the window even though there is a thin drizzle. He squints at the strange mineral eyes of a crow sitting on the headstone until he hears himself beginning to shout, shout, though there are no words, and he climbs slowly into bed, pulling up the thin pink sheets around him.

11.

Late into the night, when there is no light at all left in heaven, no moon, no stars, not even a single firefly, just an overarching wave of black, he leaps into the gloom, and at his heels hounding, a quiet desperation. He runs, his feet pressing on both sides of the earth, his hands flailing against the world until his skin begins to burn. Branches of the lignum vitae trees hook onto his shirt, and the twisted vines lay traps at his feet, and still he runs until he hears a rumbling on the road, hooves beating down the dirt, galloping toward him, oh God, oh God, he cries, as the hooves come tumbling down on him and a man wearing a cowboy hat cries *Excuse!* and rides through him on a horse with a white star branded on his forehead and immediately he has to piss; he almost wets himself, tearing the zip on his trousers as the piss gushes out steaming and rank, and his breath runs ragged in his ears. Around him now there's only the gently brooding black, hardly a sound. He tucks himself away and wipes his wet hands on the thighs of his trousers. His heart in his chest has slowed its screaming. But what the fuck was that, Jesus Christ, what the fuck was that. He stares into the night. But it is so black, there is absolutely nothing to see. Not one single solitary thing. Little by little his eyes grow accustomed. A mongoose, hungry and thin, slopes past on his way to Deacon Roache's chicken coop in search of young pullets. A pack of rats slows to observe him for a while and then turns left at a clearing. A toad hops over his shoes. Still he has no idea which direction now to turn. At first the trees look like soldiers, then like houses then like trees again. May as well lay here until daybreak he tells himself, sitting down at his feet and stretching out on the grass, the tough earth. Hopefully it won't rain. And the mosquitoes won't bite him to death. And all will be well till the morning and he can find his way again. All will be well. He dozes off, overcome with confusion until he hears footsteps again, and in his chest, the awful screaming again; he leaps to his feet again, and spins.

Winston is that you?

He is so relieved to hear his brother's voice, to see his brother; he grabs him hard and pulls him to his chest. Septy, he says weakly.

Everybody's out tonight, Septy laughs. Did you see the man on the horse.

Winston has nothing to say to that. They are standing in the middle of the road in the middle of the forest surrounded only by the listening trees and God knows who or what else.

Septimus lights a cigarette and hands it to his brother and lights another for himself and drags down deep on it and looks out at the night with wild eyes. They start to walk again. Winston cannot begin to imagine how his brother can find his way, but it's as if his feet have a mind of their own, and within seconds he's even able to pick out the pointed A-frame roof of the house. He had not wandered far after all.

Did you ever get my letters? Septimus says. I wrote you seven of them. He stops to light another cigarette and to inhale deep into his lungs and to exhale. I wrote them…

I still have them. Winston sighs into the night.

You still have them.

For years I read them and read them.

Then why didn't you reply; even a post card…?

And Winston cannot say why. His silence was his weapon and he was ruthless with it.

His brother says no more. They walk, the only sounds the steady heels on the grass and the smell of aftershave and the black of the night no longer a threat now that his brother is here. He is feeling sorry as hell now, sorry that he never replied to any of those letters. But he does not say that out loud, he says nothing at all.

Did Mama show you the will? Septimus asks, he left you land.

What, Winston says, for this piece of news is a stupid surprise to him. And then he hisses softly under his breath; what the hell was he going to do with his father's land.

He left you his gold watch chain; it was his father's.

He left you books, Septimus says. They were his brother's, the one who went to Panama to build the canal.

And Winston says nothing at all. He keeps abreast of his brother until they are at the verandah and then they climb up the steps slowly, and quietly enter the sleeping house.

12.

He calls Silas who's been watering his plants and feeding Ernest and sorting his mail. He's not spoken to Silas in weeks.

Everything all right? He means the three orchids and the cat Connie left behind which he hadn't had the heart to bring to the pound and of course Silas himself, and whoever he's dating now, and his two sons.

Everything's fine, Silas says, just cold as hell.

I think I made a mistake, he says to Silas. I think I should've come back sooner. I should've written. I think...

But you're there now, Silas says and you can repair so much.

I know, he says, I know. It's just that I feel so, I don't know. That place, I can't get there. Marie Jose has always said I'm frozen.

Women say a lot of things, especially when they don't get what they want. Don't start swallowing that now.

I know he says, I know. It's just that I can't get to my father, you know, there's a wall.

He imagines Silas nodding, the face like a boy's still, big and round and full of wonder, Silas who went home to Cape Town a year and a half ago to bury his father.

Can you touch him? Silas asks.

What? he says. This he cannot imagine.

You know, make contact. Sometimes when you can't find words, you put your hand on his shoulders, on his knees. That's what we did with my father when he was in the coma. We just touched him.

Winston says nothing. He cannot imagine himself in his father's arms at this late stage of life, or his father in his.

Anyway, just a thought, Silas says, Silas who is his age mate, but who feels like an uncle on most days. After they'd met, that first September freshman year at the foreign student reception in Watson Hall, the two of them turning thick right away, summer after summer he went home with Silas to South Africa, looking for a country and a people to claim him, because even then he'd already cut the ties to his own. He wrote his senior thesis on slavery, his dissertation on apartheid, and later on he published three books, *White Nationalism and the Rise of Apartheid in South Africa* which grew out of his dissertation; *Resistance Movements in South Africa* which gave him tenure; and *Truth and Reconciliation* which promoted him to full professor.

I just wanted to call, Silas. Wish you season's greetings, man, and your family back home as well, and Christopher and Marcus.

Merry Christmas, Winston.

13.

In the middle of the day when the sun is at its zenith, the light at its whitest, when there is no breeze at all stirring the world and all God's creatures have come to a complete full stop – the dog is fast asleep under the mango tree, its mouth bubbling with foam; the cat is curled up underneath the bed licking herself slowly and yawning; the birds have taken refuge down by the river; the rooster is too stunned to crow; the cows have fallen to their knees in the fields; the flies don't even bother to move out of the way of the swatter; the mosquitoes land on your arm and forget to sip – this is when they come to the willow trees at the bottom of the garden, his mother periodically dozing off and then picking up the conversation again, mid sentence, and Rosa, home early from school, is engaged in a deep and complicated conversation with one of her dolls, a cloth one named Stella. And he, too, is there resting on a bed of soft dried needles, trying to read.

You disappoint me, his mother says, closing her eyes again after staring into the middle distance for some time.

Winston raises himself on an elbow. He hates when he can't please her, when she criticizes him.

How do you mean, he says watching her large and soft lips, inhaling her smell of camphorated oil.

If he dies and you haven't made peace with him, then what, she says, then what?

He looks at her sharply, and then he looks away.

I did not send for you just to come and bury him, she says; I had a reason.

What the hell am I supposed to do, he says, what the hell?

You cannot hold on to anger all your blasted life, she says, it's like poison, it kills slowly. It brings on cancer, all manner of diseases, she says. Make an effort. We hire people to find you. It wasn't 'cause we wanted to see your face only, though this is nice, she says, it's good to see you. But if he dies there and....

Leave me alone, he snarls, rising up off the ground.

All right, she says. I wash my hands, you hear me. I wash my hands. She dozes off. Just so, she puts down her head again on her towel and starts to snore heavily.

There's a Graham Greene novel he's just started, but reading is out of the question now entirely. He puts down the book, and sits up slowly, massaging his neck, which is hurting like the dickens, as if he's cricked it. Jesus Christ, that's all he needs now. A mosquito sings lazily about his head and he strikes out wildly and in mid snore his mother stops suddenly to stare at him and then to pick up the great throttling again. Rosa has disappeared, he doesn't know where, but there is no sight of her. Just as well, he thinks, getting to his feet, unsteadily at first, for his gut is like a drum, hard and tight, but he finds his balance and he weaves his way up the short hill to the house. He enters the room where his father sleeps lightly under a white sheet. He sits on a chair where visitors one by one have sat. He could touch him he's thinking. He could get up right now and go over there and hold his father's hand. It's not as if the hand could shoot out and box him. The hand is probably hard and rusty now and cold and withered. Maybe tomorrow, he is thinking, maybe tomorrow he could hold his father's hand until it warms up and fills with life. In the end he steps in closer, and a sweep of peace descends on him. His father's face, smashed into the pillow, has no edges left, it is round like the moon and softly gleaming. Having never seen a thing such as this, nor felt a peace like this, he leans in even closer, so as not to wake him, and again he is struck by the same thought that had come to him earlier. Couldn't they in fact fly him to Boston to see a cancer specialist at Beth Israel, or one of the first class hospitals in the area. I mean it could be nothing at all. In two twos they could have him patched up and on his feet and walking again, in two twos. And he could have his father again, the two of them sitting out on the verandah and talking he knows not what about, but they could find things good and safe like politics, how the government just mashing up the country or they could talk about the land, or about his people who lived up in the hills.

Back inside the drawing room, he calls his brother at the funeral home. It's the day before Christmas and his mother and the housekeeper have strung coloured lights over the windows and doors that flicker on and off once it gets dark. There is a goat tied out back to be slaughtered for the big dinner and all the family who will come tomorrow to see their father. Mrs. Gladison has been busy at the stove making puddings and black cakes and stirring the bowls of rum punch.

You still working, he says to his brother.

A whole vanload just came in, his brother says, some kind of shoot out there in the city, gangs and things. He hisses his teeth. We make so much money out of people's misery, he says, it's no joke.

No Christmas for you then.

Christmas night we will come, he says. Me and Fiona and the kids.

Fiona is the second wife whom he likes.

I was thinking, Winston says, we could fly Pa down to Miami, it's not far, but at least he'd get good medical care, maybe they could even remove the tumour, have him on his feet again in two twos.

What's wrong with Anglin?

Nothing, Winston says, his voice failing him, nothing. I just thought, you know, they have good surgeons, they have…

No, his brother says, right here is good enough. All that flying now could shake up things, make it worse than it is. Let him stay right here so we can see him and he can see us. No way, sir.

14.

Christmas Day he hires a car and spends the day in the Blue Mountains with Rosa. For hours they walk and talk and eat the sandwiches the housekeeper prepared and, when fatigue lays them out, they nap in the tall grass, her head leaning against his chest, his nose buried in the coconut-oil smell of her hair. It is not as hot as it could be; overhead a light breeze blows, crickets and grasshoppers circle them for a while and then disappear; spotted turtles crawl out to bask in the maternal heat, and far off in the distance there are the muted cries of boys plunging into the long winding cleft of a river. He teaches her all the hand games he played with Althea and recites all the long poems he remembers from high school – Hamlet and Macbeth soliloquies – and the bible passages he used to recite by heart in Sunday school – The Sermon on the Mount, The Ten Commandments, the books of the bible. She recites everything back to him perfectly and this pleases him no end; he likes her mind, her inquisitiveness, her spirit; h   Perhaps his father has done well after all, keeping   see good things in his father, but here is one   to that. There comes a point when a man m   he, too, treated them badly, punish   He should've come earlier, he should've sent them a card, look his poor mother, wizened now, half blind; look at his brother all day long burying the dead over and over, look at…

Uncle Winston?

He turns to face her, glad for the interruption.

Can you tell me about Africa?

Africa, he says, thinking immediately of Silas's sisters, whom he must call tonight and wish Merry Christmas, and the house-keeper, Lothohonolo, whom he must call as well and send off the cheque for her children's schooling. He is so pleased with Rosa for asking, his face twitches with smiles. What it is about her that makes his heart glad, he does not know. Perhaps it is Althea he sees all over her face, in her teeth and her smile, the way she holds her back, the turn of her neck, Althea in her walk and in her talk. He pulls paper and pen from his backpack, draws a map of the continent, shows her the very tip of the horn where for years he's travelled and carried out his research. Then he takes her over to its western edge. All our ancestors came from here, he says, and he pencils in names for her to remember: Ghana, Ivory Coast, Mali. Drawing an even bigger world map for her now, he outlines the route the slave ships took, carrying their people from Africa to the Caribbean, to the Americas, to Europe. He draws a map of the United States, shows her the north east corner there on the Atlantic where he lives, tells her about the frigid winters, like living inside a freezer all day, he says, for months. And then he thinks of poor Marie Jose plodding through that snow everyday to work, shovelling out the drive so the car can move.

Can I come home with you to America?

Her wide brimmed hat is slightly too big; he can barely see her eyes, but he can feel them beaming on his face. You want to come and live in America with me, he says, slowly turning to look at the wilderness closing in on them and then at her face again, at Althea's face.

Grandpa is going to die and then it'll just b̶e̶
think they want me, she says. S̶o̶m̶e̶
Grandma is too old n̶o̶
know, sh̶e̶ s̶a̶y̶s̶

W̶h̶a̶t̶ t̶o̶ d̶o̶ n̶o̶w̶ w̶i̶t̶h̶ t̶h̶e̶ l̶o̶v̶e̶ b̶l̶o̶o̶m̶i̶n̶g̶ i̶n̶ his chest?

U̶p̶s̶t̶a̶i̶r̶s̶ o̶n̶ t̶h̶e̶ t̶h̶i̶r̶d̶ f̶l̶o̶o̶r̶ o̶f̶ t̶h̶e̶ rambling old house he b̶o̶u̶g̶h̶t̶ a̶ y̶e̶a̶r̶ a̶g̶o̶, t̶h̶e̶r̶e̶ are two little rooms with sloping down r̶o̶o̶f̶s̶. O̶n̶e̶ of them he painted a very tranquil green and offered to Marie Jose as a meditation room. Since then he's added a flat screen television, a treadmill and a set of weights he hardly uses and a punching bag. The room next door is still empty, except for the boxes of books he hasn't yet unpacked, framed prints he has yet to hang on the walls. He keeps an orchid at the window that puts out a bright pendulous spray of red-spotted yellow flowers every spring. That could be her room, he thinks, and then he smiles at the subtle and profound way things unfold.

Why not, he cries, throwing up his shoulders. Why not come and live with me, indeed. Isn't this what he's always wanted, family, children. And isn't this what has fallen into his lap now. Of course, he hadn't intended it quite like this and he has no idea whatsoever what any of this means, what it will entail, but why not, why the hell not. She's his sister. She's Althea through and through. And what could be better than that. What could possibly top that? And immediately he starts to plan, for there is the visa to be got, and the passport he must apply for, there is the permission he needs from his mother and his father, and the money he must scrape together for school fees.

There is only one thing, she cries, something in her voice sobering him at once.

What's that now?

Can you find my mother?

Her eyes are boring through his, and he drops his head and begins to nod slowly like a gecko, annoyed with her suddenly.

I don't feel she's far. They say she was sick. I want to see what she looks like, see if we resemble. I want to know her name.

Okay, he says tightly, though he has no earthly idea how that is going to happen, finding her mother, opening this damn fool hornet's nest, stirring up his father's shit now.

Grandpa said she was sick, she couldn't care for me. But I don't think she died; the old woman would've said something.

Rosa, he asks quietly, who's this old woman you talk about?

Oh, she says, a friend. And she smiles at him.

And it's a smile so beatific, he forgets completely about any mention of an old woman.

We'll look into this thing with your mother, he says to her smiling, though it's no real smile at all, just a very wide line drawn across his face. And then he grows very, very quiet.

1 5.

Boxing Day, all day, they've been playing dominoes with cousins who've come to visit his father, but now the cousins have left and Septimus is famished and they're in the kitchen and Winston's at the stove, frying plantains in a pan and in another pan, with strips of onion and crushed garlic and scotch bonnet already turning brown, Libby's bully beef. There's a pot of milk boiling, there's a loaf of hard dough bread he'll slice for their sandwiches. Beside him, Septimus is setting the table, putting out their plates and mugs, their forks and napkins. He has lit the wick on a lamp and switched off the overhead electric. The lamp puts out a moon glow.

He wants to ask Septimus about the mother, Rosa's mother, and he can see already how this will crush whatever closeness he's gained with his brother over the last few days. This is the white elephant their father brought in, sitting on top of them and no one wants to look at it. It is almost two in the morning, the entire house is breathing deeply around them, including Septimus's family, and even Rosa's green parakeet, Lambert, is fast asleep on one foot in her cage.

Rosa's been asking me about her mother, Sept, you know anything, you know the girl? He asks the questions as gently as possible, he knows this is not easy for Septimus who likes to pretend she is not his sister. He is never happy to see her when he comes to the house, he doesn't lift her in the air and swing her. He doesn't have a smile ready. He wants to pretend she doesn't exist.

All of a sudden, his brother does not look so good, his brother seems to have broken into a sweat, his brother is busy at the sink, rinsing out glasses, his brother does not respond.

71

I figure more than anyone, you'd know who he kept company with, where he took his rum in the evening, you'd know the girl.

And still his brother says nothing at all; he stands there, unblinking.

Just now the milk comes foaming out of the pot and bubbling on the burners and there is a loud hiss and a terrible smell. The beef, too, is beginning to burn and the yellow plantains are turning black.

They fill their plates and take a seat at the table. They eat slowly, quietly, just the clicking of forks on the plates, and the slurp of their lips on the rims of mugs. But now the hunger has gone, and in its place silence is bright and heavy between them.

Isn't that assault and battery, Sept, a girl so young? I mean what did her parents say, I mean that's how old Althea was before she died, no, thirteen or so.

His brother's face only hardens with what looks to Winston like hate, though he could be mistaken, for he looks, too, as if he could explode all over the room, stuffed as he is inside that white shirt. Winston decides to leave it at that; he's pushed enough, needled enough, but the injustice is what he's thinking, the utter injustice.

Four weeks their father has left now, according to Dr. Anglin. Four weeks. He is completely incontinent now, and his mind should be gone, but still he hangs on, speaking in complete sentences when he does speak, asking for things, ignoring Winston altogether at every encounter, the hostility coming from him even greater it feels. Winston, since their meeting, has shrunken even further away.

You left, his brother says finally, and for twenty-five years you didn't even call. Not even a letter. I wrote you seven. Jesus Christ, Winston, I missed you. It was like a hole – and he grabs his side – it was like something tore out a whole piece from here. And he points to his side and moans out deeply into the night. You come, he says, quieter now, but you didn't even come alone, you came with Marie Jose so we couldn't get close to you and now you pick up with the little girl, obsessed with the little girl this woman drop off, because she can't mind her child. What about me, he cries, what about me? I don't count? I don't matter? He lights a cigarette and smokes it down rapidly and then lights another one.

Look, Winston says, and he opens his mouth to speak, but only hot air shoots out. So he closes it down and then opens it again. Look. He touches his brother's muscle-bound arm and he holds him there, trying to find just the right words. Look, he says again, I didn't really forget. I mean, how could I forget? Late at night when I can't sleep, when I'm flooded with memories, how could I forget? But still, I didn't call, I didn't reach out. I didn't make the connection. And so how would you know, right? How would you know all those years that I was missing you too, right? He grows quiet. He feels awful.

Outside a car growls by and, even further away in the night, a cat moans. But besides that the house is in utter stillness. In a few hours it will be dawn and the world will be dappled with new light and life will again be in full swing.

I know this is sudden, he says, but Rosa asked me to take her with me to America and I said yes. So I will take her, he says, and I will raise her and I will send her to good schools, help her make something of her life. Mother is too old and when Papa goes, there'll be no one.

He sees his little house shuddering with her shrieks and her laughter. He sees her at play in the sand box at the left of the garden, though she might be too mature for that; he sees himself pushing her in the swing he'll attach to the cedar tree. He sees himself crouched on the ground outside, on the pavement where he parks his car, pitching marbles and playing jacks with her, teaching her to throw a baseball out on a nearby field full of soccer moms, teaching her how to hold a tennis racket for a perfect swing.

All the while his brother only stares into the dark window and sucks silently on a cigarette. Now and again he looks up from the darkness of the window and turns his head to study Winston's face and to study Winston's movements as he clears the table and washes the dishes, wipes down the stove and sweeps the red, polished floor, puts out the garbage and waters the crotons and hibiscus. All this time Septimus says nothing at all, he only watches Winston, silently sucking on his cigarette.

Finally, he says to his brother, she is not Althea, you know. She is not going to bring back Althea. This is now. NOW. And he spells it out in a voice loud and precise, as if he's saying it for himself too, as if he, too, needs to hear this. She can stay here, keep mother's company; the housekeeper can raise her, and I am here. Why you want to take her? Why? Septimus cries.

I've always wanted a child and here's a child nobody wants. I mean, do you want her, Sept? Are you going to sit up with her and help her with spellings? You going make sure she's safe, no old man will rape her off? Mother is there – she can barely walk, her ankles so swollen, she can barely see. I mean who's going to care for her. All of you sit down there pretending she's not growing up, pretending she's not somebody too, all of you sit down there fucking pretending. That selfish bastard brought her here and now he's about to die and leave her, and who will be there now to take care of her, he cries, who?

He switches off the lights and blows out the lamp leaving his brother there in the dark, just the smoke swirling out into the room, and the tip of the cigarette brightening and then dulling. He is exhausted to the bone. He is scared as hell, scared and yet, strangely invigorated, strangely calm.

16.

The next evening, he tells Marie Jose.

Are you sure, she says, slowly, carefully, and with all kinds of question marks and exclamation points in her voice.

And he takes that to mean that she is not sure, she's not ready, this is his project alone. I'll never be ready, he says, I just have to take the plunge.

Will she come back with you?

Yes, he says; Septy is looking into her papers. It will bring me closer to everybody, he says, though how true this is is highly questionable.

It's a strange idea even to him, it's quick and he wishes somehow that she could be more a part of it. I've always wanted to make a family with you, he says, careful in his tone not to push or to pressure. Maybe you can be a godmother or some such. Play as big or as small a role as you'd like.

There is no response for a while. He hears chanting on a CD in the background. He hears Enid barking, demanding a cookie before bed. He hears the flat silence on the phone.

Finally she says, this is a big leap, Winston.

I've always wanted this, he says, the iron seeping into his voice.

And this is not a stand in, this isn't some way to punish your father, fight him, take away something he loves, something that belongs to him?

She is my sister, he says firmly. Outside his window, there is only the long unrelenting night. Inside, on his dresser, the clock ticks away steadily.

It feels rushed to me, she says.

She is my sister, he says, my half sister. I'm asking you to help me with her, but only if you want. No demands.

Yes, she says, but you're asking me to move closer, make a larger commitment when things between us... I don't know, she says.

We haven't even been connecting she says; you don't know what's going on in my life. When last did you inquire about me? When last have you said, okay, enough about Winston and his father and his half-sister, how is Marie Jose? When last did you inquire? And now you want me to take on your crazy ideas.

Nobody wants her, he says.

She is quiet.

Why don't you wait, she says slowly, why be impulsive? Why don't you wait and see how you feel in a few days, a few weeks?

I cannot wait, he says. I've waited long enough. This is for me now, he says.

She says nothing more. He waits. He begins to suffer. For a second he wonders, what is the rush, what has overcome him, what is it?

Do what you want, she says. It seems you're going to anyway, so why ask me, right. Why call me at 11 o' clock at night when you've already decided.

I need you, he says.

Oh Winston, I'm so damn tired of your needs.

17.

The night is not good.

He goes to his father's room. The lamp by the side of the bed is turned down low and he hears the ragged breathing in the dark, almost as if he's choking. He's covered under a white sheet. Underneath the sheet he is naked, and there's a diaper tied to him. Winston sits on the chair at the foot of the bed. He watches the steady rise and fall of the sheet. He hears the crickets outside, the wind moving through the trees. He hears the dogs. Somewhere a rooster is already making his morning call. He begins to talk to him. Can his father even hear on top of all that racket in his chest?

I am taking Rosa, he calls out into the room in a small voice. He was just starting to soften, but now he has grown wooden again. I am taking Rosa back to Boston to live with me, he says. There is a radio next to the lamp and on top of the radio, a bible, the cardboard covers gone. The window on the other side of the room is half-open. The curtain moves slowly, at the same speed as the slow moving overhead fan that stirs the warm air. I don't know anything about parenting, he says, but I am going to learn. I want to be the kind of parent she can look back on years from now and still respect, still want to spend time with. Still love. This last part comes out a croak. He stops. His father has gone deathly still. In the near dark he has to strain his eyes to see if the sheet is indeed moving. He hears his mother's house slippers sweeping the floor and he is relieved to see her shadow in the doorframe.

Stop fatiguing him, she says, waving him out the room.

Then she turns to his father and puts the back of her hand at his throat. Sam, love, she calls gently, and the crackly breathing starts up again.

18.

With you, there's always something, she says.

He doesn't answer. He sits out on the verandah in the dark, the phone cradled by his ear. Inside the bowels of the house, he hears his father's deep moaning.

I mean it's not enough for you to just go home and be with your father who is dying. There has to be a big drama. First there is your hate, and then you fight your brother. And as if that's not enough, now there's a child. I mean, don't you want to breathe a little? You're just spinning and spinning out of control and wrecking everything in your way? Why, she says.

She's my sister, he says.

But can't you wait, she says. What's the big hurry? I've just come out in the clear with this illness.

If not now, then when?

What is the rush, Winston? Don't you want time to just be with me? Don't you want time just to be?

I've lost one child already, he says.

And you think Rosa will replace him, Rosa is the answer?

I don't have anything, he says. You have your healing and your prayer circle and your crystals and your conings. You have your family there in Spain, and your stepchildren if you want them.

And so Rosa is going to help you fill the hole in your gut, she says.

When you got sick, he says, we weren't ready. But there it was, we had to face it. I know you're not ready yet for another child to raise, but if not now, then when? Give me a chance.

I did not choose my illness, Winston.

I didn't come here intending to choose a child. I came to bury my father and to get home as soon as I could back to you, back to our life. A child was the last thing on my mind when I came down here, he says. But here she is. This is what I asked for in that coning of yours, he says, those conings you go on and on about. They sent me Rosa, he says, they sent her to me.

Oh, please, she says and hangs up.

19.

You are going to take her then, his mother says to him on the verandah as they take tea and crumpets lathered with home-made guava jelly.

Yes, he says. There are good schools near me. And I have her room ready.

You're going to need money, she says. I'll sell off more of the land in Katie so you can pay her fees.

He nods. His mother has always been good at the practical application. Not much else.

You won't miss her, he asks.

Of course, I'll miss her. But I'm old now. Can't run around after a child. The eyes don't see well, even with the operation. She needs someone robust. There is the housekeeper, Mrs. Gladison, but even she is getting hard of hearing. I have to find money now to buy her hearing aids, and her granddaughter there, the last one, is starting big school September; I am going to have to find money for her fees. It never ends, she says, it never ends. Then she is quiet.

And he thinks she, too, can't wait to get rid of Rosa, can't wait to get this shame off her hands.

He tries again. You think she'll be able to handle it, he asks, moving to a new place, leaving all she knows behind?

His mother bursts into noisy laughter that disturbs him and then just as suddenly she stops and wipes her face with the tail of her house-dress. The house-dress is embroidered with little purple flowers and it has a scoop neck.

Rosa's stronger than you and me put together. I wouldn't worry so. Of course, the first few days she'll miss us, but young children are hardy. In no time she adjusts. Mark my words.

I didn't adjust so quickly, he says.

She looks across at him quickly as if to say, and whose damn fault is that you didn't adjust in America. You were so blasted selfish, punishing us with your big hate. Whose damn fault is that? She turns away.

Rosa is hardy, she says. Bring her back once or twice a year. Show her how to write letters. She can write me or Septimus or her friends at the infant school. She can call once a month collect.

She makes as if to get up. She wants an end to the conversation, he can see that. She does not want to hear about his loss. And he does not stop her. He cannot blame her. He makes as if to get up himself and she leaves.

20.

He calls Silas. He wants to get her into the Quaker school where Silas already enrols his two sons, sits on the board and has some clout.

And Marie Jose, Silas says after a long pause, does she want this, Winston?

This is a recipe for complete destruction. You know that right. Because this is not play, Winston. Take it from me, your life is over, your writing life, your sex life, your leisure life – forget it. Your bank account, finish.

Come on, Silas. Your life isn't over.

I share them with their mother. But Marie Jose doesn't want to raise any more children, which means you're alone, brother. I can baby-sit now and again, but you're alone. ALONE.

I want you to support me on this, Silas. Plus, she'll come around. Marie Jose will come around. She loves me. He really can't believe he's saying this.

I can't believe you're saying this shit. Love doesn't work that way, friend. You should know that by now.

I do know. It's just that... I shouldn't have said that. He sighs loudly.

I want you to support me on this, Silas. This means a lot to me.

Okay. Okay, Silas says. I'll look into the school. It ain't cheap. I can tell you that. That little Quaker school ain't cheap. I'll help you out for the first six months, but after that you're on your own. You hear me brother, on your own.

Silas, I can't thank you enough, man.

It's all right, brother. It's all right.

21.

In the blinding sun, he walks the half-mile to meet her at school. Usually she takes the taxi home, but today he's made arrangements with the driver. He's careful around the big bend; he walks on the banking, listening out for cars. He walks on the shady side of the street, careful not to step into the stinking water in the gutters. The sun is harsh and bright; it beats down on him and scorches up the grass. A dog with only three legs limps by; another one with its teats reddened and distended stops to sniff the legs of his trousers and slopes away. A cat in a doorway looks at him and yawns with tremendous boredom. They've paved the road; Miss Blossom's house is long gone, just rows and rows of potato slips now.

She's waiting at the doorway where she usually waits for the car and for a second he begins to doubt. I mean what the hell is he getting into, he knows absolutely nothing about raising a child, absolutely nothing, and poor Marie Jose, what is he doing to his relationship. He straightens the collar of his short-sleeve shirt nervously; he clears his throat which is full of phlegm; he runs his hand over his head which is damp with sweat.

I thought we could walk, he says.

In this heat?

He looks at her face covered in a scowl and he looks upward at the sun. We'll have a drink first, he says, and he takes her bag and helps her with her hat. He pictures Althea in her green tunic with the stand-up collar. They walk quickly to a nearby bar.

At Cappy's they sit out on one of the benches in the mangrove shade. We'll carry on once the eye of the sun shifts, he says, sipping a bottle of cold beer and studying her.

She wears a green-checkered tunic and a white blouse with a big sailor collar. She has the hair scraped into a bun today. Unlike his sister, Althea, she is quiet and solemn and neat.

Grandpa has eleven more days, she says between licks on her Popsicle.

He doesn't ask her how she knows this. A taxi flies by stirring up the red dust, which settles down again quietly on their skin. He gulps down the entire bottle of beer and burps noisily. In the distance, there is the sound of a truck switching gears as it groans over a hill.

You'll come with me when he goes, he says after a long sigh. Septy is helping out with your immigration papers, he says; he has a friend.

She does not say yeah or nay. Instead, she turns to him; you sure? she says. Her face is light and clear.

You'll settle in quickly, he says brushing away her question, took me years and years, but it'll be quick with you. You're young, he says, resilient. He is talking like a machine, why is he talking like a machine? Why is he rushing everything, what is he trying to stave off? What is underneath all of this?

A thrush sings in a tree. A dry wind picks up, rustles the leaves and dies back down. Deep in the wide flat fields, a cow lows.

Marie Jose isn't young and resilient, she says.

What, he says, irritable now, for he does not know what to think about Marie Jose.

Her tongue is purple, the Popsicle almost done and the sun has shifted, the shade has moved. The dried sweat at her temples leaves trails of salt.

We should go, she says. Friday. Fried fish and bammy, my favourite.

A morning dove watches them from a wrought-iron fence.

Are you a good cook? she asks when they're shambling down the narrow road again, and the wide-brimmed straw hat is fitted back on her head and the satchel latched to her back and her hand finally grasps his. A schoolgirl waiting at the corner for the bus with a blue vinyl folder in the crux of her arm eyes him brazenly and he winks.

Fair to fine, he says. You won't starve, that's for sure, and you may even put on weight. He points to her skinny legs ashen in the empty street. Like Mrs. Gladison, he says – the housekeeper who is short and rotund.

She cackles with glee. Very funny, she says.

22.

His father has taken a turn for the worse. Fever and vomiting and bloody diarrhoea and cold sweats. It is a strange thing to see his father frail and poorly like this, and like a child weeping. The entire house comes to a standstill. The hour hand on the clock does not move. The DJ on the radio plays the same sad songs. His mother at his bedside reads verses from Isaiah, Luke and Revelation. In the house, there is no peace whatsoever. There is a steady stream of visitors they must offer a taste of rum; the phone rings incessantly, and what is there new to report: he called for a glass of lemonade this morning instead of plain water. His breathing took on a fierce ragged tone for a good three minutes and then it went back to normal. He wants us to remove all pieces of clothing from his body, even his drawers, every striking thing except his socks. Leave the sock, he commands in a weak voice. Those he wants pulled up to the middle of his calves. This afternoon he woke from his nap and called out for Selvin White who's been dead now six years. Two days now, going on three, and not a drop of food has touched his lips.

23.

According to Septimus, the bar belonged to the old woman whom their father had known for years and a place he frequented just about every evening. But after the episode with the girl, the old woman, the girl's grandmother, had barred him from coming. You can't miss it, Septimus had said, it's near Chin's Patty Shop and it has a green awning out front.

At about five, he takes Rosa's hand and they climb slowly up the narrow stairs littered with empty peanut shells and plastic wrappers and cigarette butts and emanating from the dark corners the smell of stale beer and urine. He imagines her dusting off shelves, polishing bottles, rinsing out glasses, arranging ashtrays, laying out change for the evening's operation. All of this she's done so many times, her hands move of their own will, picking up a rag, putting down the broom, twisting the cap on a bottle of rum, filling up the ice trays.

She doesn't look up when they enter. There are bottles lined up neatly on the counter and she's pouring brandy and rum into flasks. He heads over to the jukebox, relieved that there's one, that there's something to do.

He has said nothing to Rosa, he doesn't know how yet or even if he should. He's been praying, never a thing he does, but he wants to do this just right, he wants it to be perfect.

Read the sign, the barmaid calls out in an impatient voice. Something's wrong with it. The man's coming just now to fix it.

He's not planned any of this. He goes over to the counter. Rosa, confused, is almost stepping on top of him.

Children not allowed in here, she says, plus it's early. The bar's not open until six.

We're thirsty, he says. Isn't that so, Rosa?

We're not open until six, she says, staring at him and staring at Rosa and the outrage is all over her face. She's still a child he thinks, looking at the round cheeks, the unlined face covered in paint. The red fleshy lips. A child with a woman's face painted on her head.

Perhaps you could give us water, he says.

Come on, Winston. Rosa tugs at his hand.

Plenty places across the street for you to get water.

Water is free, he says. You must can give us a drop. He is annoyed. Even he could be her father, he is thinking. Even he! He shoves his hand nervously through what little hair he has left. He twists the ends of the moustache he's taken to wearing now, which makes him look morose.

You want me to call police. She moves towards the phone.

Winston, I'm not thirsty. Rosa behind him, the voice of reason.

Thank you, he says to her; his voice is hard. Thank you for your hospitality. He gets up off the stool.

She slams the door behind them and locks it.

They drive home quietly. He can feel all of Rosa's questions pointing at him and he says nothing to quell the confusion.

Two days later, at five past six, they are back there again. He's found a space right out front, next to Chin's Patty Shop. It's been raining nonstop all day and the sky is low and grey, the air thick, and he grabs Rosa and they run for cover inside the building, their shoes clattering up the dark dirty steps. He still does not have a real plan. He thinks that if he just springs the news on the girl, as Septimus suggested, she'll just run. She'll just shut the door. He wants to wear her down, wear down her defences until she really sees them. He's told Rosa nothing, he still can't find the right words yet, and he doesn't want to disappoint her, and as if she too understands all of this, she voices no questions, which he has to admit is unusual. These days now, he's taken her out of school, and they've been driving back and forth to town in order to pick up passport and visa and whatever other travel documents are needed. He's been trying to do everything as quickly as possible. The lines have been notoriously long and the service slow. But she has a good attitude, Rosa, and all this helps.

The barmaid is alone; she's wiping the floor with a mop. He sops his face, and Rosa's, with a white handkerchief. At the counter he orders beer for himself and a cola for Rosa. There is no expression on her face as she serves them. As Rosa is almost nine, he puts her age now to be around twenty-three, twenty-four. He cannot even begin to imagine what it's like to make love to someone who's fourteen; someone who is not even inside her own body yet. He remembers himself at sixteen, his face full of pimples, his limbs long and slim and with a mind of their own, and his cock raising its head at the slightest provocation. Her face says she's fed up already with life.

Is the jukebox working now? he asks her, filling his hand with nuts from a bowl she places on the counter.

You see a sign on it saying otherwise? She looks at him.

He's encouraged by a smile beating around her mouth. Her tone, too, is different. I don't think you like me very much, he says.

She kisses her teeth and smiles openly this time and in that instant he sees Rosa all over her face.

Rosa, he calls from the machine. What would you like to hear?

He studies the songs, puts coins in the slot, wanders back to the counter, and nibbles at his beer. What about you, he says to the barmaid who is wearing a short low-cut backless orange dress that shows the cleavage of her breasts and her muscular thighs. What would you like to hear?

My desires don't concern you, she says; play what you want.

She carries a self-satisfied confidence about her. Saucy. This is the word that comes to mind. Rosa, he says, do you think this lady likes me?

At the counter, Rosa sucks on a bottle of cola, the stillness about her almost deafening as her entire body studies and listens and assesses everything that's going on in the bar.

A couple hanging over each other comes in, a couple the barmaid knows, and for a while she is busy with them, laughing and talking and mixing their drinks and he notices Rosa's eyes on her face and her movements and her gestures and sighs.

When he gets the barmaid's attention again, he orders another beer and cola.

This is the last one, she says, opening his beer and setting it before him with a glass. Then you leave with the child. People come, they curse, sometimes fights break out. It's not safe. Plus, that cola is pure sugar. It will only drop out her teeth. She pours a glass of tomato juice for Rosa who is already knitting up her face.

Okay, he says, I'll bring her home and come back on my own.

She does not respond, she's over at the till, working out change for the evening's transactions.

She's attractive, he decides, with her big expressive eyes like Rosa's, the light beaming out of her face when she half laughs.

You from America, she says; I've people in Brooklyn and in Miami.

My father is sick, he says; that's why am here.

He is going to die, Rosa says. He has only days. And it's going to be bad.

He pulls Rosa over to him. Rosa is my niece, he tells the barmaid, the word niece like sharp shards in his mouth.

The barmaid looks at him. Then she looks at Rosa. I'm sorry to hear your father is dying.

He sighs. All great things must come to an end, he says.

Who is your father, she says, maybe I know him. This is a small place.

He looks at her with a stiffened mouth and then he stares into his beer. Beside him Rosa has stopped breathing.

Suddenly a gang of men enters the bar and she is busy again, mixing drinks, digging ice with a pick, talking into the phone, which has just now rung.

Relieved, he puts money on the table and heads out into the soft warm rain.

According to Septimus, their father went there every evening for a drink after he locked the bakery. He'd seen the girl grow up, he'd seen her put on hips and fill out her frocks and seen the nipples rise underneath the midriff blouses. He never saw his own daughter grow up. His own daughter died at thirteen. One afternoon, she ran across the road not thinking, not thinking, and just so, a goods truck flattened her, crushed the body to pulp. When the grandmother left the girl to run the bar and the girl handed him his change he would hold on to her fingers with his big hands.

You behaving yourself? he would ask, with the lopsided mouth. How is school; you passing your subjects? You staying away from these worthless boys out here who just want to put a baby in your belly? He tilts his head back and laughs.

She loved him. She has known him for as long as she has known her grandmother. And the old woman knew his family; she remembers his brother who went away to Panama and never came back and, out of affection, twice a week, he drops off a loaf of sliced bread, a bag of donkey's jaw bones, a bag of sugar buns for the old woman. The old woman calls him Sam-Sam, and if she needs a lift to the hospital or to the bank, if she's having trouble with a creditor, she calls Sam-Sam. Sometimes, on a Sunday evening he'd go over there, after the big Sunday meal at his own house with his own family, he'd go over and spend time with the old woman, who knew his brother Harold, and her granddaughter and he'd sip a glass of sorrel laced with rum while the old woman pours out her sorrows and the little girl suffers over her multiplication tables.

Hello, Rosa, she says, when they go in again, two days later.

Hello, Rosa says, a little darkly. She is tired, he can see that. Poor Rosa is tired. He has continued to say nothing and she, too, has refused to ask. It is an unspoken acknowledgment between them and it feels like today it might come to an end.

The mother is wearing a black linen dress with a scoop neck. Very tasteful he thinks. Her hair is done up in some kind of attractive twist, her eyes are ringed with kohl and her lips are large and red. Had she been expecting them, he wonders.

What's your name? Winston asks her. He has never been attracted to young women. He likes them older, mature. He wants an equal, someone with whom he can always have a conversation.

Bev, she says, Beverly Johnson.

I am Winston, he says, Winston Rowe. My father is Samuel Rowe. And this is Rosa, my father's last daughter.

At that moment, the world comes to a standstill.

The barmaid looks at him, as if truly seeing him now, and then she looks at Rosa. Rosa's face is as blank as a slate. Suddenly the barmaid is at the other end of the counter wiping it down and then she is at the sink, rinsing glasses, unable to meet his eyes. Inside the bar, it's suddenly quiet. And he thinks how odd it is that she's never wanted to see Rosa, she's never wanted to know how her daughter fared in life. Here she was with this appendage on her stomach all those months and the minute it was born, she only wanted to erase it. And then he thinks how he too had attempted to erase his own family all those years until they tracked him down. Look how difficult it is, he is thinking. He feels terrible for the first time since he's been coming here to see the girl, to interfere in her life, to put things before her, force her to look at them before she's ready. Not to mention what he's done to Rosa, but he so hates the God-awful lies and the cocoon in which they've shrouded themselves.

He orders the usual, a beer for himself, a cola for Rosa. Would you like a drink, he asks her, heading to the jukebox. His entire body feels a great weight of exhaustion.

No, she says with a steady voice, pouring tomato juice in a glass for Rosa. No thank you.

Her pronunciation this evening is precise and there's no joy at all now in her voice.

Why you keep coming in here? she asks, after he's sitting again at the bar. What you looking for?

He looks at Rosa who's studying them, her head suddenly large and bright to him now as if it's glowing.

You here to cause trouble, she says, you here to stir up something.

He tries to laugh, to play it off, but his face does not move. Inside his shirt, his stomach, too, has turned to lead.

I want to go home, Winston. Rosa hops off her stool.

Okay. Okay. He searches in his pockets for his wallet. He smiles at Beverly but she is not smiling and the customers are starting to trickle in.

If you're trying to start something, she says. Her eyes are like coals.

No, no, he says, taking Rosa's hand. None of that at all.

Outside, where it's still pissing down rain, he feels eyes on him and he looks up at the building he's just left. He can't tell out of which window the eyes are staring him down. Paint flakes off the crumbling walls and all around him there is the smell of urine. His hands are shaking when he gets in next to Rosa and starts the car. The wipers begin to move.

Oh, well, Rosa says, wedged into the door of the car, staring down the afternoon with her thumb jammed into her mouth, what's done is done.

He takes her other hand that's been balled into a hard little fist and squeezes it.

It's okay, she says in a tight voice, what's done is done. We should come back tomorrow and tell her everything. Tomorrow is another day.

Yes, he says, pulling her into his chest and holding her head against his heart and cradling her back with his hands. He rocks her for some time, before he slowly puts the car in gear and moves away from the curb. Tomorrow we'll straighten out things, he says, looking into the sky at the rain which is tearing down harder and will probably flood out some of the dirt roads making it impossible to pass. Tomorrow, he says again, squeezing the hand balled up into a fist in his.

It's after midnight. His father is driving home from a function and he sees that there is light beaming out of the bar, which means it's still open. His father stops the car out front and inside there's nobody at all on the stools. She's locking up, putting out the lights, emptying the till, washing out the last few glasses, straightening out the bottles on the counters, filling up the ice trays with water.

You alone? he asks.

Yes, she says, without even turning. She knows his voice. He is like a father to her. Where is her father? Who's to tell? For that is how it often is around here with these men. Her mother is in the capital trying to make ends meet. Every few months she sends an envelope with money, a box with clothes.

I will drop you home, he says.

And it's nothing. Nothing at all. It's not the first time he's given her a lift home. It's not the first time he's stopped by the shop on his way home and she's the only one there locking up. She doesn't always like what she feels when he looks at her sometimes; it feels dangerous, but he's the closest thing she's known to a father and she loves him.

He's just come back from a function in Auchtembeddie. He is dressed in a nicely starched and pressed long-sleeve shirt, turned up at the cuffs and his trousers, too, are nicely starched and pressed. His hat, like the clothes and the shoes, is white. There's a red feather in the band. Her back still turned to him, she reaches up to turn off a switch; he sees the dress riding up her hips, he sees the strong thighs, the strong calves, the firm round bottom. He swallows. A knot springs up at the base of his gut and he shoves his hands in his pocket and jiggles the coins there. He takes them out again. He walks up to the girl and puts his hands on the girl's bottom, puts his mouth on the girl's neck, which is warm in the night, and on the girl's cheeks when she turns around, on the girl's throat which has the scent of rosewater. He does not meet the girl's eyes, which are like new coppers in the night, he cannot meet the girl's eyes. Instead, he leans her against the counter, lifts the green dress. And in his chest, there's just the old heart battering away steady and sure, and the old lungs wheezing out as much air as they can muster.

The whole thing finishes in minutes.

In the car, she is quiet. He takes her hand and she pulls it away. He takes it again and it just lies there limp in his lap and damp. She is stuck to the door, her eyes far far away. There is a sadness in the car that overwhelms even him, and he's a man who absolutely cannot bear to be anywhere near that emotion.

Is nothing, he says gently, is nothing. He pats her leg next to his; it is like stone. He pats it over and over again. Impossible to think now of the future ahead or of his past with the girl, of all the things he has meant to her. I have deep feelings for you, he says in a hoarse voice, you must did know that. You're so pretty, he says.

She says nothing. For what can she say? She is twelve, maybe fourteen. She has her whole bright future ahead. She has her whole bright future.

Is nothing, he says again, into the gloom. Don't let it trouble you, okay, don't let it trouble you.

All morning long, she follows him up and down, through the house, outside in the yard where he feeds the chickens, at the bottom of the garden when he goes to calm himself under the willow trees. Rosa he cries, wrapping her in his big arms. Over and over again, he tells her all will be well, over and over, he tells her, he loves her, and that he'll take only the very best care of her. But her face has nothing to say to that, her face is a closed door, as if the Rosa he knows and loves has disappeared, has gone inside somewhere to rest. He looks at the eyes staring out at him like marbles and he wonders if she believes him.

He has already described for her the room waiting on the third floor, the skylight in the sloped ceiling so she'll see the stars at night and the windows looking out into the trees full of blue jays and cardinals and squirrels. He has been living there over a year, he tells her, and so much is still to be done, a garden to put in when Spring comes, he says, carpets he has to pull up so he can get at the polished pines underneath. It was a fixer-upper, an old Victorian farm house with a barn in the back that looks out onto a field full of milkweed that comes up to his waist in the summer, a barn he'd like to one day turn into a studio.

She's not impressed with this talk of his house. She sits on a warm, flat stone in her bathing suit, their clothes in a nearby heap, thinking and chewing a long blade of grass and studying him, though he gets the feeling, lying there beside her in his trunks, that she's not really seeing him, she's looking off him for something else, some other means of communication she can read more clearly, not his voice, not the things shooting out of his mouth, but some other truth that she alone can perceive, that she's come to rely on more than words.

Look, he says, I probably should've waited until you were much older. I just hated the lies and the deceit, he says, I just wanted the truth once and for all, I just wanted freedom for all of us.

At the counter, Beverly is thumbing through a ledger of accounts.

She puts it away when they enter. He orders a beer for himself and a tin of apple juice for Rosa. He's not rehearsed a script. He sets Rosa next to him on a stool.

That life is behind me now, she says, looking at him.

I understand that, he says. But she'd like to know you. I'm taking her to America. I don't know when I'll...

That life is behind me now, she says again, her voice tilting.

Yes, he says, but she's here now, she wants to meet her mother.

She turns away from his face. She looks at Rosa. She looks not much older than Rosa does. Something awful appears in her face. Hi, she says to Rosa in a tiny voice.

Hi, Rosa says in a voice, deep and flat.

She lifts the trap door and comes around to where they are seated. And with eyes that can see deep into the future, and way way back, Rosa regards her. Beverly regards her too. Just as intense. As if the two are sizing up one another, or maybe just talking in their own special way. He touches his face and feels that it is wet. He wants to protect them both, these two children, he wants to hold them both.

I would like to be your friend, Beverly says to her. It's too late now to be your mother. Maybe I could be your big sister, she says, or your auntie.

You could be my godmother, Rosa says, in a voice that sounds as if she's been rehearsing this all her life.

Yes, Beverly says, I could be your godmother. She takes Rosa's hand and she pulls her off the stool and holds her against her waist and Rosa's face is buried in her yellow dress nipped at the waist and they remain like that until the first customer comes in.

24.

That night after his father dropped her off, did she go right inside the house she shared with her grandmother, or did she stay outside for a while, long after the car drove off and she could no longer see the tail-lights or hear the rumble of the engine over the hills? Did she stay out there in the dark listening to the insects shrieking near her ears, her body in knots, her body in confusion, her mind, her mind, what to do with her mind? And did the old woman finally open the door and call her in, Bev, that you out there in the dark, dark night?

Yes Mam.

Uncle Sam drop you off, I heard a car.

Yes Mam.

Everything all right down there at the shop.

Yes Mam.

Somebody trouble you, Bev? The old woman is no fool to the world, the old woman could hear her voice smashed in the night, she could see that something was not right in her granddaughter's face, in her granddaughter's gait, even under the pale skin of the moon.

Somebody trouble you? the old woman asks again, tempering her own hysteria, for she knows a girl child is never safe in the world, never safe, no matter how you protect them and shield them from life. The old woman turns up the wick on the oil lamp, she brings it closer to the girl's face and she can see that indeed, it is her granddaughter standing up there before her, standing there tall and straight like her mother in Kingston, with the same bandy legs, the same forehead flat like a board, and the eyes wide and bright, her mother in Kingston working so hard, and not a word from that worthless police man who is her father, his mouth so oily with promises, yes man, yes man, I going to send money for school, yes man, I going to send for her to come and spend time with me, yes man, yes man, and she sees that indeed her poor Bev is standing there, but in truth her Bev is not there at all, her Bev is hiding somewhere underneath the bed, squeezed far against the wall, and holding herself, holding herself tight because she has been torn open, mashed up, intruded upon by this awful awful world,

Come, Bev, come. She is an old woman, not long for this world, she turns the key in the door behind them, she shuffles into the kitchen, drawing the duster tight round her waist; she boils a pan of hot water on the stove and fills the big plastic tub with cool water, all the while mixing the two, stirring with her fingers until the temperature is just so,

Take off your frock and sit down, she beckons the girl; just heap up everything there in a pile, baggy and shoes and slip, heap up everything there in a pile; tomorrow daybreak, I burn it all. Sit, sit, she cries, the water ought to be nice and warm now, and she takes her little vials of oils and herbs and little packets of white powder tied up in her handkerchiefs, and one by one she sprinkles them into the water; this one to calm nerves, keep them tranquil; this one to let bad thoughts dissolve, no matter from where they come, past, future or present – no matter the dimension; this one to unlock the heart; this one to connect with spirit so that the outcome of the damage tonight will already be reversed into goodness and love.

She draws up the little stool next to the tub, sits down and begins to wash the girl, her granddaughter, who is eleven now, about to sit for common entrance examination, which if she does well, will get her into a good school and give her a good lead in life. She has a good mind, her granddaughter, she hopes she doesn't lose it with this pestilence that has beset her tonight. The young girl begins to weep; yes, the old woman says, yes, bawl it out, bawl it out, louder and louder, she tells her, and the young girl wails into the night; yes the old woman says, bawl it out, for when I was a young somebody like you, ain't nobody to tell these criminal acts to, nobody; we carry them with us all through life, burdening weself with them; can't tell your mother, she doesn't believe you, tell you is your own damn fault, what you doing out there in the first place, but in truth she knows the heartache you carrying, for she's there carrying it too, but she doesn't know how to help herself, doesn't know how to help you, and you can't say a word to your father, when he's the very culprit, coming night after night, and what you going to say or do, but to run away, run away, and hope you fall into good hands, for life is there at every turn to trip you up sometimes and sometimes to catch you, but still you must continue to trust life, trust life, even if wrong things come to you, you hear me, trust life for you are a strong girl, you hear me, don't let this cripple you, for it can, and at first she starts with her granddaughter's face and her back, soaping up the rag with castile soap and with Dettol and the Canadian healing oil and soaking all over her arms, her throat and chest, with the warm rag, up and down her legs and along there where the old animal hurt her, push up himself into her and tear her, bawl it out, she says again, her own self starting to weep, now, bawl it out, me child, bawl it out.

25.

I can't do it, Marie Jose says.

They're on the phone again.

It's too much. I'm not ready. There are things going on here. I just can't do it, she says again.

Okay, he says sadly. Then he waits. He doesn't think to ask what things are going on there. The truth is he cannot imagine a future without her.

I don't get it, she says.

I will raise her on my own, he says. He has finally come to this conclusion. And we'll continue to have our relationship, he says.

Don't be ridiculous, she says. I've done this before, I know this, and it's virtually impossible.

Okay then, he says. Let's give it six months. He can't believe he's giving her an ultimatum. He can't believe what's overcome him. Still he presses on. If you absolutely don't want me with Rosa, then let's end it, he says, but let's give it six months.

He hears the sharp intake of her breath, then the dead silence on the line. He, too, is frightened by the decision he's just made, frightened by the limb he's just walked out onto, the precipice that lies before him, the sharp unending plummet. In a strange way, it feels like it was Rosa, not his father's dying that summoned him here. But how can he explain that to his girlfriend?

You're choosing, she says, finally. She's been weeping.

I don't want to, he says, I want you both. I love you both. You're the one choosing, he says.

I can't do it again, she says. I've already done it once. I lost everything

Okay, he says sadly. Okay. And then he waits. I don't want this to end, he says, finally.

I have to go, she says. I have to go to yoga.

Okay, he says. Okay.

26.

Early morning, he has not slept, he goes to breakfast, and his mother is there. He takes coffee and a slice of hard dough bread lathered with Anchor butter. He sits next to her, he does not speak. He knows that when he's anxious like this, he needs to go for a walk, which will calm him. He needs to write in his journal, take a bath. Spin. Clear. Open a coning. Send himself a Reiki as Marie Jose would do. But these are Marie Jose's things. He wishes he had something of his own – meditation, prayer, anything, just something in these moments to support him. Instead, he sits at the kitchen table, watching his mother. Her glasses are foggy with dirt; no wonder she can't see, and the ankles spilling over her shoes – isn't that from too much salt in her diet, her body holding onto all that water, or is it the heart? She needs care, his mother, she needs to see a proper doctor instead of that Anglin. Her hair could use a nice rinse, maybe even a cut, her whole damn house could use some big windows to let in more light.

He wants to tell his mother about Marie Jose; now more than ever, he wants to talk about love. In these two months she has wanted to know nothing about Marie Jose. She has ignored every attempt he's made to tell her, rerouted every conversation. She has not asked one question, not even how they met, how long they'd been together. Not that this should matter. What should it matter what his mother thinks about his girlfriend? What should it matter? Isn't this the same woman who takes in his father's outside child, who rewards his father for philandering, rewards him for molesting this young, young girl – could've been his own daughter – and who knows the countless others.

The morning is not good. He has sadness slathered all over him. She does not answer his calls, five days now, and he cannot find her best friend, Margo. At her office at the press, he leaves a million messages; she does not return any. It is not like her to cut him off like this. Something must be desperately wrong. Could it be the cancer again, for she'd complained of swollen glands, swollen lymph nodes? He cannot tell what it is, he only feels it, the great pervading dread.

Mother, he says finally, I met the mother. This, too, has been on his mind, pressing him. I met Rosa's mother. I tracked her down, me and Septy, and I introduced them. Rosa wanted to meet her.

His mother is over at the stove, stirring something in a pot, cornmeal porridge it smells like, perhaps it's for his father, or for Rosa. His mother does not look up. He doesn't know how to read her back in the white summer dress he bought from the discount warehouse. Has she even heard him? He does not know.

And I told Rosa, Papa ain't her grandfather at all, he's her father, her flesh and blood father. Finally out of his mouth, he breathes a sigh of relief and slumps even deeper into his chair. Still his mother does not turn, and whether she has heard him or not he has no earthly idea.

Get out of this house, boy. As if out of nowhere his father appears in his wheelchair, his sentence frighteningly coherent.

He turns briefly to look at his father, to make sure he's in fact there, not just some spectre, not just voices in his head. And indeed it's his father wheeling toward him in his chair, his face puffy and strange. When did his father recover strength? When did his father find voice again? He'd been so busy with Rosa, so preoccupied with Rosa and visa and Rosa's mother, when did his father come back from death?

His father is before him now and he's getting ready to strike. I'm going to kill you, his father cries, I'm going to fucking kill you.

Mr. Sam, the mother warns, lifting a restraining arm. It's okay, it's okay, Mr. Sam. Calm yourself, calm yourself. Mrs. Gladison, she calls out for the housekeeper, her voice starting to break. Mrs. Gladison.

What happens next happens quickly, in the wink of an eye.

One minute the old man is in his chair, the next he is leaping, the entire six-foot frame, with deadened parts, is leaping, knocking Winston from the table, the chair flying out from under him, the old man and Winston on the floor.

And in that moment he's three or four, as in the dreams, he's fallen off his bike, his knee is broken open, his father has him in his arms, he's running across the field: shit, shit, shit, his father is saying, as fluids spurt out the wound. His father's face is dark and wet, it's sculpted, his fat lips are trembling. He smells of dirt, of grass; they've been out in the field all day; he's without a shirt, his breasts jiggle as he runs, his breasts are circled with tight curly hair and there's hair, too, all over his massive chest. Now his father smells of shit, of Castile soap, of Dettol, now he smells like an open sore, a man rotted to the core.

On the telephone, his mother begs Mr. Post to bring his ambulance. Then she disappears into the bedroom to prepare bags. Rosa is weeping in a corner; he takes her in his arms and brings her outside. He can't tell where her grief begins and his ends. The crickets are noisy and busy in the yard. Overhead a plane. The wind whistles through the grass. A yellow butterfly dances by daintily. There is a slight chill in the air, and down the road, traffic zips back and forth.

He hears the wailing siren from miles away. His mother brings the bags to the car. Her back is straight as a rake handle. Her back says she can face just about anything in the world: adultery, betrayal, her son's absence for years and years, heart attacks, comas, strokes. Her back says she is way stronger than you think, though she is eighty, suffers from high blood pressure, from diabetes, has arthritis in both hands, the fingers gone crooked. She has been doing this for the past two years. Picking out white briefs and merinos, thin black socks, shirts he can slip into easily. And for herself: slippers, ready-wear cotton frocks, a sweater, a novel from her book club, her Bible, a piece of embroidery to finish, a deck of playing cards, and a flask of brandy.

SEPTIMUS

1.

Outside in the carport, he moves quickly from one corner of the lot to the other. Just a sip of fresh air, he thinks, just to hear the birds chirp and to stretch out his legs, stiff and cramped from all that bedside sitting, just to feel the sun drenching his face and neck, and to smoke one stick of cigarette. One stick. Bam!

He comes back to find Winston on the bed, next to their father, holding him, trying to bring back life, playing God. The nurses have already unhooked the tubes, turned off the machines and the room is now washed in a silence, palpable and strange. What can he say to his brother, what can he say after everything his brother has done, after everything. He can't find his mother whose book is on the floor. He picks up the book – *Palace of the Peacock* – and stuffs it in the side of her bag. He takes a deep shuddering breath and for a second he feels the anguish in his ankles rising up and he knows that it will only be a matter of time before the whole damn thing engulfs him.

Did he say anything? he asks Winston, the snake who is tangled in his father's tubes. The room is washed in the smell of astringents.

He said the man in the chair was calling him.

What, Septimus cries, his brow furrowed, and then he turns away; it doesn't matter, he thinks; his mother is back in the room and she is picking up her bag and jiggling the keys to her car. The nurses are back too, and they are wrapping up his father in a white sheet, they are wheeling out the body.

I'm going, his mother says, his mother who seems to have grown much taller all of a sudden, and whose back has straightened and who carries now a blue glow around her head.

So much to do, she says. So many calls to make to his people and to the people at the radio stations and the newspaper desk. She reels off a list. She sounds happy to have all these things to do. She sounds relieved. She must call Mass Stephen, who is to butcher the goat and the three pigs, she says, and Miss Cynthia, who is to arrange the cooking, and Mr. White, who is to organize the nine nights and the singing. She has to stop at the supermarket and buy rum and beer and cigarettes and at Miss Imo's shop for several yards of tobacco for the men who will come to dig the hole behind the house. She must call Mass Raphael who is to build the coffin.

I can't even choose a box for my own father, he shouts at his mother – something he's never done, raised his voice at any of them. Why you think I have the funeral home there?

You know your father, she says in a low voice, cutting him with her eye. He's always wanted Mass Raphael to build his box.

His mother has left him with not one single thing to do. She's left him with his empty hands dangling beside him, with the anguish swiftly creeping up his thighs and the day of his father's death slowly unfolding.

Back at the house, the helpers have already boxed up his father's clothes, except for a felt hat his brother Winston is able to abscond with, and an embroidered bush jacket. In the bedroom, he finds his brother rifling through musty old letters, through a chest of drawers full of their father's rat-eaten handkerchiefs, his silk scarves. His brother picks them up, he presses them to his face, he fingers the tissue fabric. His brother packs up the exercise books their father used in third standard, his Bible, his hymn book, two copies of Bunyan's *Pilgrim's Progress*. His brother puts all the pictures he can find in a folder, brown sepia shots of his father as a boy, and of his father's only brother who went to Panama to build the canal. His brother stuffs the handkerchiefs and the scarves into a cellophane bag. All these he'll take back with him to America – and his father's fountain pen, his stamp collection, his fluid lighter, his pipe, his pig leather wallet. For the eight whole weeks his brother has been there, he did not try once with their father; he came instead with resentment and hate. He came to stir up things that did not concern him and to create a big ugly dirty mess. How are these things going to help him now, Septimus wonders.

His mother is on the cellular with this person, that person. He's never seen his mother so busy on the phone. His mother is talking with a contractor now. He can't believe what his ears are telling him. She wants the ramps taken away, she wants the master bedroom rebuilt. She has already ordered a canopied bed with curtains drawn around it. The van is dropping off everything next week. She has already ripped off the drapes and ordered new ones, she has reorganized the room, removed every trace of him. Just forty-eight hours into his father's death and he overhears his mother telling someone how she's never liked the bush, how she'd always wanted to live in the city near her red people, how it was because of him, all these years, she stifled so much of herself. His mother!

The house is crawling with people. There is no peace whatso-ever, not even in his old room. He wakes up sometimes to find complete strangers stretched out next to him, their arms wrapped around his neck, or a baby fast asleep at the foot of the bed. From morning to night, the workers sing their awful mourning songs as they tear up the ground for the grave. The kitchen is full of strange women he's never seen before. They come with bundles of food wrapped up in white cloth. They come with nostrums for his mother's sudden onslaught of ailments, all of them imaginary, he decides. They come looking for dead-left things, their hands stretched out. They come with their oily mouths full of condolences. From the villages and towns where his father had opened bakeries and from the district lost in the hills where he grew up as a boy, people pour in. He meets cousins he didn't know existed. All night long, they recite stories about his father, all the while gorging themselves on the curried goat, the stewed beef and the cow-cock soup, the pig skewered over a spit. There is so much food even the dogs are joyous, and in their excitement they bite furiously at each other.

Again and again, complete strangers walk up to him with wet faces, pumping his hand, clapping his back. They say to him, you're lucky to be his son. They say to him, oh, what a good man your father was. Did you know your father did this good deed, that good deed? For four years he gave money so So and So's daughters could study at university. He helped So and So's business so it wouldn't fall to pieces during the early days. He helped So and So to rebuild his house after the last big flood, and So and So to rebuild his church after the terrible raging fire. He wishes Winston could hear all these things about their father.

During all this his mother says nothing at all. She does not laugh when they give their big jokes, when they recite the long winding tales about his father. She glides through the ceremonies tall and grand and covered in black, followed by a train of women with white scarves on their heads who weep openly. His mother is not in mourning. Her eyes are big and clear and bright and her face says, I can't wait for all of you shits to clear out of my house so I can have my peace again. Her face says, this is the happiest moment of my life and yet I'm not supposed to show it. I'm supposed to look mashed down and destroyed. Well, watch me. Watch me! the glittering eyes say. The blue light is still swirling around his mother's head, and he thinks he doesn't know her at all. She did not look like this last week or the week before. His mother is a complete stranger to him.

Winston is busy packing up his things and making flight arrangements, and packing up Rosa's things – Rosa whom he's taking with him to America to raise on his own, without a woman, for Marie Jose, it seems, won't put up, and so there he is, picking up Rosa just like that and taking her away. Just like that, breezing in and destroying every fucking thing in his way and blowing out again. He cannot find words to speak to his brother, he cannot find words.

At the funeral home he cannot face his father stretched out there on the table, his chest refusing to heave up and down, his mouth refusing to open and advise him about a thing, his ears plugged up with cotton instead, and his nostrils too. At the funeral home he cannot even answer the phone without his voice breaking up into pieces. In the mornings at the breakfast table he dawdles over his mug of ginger tea. He cannot finish the plate of ackee the housekeeper sets before him. He sees his son's mother, the first wife, April, everywhere he sees the boy now. He sees her in the boy's mouth, in the row of teeth when the boy grins. He

110

sees her in his throat when the boy rears his head. She is there in his small round shoulders, in his thin arms, in the slight bow of his legs, in the dimples on his chin. In the end he begs Raul to take over things for a week, to run the business, to wash and dress his father's body for Mass Raphael's embroidered coffin.

At night, desire is rife in him; he wants his wife, Fiona, and yet he's afraid of the violence boiling his limbs. He comes to bed, he peels off his clothes. The frenzy must be leaping off his skin because she stirs at once and puts on the light and looks at his face smashed with pain.

Come, she says, come. She takes his head into her arms, she puts it against her breasts. Talk, she says, talk. Tell me.

He doesn't have words to describe anything. He's up to his chin now in the anguish. Soon the damn thing will drown him. He wants to be crashing away inside her so everything else recedes. He wants to be crashing. This is the only language he knows. But she doesn't want any of this. She hasn't wanted him like this in weeks. She turns her face when he meets her with his lips. She holds his hands in place when he tries to remove her nightie. She slips out from under him when he tries to mount her. He could force it, he thinks, he could force it, but what is that, what is that. And he thinks of her in the Chinese man's arms, he thinks of her fucking the Chinese man and he doesn't know what to do with the rage clamouring inside him.

At the service, the church is packed with people and at the pulpit, when it's his turn to say a few words about the deceased, not a single thing comes out of his mouth when he creaks it open, even though the jaw is moving back and forth like a saw. Somebody, he doesn't know who, comes up and takes his hand and leads him away like a drunkard and from the corner of his eyes he sees a long thin scar on the face of a man, who has the same face as his father and he grabs his eyes away at once, but something in the next man's face pulls him and he sees his father again and again repeated in that row of men standing there in black suits, holding hymn books and standing there with his father's puffed out chest and his father's high bottom and his father's long, long legs that could mento and meringue and ska and salsa, for he had been a champion dancer at

111

all the street fairs when he was a teen, and it was to a street fair he had gone that night with his father when he was boy.

They were driving back home when the van broke down and it was late and the road was dark without street lamps, a narrow and perilous road with a battery on both sides and cars drove by only every half-hour. There were neither moon nor stars in the sky that night and it was impossible to make out his father even walking next to him. But his father was happy and therefore he was happy; he loved his father's big, strong presence next to him. For about a mile, they walked hand in hand, the broke-down van left back there. He was not tired, his mind still jingled with the tunes from the festival and now and again his father broke out into one of the songs and stepped away in a jig. They finally flagged down a car and the car dropped them off two towns over at a mechanic named Sammy.

A grey light the colour of steel was just coming up over the horizon and all over the hills the roosters were starting to call. His father rang the bell until lights came on in the apartment above the shop; a dog started to bark and a curtain was drawn. The door scraped open and when Sammy came out, Septimus's lips trembled; he looked up at his father, whose face was impossible to decipher in the light, but he could feel him stiffen. Sammy pulled out his wrecker, they climbed into the cab and drove to pick up his father's van. His father was solemn as he explained to Sammy how he had been driving and then the damn thing just shut off like that. Bam!

Sammy was not a talker. He had a long knife scar etched into the side of his face and it made him look old and mean. Septimus sat on the steps of the garage and watched his father pace up and down in the yard, while Sammy lit up the garage, hoisted up the van and with a magnificent light peered up into the van's belly. He must have been in his early twenties, the boy, Sammy; he was thin and wiry and extremely serious. By the time the sun had thoroughly pierced the sky, the van was ready.

He could barely reach the counter. Still he stood up next to his father as he pulled out a wad of money from his pocket. How much? his father said gruffly. He was no longer happy, his father, which meant that Septimus, too, had lost the light.

112

Velma Pringle is my mother, the boy jerked out, looking at his father with a face sullen and mean.

And what does that have to do with me, his father growled, and Septimus saw something shriek across the boy's face and he felt suddenly afraid for his father.

There were just the three alone in the shop and from the open door he caught glimpses of the clouds moving rapidly across the sky, running away it seemed. As if called, a dog, which they had only heard before, burst into the garage and stood next to the boy and rubbed his head against his thigh. It was a St. Bernard. Septimus knew this for his godmother had just given him a book on dogs for his birthday and he had memorized them all.

How much, his father asked again in a softer voice. Septimus could feel sweat building up underneath his arms and he could hear through his shirt the furious beating of his own heart. There was a smell moving off his father he has not smelled since.

There's one more Samuel Rowe, the boy said, he work at a bank over in Troy Square. His mother's name is Pauline Block. She married to a Reverent Block, also from Troy.

His father swallowed. There was already a pile of bills on the counter and his father was still counting out more when the boy swept them off the counter with his fist and rammed the keys to the van into his father's chest.

His father's Adam's apple slid up and down in his throat.

Get out, the boy Sammy said, looking at his father with deadpan eyes that had in them a pure raw rage.

Look, his father said, in a voice that was about to cry. I don't know this Velma Pringle you talking bout. I don't know you mother.

But the boy was already walking out through the back door, slamming doors, turning off lights, and the dog at his side had started up a low nasty growl in its throat.

They drove swiftly. They did not speak. A mask had come down over his father's face. The face he had now was unreadable. The lips turned down and tightly drawn. He knew this mask; he'd seen it many times before. It was there seconds before he flew into a rage and went after Winston. When they travelled together in the van and the mask appeared, he knew to appear as invisible as

113

possible, not to cough or breathe heavily, to sit absolutely still. It was the worst time to ask his father if he could stop the van so he could pee. He knew that the boy back there was his father's son and that the boy had been waiting his whole life to introduce himself to his father, to do something for his father, to show his father what he'd made of himself, to show his father he existed. And this was the unfortunate way it unfolded. They pulled up at a bank.

Stay here, his father said.

But he followed him inside anyway.

The other Sammy sat at a desk in a tight blue suit behind a sign that said loan officer. He was attending a customer and two others waited in stiff straight-back chairs. This Sammy did not look like his father; his lips were like plums and his face too round, the cheeks too big, but everything about the boy's gesture belonged to his father, the way he cocked his head to listen as if waiting for more than just words to reveal themselves. There was the way his father's face could be still, almost wooden or like stone, and yet the eyes were jumping around. The boy, Septimus had to admit, had his father's ears that jutted out of his head like wings. They drove home with the radio blasting between them. His father drove recklessly, swinging quickly around dangerous corners, tailgating and over-taking others on the wrong side of the road, and cursing them on top of it. The van dropped down into potholes and tumbled out again. They never spoke of it. And somehow he understood that this was to be their secret. His and his father's, and he never betrayed him.

Eight weeks ago, his brother arrived from America. Eight weeks later he is driving his brother to the airport. The trunk is full of suitcases. Rosa is in the back. He cannot read what her face is telling him from the rear-view mirror. He thinks maybe she, too, is uncertain; she can't begin to imagine the life set out ahead. He will miss her even as he'd never rested in his feelings for her, even though he could never swallow how she'd come into their lives. If she didn't look so much like Althea, he'd say the mother was just looking for a fool to mind her child. Eight weeks ago he himself was more certain about things, about his life and how he would live it, and about his marriage to Fiona. Now he doesn't know. He is driving his brother to the airport and he thinks they should have more things to talk about. But they are quiet in the car, each in his own private place. He feels as if his whole entire life he's been burying things, burying body parts, pieces of himself. His whole entire life he's been holding on to things and all around him are the remains of a losing battle.

Two days ago they went swimming. He asked his brother, how exactly was he going to raise Rosa there in America without a woman to help him.

Women do it all the time, his brother said.

If they have to, he said, if they have to. You don't have to. Rosa can stay here with mother.

Mother doesn't want her, he said. She is a throwaway, like trash. Then he started to cry.

He had not seen his brother cry like this the entire time he'd been home. He did not cry even at the funeral or at the nine nights celebrations. He cried the way he did when he was a boy, his chest heaving. He cried like he'd heard him cry many times when he was a boy and their father lashed him. The sound of his brother Winston crying made him want to cry. They were sitting on a stone heap near their clothes, drying off. Beside him his brother wailed and he did not try to comfort him the way he did every day in his profession. He was tired of holding everybody up. He felt like something inside his own chest had fallen down, something had broken. Who is there to hold him up? His wife feels like a stranger to him these days, now that the great wall has come again between them. He sat and he listened to his brother's soft moans and then his brother was quiet. All around them there was just the stillness of the woods. The surface of the water was still in some places and in some places full of ripples. Bangas darted back and forth and trembled the water. Close by a woodpecker hammered into a tree. Soon the sun would drop and the sky would turn a deep blue and this blue would deepen into night. They took off their wet trunks and put on their trousers and shirts. They slipped their feet into slippers. They did not speak. They walked back through the woods, past the clearing where Althea was buried and most recently their father, and back to the house.

Beside him, his brother felt lighter as if something huge had been unburdened.

He, Septimus, is still carrying the weight.

Maybe you'll come and visit, his brother Winston is saying to him in the car on the way to the airport.

You can come more often as well, he growls. The whole world doesn't have to jump for you.

After Winston left the first time, for months – it seemed like for years – he was to his parents like the cassia tree they saw out of the window year in, year out. They saw it so often they stopped seeing it altogether, they saw right through it.

Look, his brother Winston is saying, all that is water underneath the bridge now. I've come and I will come again and Rosa will come again to see her mother. And you, he says, you I have missed. And you I will always want to see. His brother Winston is saying this over and over and over again.

The pressure is building up in his head and in his face and spreading behind his eyes and nose. And to top it off, he is out of cigarettes, completely. Can you imagine that? What can he say to his brother, Winston? There is nothing to say to that, absolutely nothing. He must swallow, he thinks, he must remember to inhale and to exhale and to swallow.

He sits all day, every day, in a chamber full of dead people. Perhaps he has become like them, deadened. Later on, when the bereaved drag themselves in, he has to hold them up, he has to find words to life them up, put them back on their feet. He has help for everybody, he thinks, and now he is lonely, lonely as hell without his father. He doesn't know how to nourish himself, that is the problem, and the dead cannot nourish him. He doesn't know how to let his wife nourish him in a good and balanced way, or his son. There is distance between him and his wife, again the great wall; his mother has turned into a complete stranger; his brother is leaving again and his father is dead. Dead. They buried him few days ago under the limbs of a sycamore. He hopes his father will visit him in his dreams, he hopes he will sense him around the house, for up until now, nothing. He thinks he does not have room in his skin to dress another dead body; he does not have room to hold up another bereaved; his own back has atrophied.

His brother is hugging him, his brother is weeping into his shirt, his brother's face is shattered, his brother is straightening up himself and wiping his face with their father's mouldy handkerchief and blowing his nose. His brother is taking Rosa's hand and Rosa is looking ahead; he cannot read her face, her face is the same mask he's seen on his father's face that says nothing at all and everything at the same time. She is carrying her dolly, and she is walking away and he sees Althea again, he sees his twin in Rosa's shoulders and in her neck and in her hair parted in two and flowing with ribbons and in her sloping walk and in the long skinny legs. After that he starts running; he is in a hurry to get back to the car, and he must push his way through the hordes of people falling on him, and he must push against the terrible mass coming at him and pressing him to their chests and he must push them away, push and get back into that car and drive away, drive fast, with all the feelings building up inside him, building up ready now to explode, ready now to cause a big ugly dirty mess.

2.

Over twenty years they haven't seen him. Over twenty years. Suddenly he blows in from America and he doesn't try with their father who has the angel of death hounding him. He came instead with his heart full of revenge. It was the white girlfriend who tried with the father, it was she who baby-sat the old man. It was Marie Jose who wheeled him day after day down the marl road through the Village Square where his father had the bakery squeezed between the post office and Lionel's rum bar. At Lionel's rum bar she ate the warm sugar bun with a cut of New Zealand cheddar and laughed at Indian Horace's bad jokes, never mind that she didn't understand half of what he said. At Lionel's rum bar, she drank the scalded cow's milk spiked with the white rum. And where was Winston, where was he? Plotting how he was going to wreck the whole family asunder, planning how he was going to rip out their hearts.

He saw Marie Jose in the rum bar towering over the old man, and he thought she could very well be family with Mass Charlie who walks past the house every morning on his way to the fields to tie out his fifteen heads of goat. Mass Charlie with his sapphire eyes, his lips like a pink stripe across his face full of freckles, and the red hair plastered to his head in the heat.

Those days he took time off from the funeral home and went with her and the old man and the driver to the sea, he could tell she was relieved to be away from the house and from Winston. To escape the flaming sun, they sat out underneath palm trees, the leaves casting lengthening shadows to protect them. She slept in the shade, and when she woke, she read, she swam; all round them the cry of the surf, the tall rocks, the silver waves, the curve

118

of the bay. The driver, who had disappeared earlier into one of the many rum bars lining the beach, brought them cassava bammies and fried fish, porgy, which she boned, serving the old man chunks of the steaming white flesh. He was touched by this. It made him like her. She reminded him of Fiona. The gentleness about her and the hardness at the same time, her no-nonsense. And it was from her he heard about his brother's travels to Africa, the many historical books he wrote. From her he heard that his brother teaches history at the university and last year even served as chair. From her he heard about the cancer that struck her two times, carrying off both her womb and her breast, the cancer that is now in remission. And in those moments he felt closer to her than to his own brother. How was that possible? How was it possible he felt closer to a complete stranger than to his own flesh and blood he loved and missed all these years? And yet that was so.

He heard them out on the verandah, his brother and his mother, kee, kee, kee, like picharies, all morning long. He heard them out in the yard, his brother and his mother and the half sister his father made with the barmaid, kee, kee, kee, all morning long. And his brother spun the half sister and he threw her in the air, and they skipped in the dust, kee, kee, kee. They sang and they danced and he walked her to Miss Iris's infant school and back and they drew on her slate and climbed coconut trees and swam in the river near the house where he used to swim with Winston when he was a boy. His brother did not speak to him. He heard them in the sewing room and he imagined his brother in there telling their mother about the books he wrote, and about his life up there in America, and he imagined Winston telling her about his friends, and filling up the twenty-five year gap, patching up things with their mother, and one day he stepped into the sewing room, for nothing had been fixed with him. All he'd gotten so far were blows to his face and an apology that meant nothing at all.

The conversation drew to a halt. They turned slowly to look at him. He stared back at them, the faces hard and glazed and he felt like a complete stranger in there with his mother and his brother watching him, until suddenly he could find no words, everything trapped inside him. He pulled out of there as fast as his feet could carry him. He pulled out of there and he found his father parked under a tree, dusty and exhausted. He could see it clearly now, how day after day his father was removing himself; the little girl he made elsewhere was all he was alive for, he could see that now. He lived for her legs scissoring his lifeless ones, her little arms superimposed on his, the orange flash of her smile, her tight little mouth gnawing his face with kisses.

He looked at his hands and saw that they were empty. For there was his father and there was the little girl, Rosa, the jacket, and there were Winston and his mother, kee, kee, kee.

3.

He couldn't stand the house. He couldn't stand the bickering between their parents. He couldn't stand the malice, how they didn't speak for weeks, sometimes months, except through the children. He was his father's favourite but he couldn't stand how his father treated Winston and he couldn't stand that there was nothing at all he could do, for fear of losing his father's affection, having his father turn against him too. Perhaps he was a coward. Perhaps that was so, back then when he was a boy and Winston was also a boy. But on the road and away from the house he did not have to be a coward. On the road he was fearless. He loved the black and silver road. The road had a heat. There were girls and there was sex and there was weed and there was Bruce Lee and John Wayne on Saturdays at the Odeon Theatre. There were the shops with their loud speakers at the window roaring out music, and the women inside their tight dresses winding up their waists. There was liquor, there was laughter, there were the circles of light under the street lamps where men talked quietly, their backs against the iron pole, a funnel of smoke around their faces. Above all, he had discovered sex, and pussy flowed easily and his cock never tired of the pure sweetness of it.

At fourteen he was already as tall as his father. He had his father's wide shoulders, his big long arms, he had his father's eggplant blackness, he had his short thick neck, he had his round open face, he had his father's smile that came quick to his face, especially when he was angry, especially when he was mistrustful. His brother, Winston, was not hooked to the road as he was. His brother, Winston, had one best friend, a slim, red-skinned, double-jointed boy they nicknamed Bone, and for the most part, his brother and Bone were inseparable. They read the same novels, they listened to the same LPs, and every Friday, underneath the tamarind tree at the foot of the garden, his brother and Bone exchanged gifts wrapped in tissue paper and green ribbon.

Then suddenly his brother Winston was studying like hell, studying furiously. Suddenly he was sitting for exams, suddenly he was being suited for new clothes, a little get-together was being held, he was saying goodbye. Their mother and father were crying, and it was rare to see his father cry. In fact if you didn't know his father, you could miss it altogether, for he did not shed tears, his father, he ground his teeth and so it was the up and down and around movement of his jaw that gave him away. His brother looked very young that day at the airport on his way to America. He was wearing a navy suit that Tailor Knight had cut, and a sparkling white shirt, a thin navy tie and black pumps. He was seventeen, but he looked eleven and at the same time he looked forty-four. He looked scared and his jaw was square and very determined. Perhaps it was a whole entire six months before it really hit him that his brother had gone, that it was just him, left there, alone with their parents in that big empty house full of malice on top of the hill.

It was a strange absence, worse even than when his sister passed away, because at least he'd had Winston to steady him. Now there was no one. It was as if he reached out to pick up something with his left hand and realized there was no arm there, that the socket was empty, and the flap he saw was just the sleeve of his shirt folded and tucked under and held there with a large safety pin. He lived his life with that missing arm feeling slightly incomplete, never fully balanced, always tilted. Some days it felt familiar and he could bear it and some days he wanted to fight somebody, anybody, he wanted to howl, to throw himself against a wall, against a tree; he wanted real physical pain that would drown out this gnawing thing in the bottom of his gut. And so he fucked. During that pounding electric moment, everything receded.

Then the road lost its appeal. Bam! Just like that. He forced himself to the bars at night, but even sex was without nectar. He missed Winston. More than he missed his sister when the truck took her that Sunday, he missed him. And his brother was every-where he turned. There was his smell of lime and of Brut, there were the shuddering jaw muscles when they fought, there was his sissy walk, for he did not walk like a man – his brother did not walk like he owned the cock and balls between his legs. There was his smile like a lantern. There were his screams when he shouted back at their father, his skinny fists trembling. His brother Winston was tall and reedy and tea-coloured and freckled like their mother, who came from a long line of money and madness. He didn't know he had loved his brother so. Then he began to hate him. It would've been one thing if his brother's body had been sent back as ashes in a tin, or even crushed up like meat the same way Althea's had been. It would have been one thing if a piece of paper had come with word of his death. It was two hundred times worse that he was alive – alive, but completely lost to them.

Not long after that he told his father he wanted to go to mortuary school. He had grown weary of the road. Under his liquor, his best friend had stabbed a man to death and was serving life in prison. He had caught gonorrhoea four times already, and women were now starting to call his name as their bellies swelled. He had grown weary of the road and the needling had not stopped. His brother had been gone three years. Their mother would call and leave a message begging him to call and she'd wait and watch the black telephone, and the black telephone never rang. He did not respond to any of their letters, yet they knew he was still enrolled at the university in America. From a friend of a friend of their mother's who had a boy at the same university, they knew he was well, he had not been struck down by illness. He had not lost his hands or the ability to use them. It was terrible to watch their mother's disappointment. It was even worse to watch his father's hurt which swiftly turned into rage. He had to get out, get away from underneath all this suffering inside the house. When he broke the news to his father, whom he'd always felt closest to, his father fired out a shrill and disturbing laugh.

It was a Sunday evening. His father had been playing cricket all day, and all day he'd been scheming how exactly he would put it to him. He couldn't explain how come he was so certain, but he was certain. It was as if he'd come to a sudden recognition, as if something that had been gestating in him for years had bubbled up.

Miss Nora, his father called, Miss Nora, come and listen to what your son Septimus is saying to me.

Night had come, the curtains were drawn, the house was flooded with lights, but the lights only made the house more desolate and the sadness inside even greater. His mother was in the kitchen gutting fish for dinner. She had been humming, but now she stopped, for there was something bitter in her husband's laughter, and he heard her sigh. He was sitting in the living room with his father who was crouched over the racing section of the newspaper. On the short-wave transistor, a tinny voice crackled out news in Spanish. Above his head, the blades of the fan turned slowly, lifting the ears of the newspaper. He wore glasses now, his father, and they made him look old and frightening, especially now that he had no hair at all, and his forehead, big and shiny, jutted out. He had grown fat and his belly swelled over his trousers and the long skinny legs inside them. His mother came out still holding the short knife, her hands slick with blood, scales from the fish speckling her face. She wiped her hands on her apron.

What, now! What? She took a huge gulp of their father's brandy. His mother, too, had aged. She'd had surgery for cataracts; she'd had tumours removed. Just the year before she'd had an operation that lopped off a kidney and a lung. She was shrunken, she was forgetful and he would always blame their premature aging, their suffering, on Winston and the way he'd turned his back. He didn't know sorrow could break down people like that.

Tell her, his father cried. Tell her! My sons are incredible! That one in America who doesn't speak to us. And now this. He sounded as if he wanted to cry and sucked noisily at his drink.

Septimus was swiftly losing his courage, but something in his mother's face, something encouraging he saw in her grey eyes allowed him to continue. It must have been this light, he decided, that had saved Winston all those years under their father's tyranny. It must have been the very same light that drove Winston away.

I want to study burial, he said, thinking of his sister whom he could patch up into one piece finally and put to rest. Every night she came to him, her body a complete scramble, the hands where the ears should've been, the eyes under her foot bottom, the nose near her backside, the teeth underneath her arms. It was driving him crazy and there was no one he could tell, no one he could talk too; it got so bad he was afraid now to close his eyes at night, to switch off the light and sleep. They have a man up near Meadow Brook I could apprentice with, he said; I could rent a room in that area. He was twenty, had long finished high school, and had passed not even one subject.

Until that moment he had not known he was leaving home, as his brother Winston had done; he'd not told his father about the room. He could see that he was disappointing his father. It was a strange feeling of betrayal and he felt a rush of love leap out from his heart and head toward his father.

Oy! His mother groaned, as if someone had punched her, and she hurried out the room, taking the glass of brandy with her. Let me turn this thing! And whatever feelings she had about losing him, whatever compunction she felt at all about the dissolution of her home, she did not show it. She was all business when she returned, though there was an edge of hysteria in her voice.

Well, Mrs. Lin has a house in Meadow Brook; I'm sure she could rent you a room. Is a nice home, I've stayed there sometimes. And your father and I could come up with the fee. It seems workable to me.

She was gone again. Now the pots clashed, and the water pipes came on in full force, and there was the little yelp from the kitchen when she burned herself.

Set the table, she roared, set the table!

He was alone there with his father still folded over his horse racing and an uncomfortable silence. The topic did not come up at dinner. It did not come up because she did not like the idea herself, she was afraid to lose him, but she wasn't going to say anything to his face and she wasn't going to upset her dinner and they weren't going to fuss. So it was settled. As if they had learned enough from Winston, there was no production at all to his departure. He came in late the night before, while they were all asleep, and the next morning, after they'd already left the house, he packed a bag and drove away. That evening he called to say he had reached. And as if to make up for everything Winston had done, he returned home once a month and spoke to them on the phone nearly every day.

But all that happened over twenty years ago, all that is behind him. Now his father is dead, and his brother has come and gone, taking Rosa with him. Septimus knows he must move forward with his own life. But he cannot move forward. He is stuck. A month now since the funeral and he cannot face the funeral home, cannot pick up the phone to call his mother, cannot even get up out of bed. A whole entire month!

4.

Jingles' shop is empty of customers when he steps in, and the transistor on the windowsill is singing out a calypso, and Jingles is sweeping up the tufts of hair covering the white linoleum floor and the place smells of powder and aftershave and shampoo.

One glance at Septimus's face and Jingles waves him over to the chair.

Sit, sit, Jingles says, putting away the broom and washing his hands at the sink.

One of Jingles's legs is shorter than the other, and so he moves in an up and down way toward the brand new chair he bought a month ago up in Miami that has a lever at the side. He pumps up the lever now, as Septimus sits down, and then he hops back a few inches and sucks his teeth and pumps it down and then he hops back a few inches, and pumps. Up and down, up and down, until he's gotten the height just right. All of this Septimus is comforted by, the up and down movement of the chair, the smell of Old Spice and tobacco on Jingles's skin, the flap, flap of the towel as he shakes and then folds it gently around Septimus' neck and then spreads it out neatly around his chest and shoulders, the feel of Jingles's fingers on his skin.

You don't look good at all, friend. How things? How your family abroad?

He has been coming to Jingles' Barbershop for as long as he's had the funeral home, fifteen years now.

But he doesn't tell Jingles he has not returned a single call. Going six weeks now. What does he have to say to his brother, what can he possibly say?

And as if in that silence, everything has been made clear,

Jingles nods vigorously in understanding and continues to work steadily on the head with the noise of the razor between them. From the mirror Septimus watches the jaw, big and square, working up and down and the eyes narrowly screwed to his head.

I don't know which is worst, all those years he was gone or now that he's come and gone again. It's like you open up a sore that's starting to heal and you can't get it to scab. It's just the open raw festering thing there. This is what he says when Jingles finally shuts off the razor.

Yes, Jingles says, nodding and pausing to inspect the head of hair, turning the head gently with one hand, the shears poised in the other. Nothing to do but to wait it out before you can move forward. Don't try to scab over that sore too soon.

But, Jingles. He feels the tears at the back of his throat ready to burst out. He swallows. He watches the face in the mirror, the face that has on its head a white hat with a blue band.

It's the only way, Jingles says, unhooking the towel, and squeezing talcum in his hands to lather the back of Septimus' neck, which he does gently, soothing him. It's the only way.

He pays and stumbles out into the terrible heat of the afternoon and wakes up Miss Icy who is dozing off underneath an umbrella by her table full of sweets and cakes and peeled oranges and peppered shrimp in a basket, and he buys the newspaper, glances at the headlines, asks for his change in ginger logs and a mile up the road he stops in a bar for a drink. They know him, he's embalmed all their dead; they call him Doctor. He orders a half flask and takes it in the back of the bar by himself, feeling like an old man already, an old drunk.

5.

Two months after the funeral, and he is driving in the old hearse with his son to see his mother at last. On the phone, he'd promised to come soon but the truth is he can't bear to face that house without the sound of his father's steps falling on the tile floors. The roadway is full of traffic and periodically a herd of cows pulls out into the street and the cars swerve to a halt and an old woman with a head tie and a bad leg hobbles after the herd with a switch. Back, back, she's crying, with the sweat drenching her skin. The cows stop to look at her and to pile up loads of steaming filth at their feet and the traffic picks up again slowly. He is driving with his son, this boy from his first marriage, this boy who has his ex-wife's jet black skin, the long lashes sweeping her eyes, her tall slim bones. He loves the boy more than life itself. He gives him clothes and money, he sends the boy to the best school in the country, and every summer he sends him to camp. But no matter what, the mother has turned the boy's mind against him, plain and simple, because the boy doesn't like him altogether. The boy is standoffish. The boy doesn't trust him completely. The boy is kind, the boy is good, but there are times when he feels as if the boy is forever punishing him for what went on between him and the boy's mother. Still he invites the boy to come along. He likes the boy. The boy is his son. He wants the companionship. It is strange to be going back to the house when there is no trace whatsoever of his father.

He wants to tell the boy what it means to him that his own father is dead. Can you imagine that? he wants to say to his son. Can you imagine losing your father? And then he thinks of Winston and their father, the hell that lasted so many years between them, and then he looks at his son next to him, his son who is probably waiting for him to die, his son whose mind the mother poisoned with her lies, her slanted version of things. He's given this boy everything. And yet, he gets the feeling when the boy looks at him sometimes, when the boy is sullen and rude to him, when the boy chooses the mother over him, he gets the feeling the boy intends to punish him forever.

Since his father's death, since Winston's departure, he's been falling apart, he wants to say all these things to the boy, even about his marriage, how he doesn't trust Fiona, he doesn't trust anything or anybody, how his whole life feels like a blasted failure. Can you imagine what it is like looking at your life and feeling as if it's all going to crap? But he cannot produce a word to his son, his chest feels too overloaded now with feelings. Sometimes he thinks it's the boy's fault, that if the boy had only kept his blasted mouth shut, if he'd not uttered a word to Winston, all would still've been well, and his father, God rest his soul, would've probably still been alive, and Rosa would've still been there reminding him of Althea, but no, his son ended up telling the truth and look at the damage.

They wait again as all around them there's a flurry of brown legs and checkered blue and white tunics and khaki suits and blue epaulets. St. Richard's Primary has just dismissed a multitude of shrieking children and they parade across the street with the uniformed guide who holds up a tall, skinny STOP sign.

They set off again, a steady stream of cars behind theirs.

He wants to tell his son that when he himself was a boy, his father used to take him along on his trips and he would ride like a man beside his father in the van to the airport to pick up goods at customs for his shops. How in those days, they went once a month, just the two of them, how he loved his father who in those days was a great big bull of a man, tall and strapping and exceedingly unattractive, yet women flocked to him. After his father wrangled with the customs officers and paid them off, they'd stop at a bar, stuffy and dark with creaking floors and rickety tables around which sat bands of old men playing checkers. He'd sit at the counter with his father; the two of them hoisted up on stools, a plate of food at their elbows. His father would smoke, he'd order a flask of brandy and drink it down slowly, he'd toy with his plate of food, he'd flirt with the barmaid, he'd disappear with her for a half-hour, and when he returned, they'd leave. On the way home, they'd laugh a lot, for his father had a deep roar of a laugh which was contagious, and his father would be slightly drunk and in a good mood, and his breath when he spoke smelled strongly of alcohol and Craven A cigarettes. It was a warm comforting feeling.

Septimus looks fondly at the boy sitting next to him, wanting to tell him this memory of his father who is gone now, whom Winston pushed into a coma and killed. But the boy is too delicate and pretty, his eyes too large and black and long lashed. Sit up straight, he yells at the boy, whose neck inside the collarless white shirt is slender like the mother's, the ex wife who ran away from him. The boy wrenches around to glare at him before jutting his chin out the window.

He understands anguish. Perhaps because he has lived it himself, it doesn't trouble him when he sees it standing up in a man's Adam's apple, when he sees it in the slope of shoulders. He can read the bottom of eyes; he hears how a voice betrays itself. He knows how to rest his hand, square and solid, on that man's kneecap. He knows how to rock a woman as she weeps, how to stroke her gently at the small of her back, how to cock his head and listen, and when to be absolutely still, giving just the great big embrace of his heart. He knows exactly what to say, what tone to use. He knows, too, that often they don't want counselling, they just want to know someone is listening, that whatever they are feeling or thinking, that thing is the most important thing in the world. This then has been his work, to tidy and dress and lay out their dead for the final passage, to treat their dead with the greatest dignity that their money can buy, and to console them in their anguish. This is why the boy's mother eventually left him. She said it was too morbid, his work: attending all day to the dead, and at night in bed, worrying over the price of coffins. She wanted to live. Live!

What could he say? He was twenty-five. But he might as well have been fifteen. What did he know about love? What did he know about how to keep a woman? What did he know about happiness? All he knew was how to be a provider. And that, he has come to learn, isn't good enough. Not even Fiona wants that. She wants something else; she wants intimacy and he has no idea how to give or even where to find this intimacy she wants.

The car ahead touches the brakes, he slows as well. He lights a cigarette and the smoke swirls out around their heads. The boy, thoroughly disgusted, almost heaves himself out the window. Septimus looks over at the scowling boy. Admonished. This is the word that comes to mind. This is how he has felt all those years he lived with the boy's mother and this is how he feels now in the car with the woman's son who doesn't like him. This boy who one day might very well turn round and push him into a coma as Winston did their father. He turns on the radio to block out the sound of snarling traffic and tries to think fondly of his mother whom he has not seen in over two months.

He parks the hearse at the bottom of the garden and steps out with his son. Breadfruit, the little pet dog his mother bought to keep her company, is bounding down the hill towards them and barking gladly, and he throws her the day-old bun he has in the glove compartment and she swallows it at once, not even smelling or tasting or chewing it. There's a car he doesn't recognize parked at the side of the house but he hears the hum of voices on the verandah, his mother's laugh trilling into the afternoon and when he's almost upon them he sees that it's Dr. Anglin.

Sept, Anglin cries, jumping up, pumping his hand, his face round and florid and full of the tufts of white hair flying off his brow and the little dent at the middle of his top lip.

You have a new car, doctor?

Yes, yes, Anglin cries. You like it? Trying to keep up with you youngsters. He is a short little man, ponderous with muscles. He reminds Septimus of a rooster, a bantam cock to be exact. And he thinks Anglin, too, like Winston, must've been impatiently waiting for their father to die.

His mother has been to the hairdresser, the helmet of hair on her head is shiny and stiff and her teeth look brand new as if recently painted, and her nails are polished a very garish pink, and the push toe slippers on her feet have a bundle of plastic flowers perched on the big toe. This is too much he thinks, too damn much. His father has just passed for Christ's sake.

132

Help yourself to a drink, Septimus, his mother says, and he's glad to escape them. Inside the kitchen there's a brand new girl stirring the pot on the stove and she titters when he opens the fridge and a torrid thought comes to him, for she has a nice face and a fleshy bottom, but he thinks better of it and pulls off the cap on a bottle of beer instead and off a bottle of cola for his son.

He takes a seat near his mother on a straight, hardback chair and he tries not to make full eye contact with Anglin, who is in a good shape for an old man. He swims and he plays tennis and he runs and he lifts weights and his stomach is flat like a boy's and the muscles ripple out of his short-sleeved white shirt and out of the short trousers he's wearing; the calves are like stones. And just the thought of Anglin there, looking like a boy, Anglin and his mother inside that canopied bed sends him choking over his first sip of beer.

You all right there, Sept, Anglin calls.

Yes, he says, blinking, for there's his father sitting on the top step of the verandah, sitting there close to Anglin's feet, smoking a cigarette and wearing a wool suit in this heat, like he's going to a funeral, a black suit and a black hat, like the one Septimus has on, except that on closer inspection, he sees that his father is wearing no trousers at all, and all of this is too weird, so he blinks, and he sips his beer, and he looks at his son who looks like April, and he looks back at his father who has no privates to speak of, a grown man sitting down there at Anglin's feet with no privates, just a smooth patch of skin where the entire package should've been.

He jumps up at once and gulps down his beer and tells his mother he's going – a half-hour after he's arrived and he's going. Take care then, Mr. Anglin, he calls behind him from the bottom of the steps. Come, son, come, he calls out to April's boy; it's making to rain, he says, studying the happy white clouds in the blue sky and the scorching light. Rain heading this way.

6.

Day after day he sees innocent babies smashed to pieces, the wives and sweethearts men turn against and murder in cold blood, the drug dons and their donishas shot up by police and by warring drug lords. Day after day, he washes the destroyed bodies and dresses them. He plucks out pieces of glass from a face that has been thrown into a windshield, he sutures on a nose that's been battered away by fists. If he lays on too much foundation to retrieve a face, an entirely different person emerges altogether.

Day after day he works in a vast and absolute silence. Sometimes two, three hours pass and if the phone rings, he does not hear. Trees dapple the curtains as the sun moves west, and he sees nothing. All of life falls away. Just his hands moving of their own accord, massaging and turning and lifting and massaging again and washing the rubber effigies. Later, when they come, the straggle of people, the bereaved, they will crowd into the hall with the grief leaping out of their faces. They will come with their voices mashed down by sorrow. To comfort them, to relieve them, he makes the dead appear again one last time as his very best self. For them he trims a beard, shaves off a raggedy moustache, daubs on face powder, glistens a woman's lips with a deep shade of vermilion, picks out an Afro, oils down a smooth balding pate with pomade, knots a tie around a stiff white collar, arranges pleats on a light blue skirt so they lay out straight. Later, when they come, howling down the house, he will receive them with grace and reproduce for them this one last indelible image.

7.

He has to find some other line of work.

This is what he's telling Jingles now, sitting in Jingles's chair again, with the towel tight around his neck and the powder dust suffused in his nostrils.

There is really nothing at all for Jingles to trim. He was just here two days ago and here he is again. This doesn't stop Jingles. Clip, clip, clip he goes with the long silver shears and his soft hands knuckle up against Septimus's head and neck and his soft hands brush against Septimus' cheeks and his chin.

Sounds indeed like it is time for a change, Jingles says. Sounds like you're at a crossroads.

Cannot even imagine what I could do now. Cannot even imagine.

How bout a supermarket or a haberdashery, Sept, something like what your wife has there, two of you expanding out, two, three here in town, one up there on the north coast, another in Mandeville, you know, like a chain.

But what about his family? This is what he's thinking to himself. What about Fiona and the Chinese man, what about the children?

The twelve o'clock news is playing on the transistor and the announcer reels off the long list of deceased and their survivors.

I could also go abroad for two weeks, he says out-loud to Jingles. He has never left the country in all these years, he'd been so tied to his father, needed to take care of the old people since Winston left.

Of course, Jingles cries with a snip of the scissors into the air above his head.

He could go up and see his brother, he thinks to himself, see his life, bury the hatchet. After all, what had his brother done but expose the truth for all of them to look at. What was so damn wrong with that? But what about Fiona, that is the thing? How is he to leave Fiona there with the Chinese man? How is he to leave?

8.

They've already turned out the lights and taken up residence facing away at opposite sides of the bed when he turns over to her as if just now remembering he has something to say. The truth is it's been on his mind, so much so that for nights he can't sleep, and he's been rummaging in her purse looking for signs, questioning her daughters, though trying not to seem obvious. Bit by bit he moves over to her side and with his arms around her waist and his face into the back of her neck that smells of white musk, he says to her in a quiet voice, so as not to break up the stillness of the night, so as not to expose the anxiety etched in his voice, the dread that's been virulent there in him, he says to her in a strained voice: Why did you go and see Robbie Chen?

Around them there's the dead of the night, the eternal blackness, and the clock on the dresser ticking steadily away like his heart and the cars whining far out on the roadway, barely audible.

It was time, she says, and then she pauses as if choosing her words carefully.

He thinks of asking her to turn so he can face her in the dark, but might as well not, he decides; what would be the difference?

It's been three years, she says, three years since we last talked. Yes, he sends the envelopes with money once a month and he's on top of the school fees and of course they see him when they want, but it's been three years since we really sat down and talked about us, she says.

Us, he says, and he can hear the trembling in his voice.

She does not say anything else.

Outside, the city, like his head, is alive now, and sirens careen down the rutted roads, and voices pass back and forth near the windows and car doors slam and bloated whores laugh and dogs yowl.

So how is he? Septimus asks, trying to stifle the noise in his head. There's a headache sliding up behind his eyes and he's trying to remember where the damn bottle of Phensic is.

Good, good. I mean, what to say? He said two of the racehorses died last year and he lost money, and that his first son, the bad one, was in lockup again. Barring that, nothing. He looks older. He has arthritis.

You want to go back to him? he blurts out. She was with the Chinese man for twelve straight years.

He feels her stiffen. She reaches back her hand to hold the steel in his thigh. It's not like that, Septimus. Then she turns to face him, but thank God, there is no light tonight and she cannot see his eyes full already with the fright. It's not like that, she says again.

No?

If you saw your ex-wife now, you'd want to go back?

She doesn't want to see me, he says weakly.

That's not what I'm asking you, she says. Anyway, she says, it's over now. It's been over, she says. And then she is quiet.

When he met her two years ago, she was looking to settle down, she was looking to marry. She had already borne two children for Robbie Chen who had no intention whatsoever of leaving his wife. So she came with her girls and with the solidity and routine of family life he had always wanted. She was not young and stylish and pretty like the first one; she didn't have April's face or figure, but she had suffered, and suffering has its own kind of beauty; it had given her weight and he liked this weight. But everywhere, all over the house, there are still traces of the Chinese man; the girls have his pictures put up on their bureau, he calls them on their cellular, and they talk to him right there in the kitchen when everybody is seated at the table. The box of chocolates Robbie Chen sent for Fiona's birthday is still on the counter in the kitchen, the flowering hibiscus he sent last year is due to bloom again in a pot near the white piano in the living room.

This plans to be regular now, he says, seeing him and such?

I don't know, she says.

How you mean? he says, you must know, you must have an idea. His ex-wife has never wanted to see him.

We didn't make any plans, she says.

What hurts me most of all is that you didn't tell me you were planning to see him, he says. What else is she planning to do without saying a word to him, he's thinking, what else has she already done, is the concern now.

None of it was planned, she says. None of it. One day at work, the feeling came to me and I picked up the phone. I guess it was time. After a while this malice doesn't make sense. I'm happy with you now, she says, I'm content.

Is he content?

He used to be content. When he first married her he was content.

Now, he's imagining Fiona with the Chinese man. Now he can't get Fiona and the man out of his head, no damn way; he's imagining her pulling the car over to the side of the road and dialling his number on her cellular.

She cannot say what it is that prompts her. Some need, perhaps, to close up things with him. Though it doesn't seem that way to Septimus, for how can you open up something and close it up at the same time. Maybe she wanted to do it right. Maybe she wanted to sort out the feelings and set them to rest, something he has been wanting to do with his ex-wife, April, but she won't have anything to do with him. He is trying to find reasons, he is trying to understand Fiona. He is trying to put himself in her position. This is how he imagines the whole damn thing unfolding.

Robbie Chen, here, the voice says and her breath spins away from her at once. It is the same voice after so many years, sounding as it has always sounded, like tin, the long, slow drawl of it.

Robby, it's Fiona.

Fee, he whispers. And there is so much joy in his voice, so much relief, and he is quiet as if allowing the sweetness of the moment to permeate him through and through. Fee, he says again, it's a long time. And then he is quiet again, as if digesting exactly how long, and then he speaks, this time with some alarm.

The girls okay? For he's that kind of man, loyal, responsible, to the bitter end.

Yes, she says, I'm down the road. Want to meet at Emporium's?

Emporium is the same bar where he used to take his beer and where they had met when she was a girl, still in high school, and had continued to meet until the pregnancy when her father threw her out of the house and he bought the apartment and kept her there like a concubine ten long years, going to see her and the children when he could escape the wife.

Now, he says? Trying hard as hell to hold back the joy.

Yes, she says.

The bar has the same old dirty calendars full of naked women with pendulous breasts on the walls and she waits for him in a booth at the back near the jukebox. When he enters, he seems like a little old man, his face full of lines, his neck lost inside his collarless white shirt. But it is still he and an old feeling, long put away, perhaps even rusty now, springs out of her as he sweeps her up and presses her close to him and he finally releases her and she sees that his eyes are big and bright and damp.

He sits beside her, his thighs brushing hers and she is weak again, and he cannot release her, he holds her arms and her legs, he leans in close like a lover, he touches her throat and her cheeks. There is sad laughter all over his face.

He calls out to the bartender.

This is exactly how I've always imagined it, he says, the air around them swirling and hot. One day I'd pick up the phone at the shop and it'd be you, your voice, and you'd want to see me, and we'd meet right here. Every day just about, I think this. He sips his stout and she sips white rum chased with vanilla Nutriment, her third. And he looks at her, his eyes filled with a shameless adoration.

She can see what she'd been in love with. How he can put into words exactly what he thinks and exactly what he feels, and how he is always affectionate, always wanting to touch her and to hold her. How loving he is. How he is not afraid of his feelings, or of hers, how he is completely open all the time, not holding himself back, not pushing her away. Perhaps this is what she misses in her marriage with Septimus, this is what she's returned for, this gush, this open admiration, this gaze full of pure love and lust, this light.

This is my happiest day, he says, his face split in two like a child's.

And she falls into his chest, his embrace. She fills her stomach with the smell of his skin, of the smoke on him and the stout and the salt.

You're hungry, Fee, we should go somewhere and eat?

She wants to know about the wife, she wants to know who is running the shop and how come he is able to escape on such short notice. But she won't bring herself to ask.

Fee? He takes her hand. He puts it to his cheek, to his neck, he covers his eyes with it, and he puts it on his throat, on his heart.

No, she says. And it gives her a tremendous joy to be the one pulling away. I have to go home to my family, she says, thinking of Septimus waiting up for her in the study, clipping his nails to bide time, reading the newspaper again from start to finish. She says the word family with tremendous emphasis. How many nights he would come at the last minute to put the children to bed, then they would make love, all the while trying not to look at the clock. Then he would pull away and put on his shoes.

His face, his sweet unadorned face, is suddenly worn and exhausted.

You know my wife left me, he says watching her.

She feels the rage in her ears like a great gathering storm and she swallows the new drink the bartender has brought in one awful gulp.

She's living with her mother now up there in Mandeville. Going over two years now.

He squeezes her arm. And then as if reading her mind, he says, I'm an old man now. I haven't been with anyone since you, Fee.

Well, you should, she says, you should move on with your life. Her voice is hard.

Fee, he says weakly, you're still angry. You're still hurt. He cups her hand and he weeps into his stout.

I have to go, she tells him, slipping off the stool and gathering up her purse and moving as quickly as she can across the floor, just in case she changes her mind, just in case, for there is her marriage at home waiting, there is Septimus waiting, and there is the new life she has built with him and away from Robbie Chen. She does not slow down again until she is outside, outside in the impossible heat of the afternoon.

He must've fallen asleep, Septimus, he must've been dreaming, but suddenly now he's awake, for she's awake and she's pushed away the sheets and climbed on top of him stark naked and her hands and her mouth are everywhere, Jesus Christ, everywhere you can imagine, and it is like a river of heat knocking him one way, knocking him another, and he is delirious as she heaves against him, as she plunges down, rocking and rocking and what is to be done, what exactly is to be done, his body is wide awake, his cock stretched and turgid and full of the heat and shadows of the night, and her eyes are glazed, her face sings in the night light looking in at the window, and above them the blade of the fan turns slowly, and on top of him, she is riding and riding, her voice hoarse with moans.

9.

He goes again to Jingle's shop and there is a man ahead of him, a man whose son he embalmed and buried less than five months ago and the man is sitting there reading the *Gleaner* and waiting his turn. The man's son used to smoke crack and deal it and then he'd torment the father, calling him at all hours of the night demanding money, breaking into the house, stealing the stereo and the television set, stealing the microwave. Then the police shot him dead in a hold up.

Just put him in any old box, you can find, doctor, the cheapest one, the father said to him when he came into the funeral home. He doesn't deserve anything special, doctor. Whatever you have there, the cheapest thing; just drop him in a hole. He dropped a blank check on Septimus's desk and stepped out. It was the man's only son, and he'd had him late in life and had doted on him.

The man looks up when Septimus enters and it's as if he hasn't slept in months, the red eyes sunken down into holes and swollen, the face with the flesh gone completely. He smiles weakly at Septimus. But it's no smile at all; a great yowl is what it is.

The boy still calls, he says, dead and buried now five whole months, and still every night when the phone rings, it's him, abusing me same way, threatening to chop us up, threatening to burn down the house, threatening us with murder.

Sorry to hear it, Septimus says, shaking his head and holding the man's kneecap, sorry to hear it, my friend. What else can he say? What can anyone say to a thing like that?

When it's finally his turn in the chair, he cannot find words to explain to Jingles what has just occurred in his house, the news his wife has just delivered to him – how she slipped with Robbie Chen. Just so, she slipped.

And yet Jingles understands all of this. He is not outraged; he doesn't tell Septy to leave her or beat her. There, there, he says, cluck clucking like a peeled head fowl. There, there.

Septimus cannot weep, cannot expose himself so. Now and again he coughs to clear his throat, and when his eyes fill, he grinds down on his teeth so the tears will not overflow. His heart is ripped up into pieces, that's how it feels, his poor little liver-spotted heart.

And Jingles. He folds and unfolds the cloth at Septimus's neck, he pushes up and down the chair, he brushes Septimus's throat and neck and then he dusts them with powder, he passes his fingers gently along his ears, along his chin and forehead and his cheeks. He daubs his throat and along the sides of his face. He hums a soft tune as he works. You all right there, friend, he cries out, you all right.

10.

He feels Fiona sliding out of bed, and he sees her in a pink nightie yawning and stretching and drawing back the curtains of the window that look out at the garden full of nasturtiums. She is opening and closing drawers at the dresser; there is the clink of wire hangers on the metal rack in the closet, the squall of the shower. She returns again, a cloud of powder dust billowing up over the room.

Septimus, she calls and he pretends to be fast asleep, but he feels her eyes on his neck, on his face. Septimus, she calls again, and he opens his eyes just a little to see her there by the side of his bed watching him. He doesn't want to, but at the last minute, he sticks out his face and she presses her lips to his forehead.

Later, she says, and he nods, listening to her heels tap across the tiles and down the corridor toward the kitchen where her daughters and his son and the housekeeper are waiting. Later, after work, she will go and see the Chinese man, no doubt about that. Later, she will go and mash up their good, good marriage.

For wasn't that what she said? She saw him again and she slipped, as if slippage was a common occurrence these days.

We should separate, he had said to her at once in a voice that was frighteningly calm, and even he was surprised by how calm he was. Everything in the room was still, even his heart was quiet. Maybe he was expecting it. He had already lost so much in his life, had already buried so much, what was this one last thing.

I figured it out already, she said.

No, he said, you go back to the Chinese man. You go and find out what you looking for again. You go and see. Get it out of your system.

I am finished with Robbie, she said.

Then maybe it's me, he said. Maybe I have to figure out things.
He was muttering to himself, muttering out into the night.

Go and see your brother in America, she said.

So you can bring Robbie here into our house?

No, she said heavily. No.

He turned, trying to look in her face deeply, trying to read
something there, trying to believe her, but the trust was already
gone. How was he going to manage now? He looked in her eyes,
which he could see clearly enough in the lamplight, but he didn't
know what he was looking for.

Later that morning, hours later, in a half stupor, he senses
someone at the bedroom door, at the foot of the bed, at the dresser
near his back, at the door again and tapping lightly. His eyes fly
open.

Who is that, he cries, from a mouth he must creak open.

You all right, Papa?

It's his son from the first wife, April's son, and the tears come
immediately to his eyes. He clears his throat. You need money?
he says to his son. See the wallet there on the dresser. Take a few
dollars.

The boy is as tall as he is, dark-skinned and peanut-faced like
his mother. He minces in his walk like her, he behaves as if this
world does not belong to him, this world isn't for him to mash
down, to show his worth. The boy is elegant in a crisply pressed
khaki suit. His hair, neatly brushed, is parted to one side. He turns
and the boy's eyes are on him, taking in the face puffy with fatigue,
with worry, with depression, the eyes listless, his hair completely
white at the edges.

You all right, Papa, you sick?

He wants the boy to leave; he can't stand the boy to see him so.
It's all right, man, he says, cross now. You're not late for school?

I can call the doctor, the boy says.

Go to school, he says to the boy, tears threatening to burst out
now. There is a brown slug slowly making its way up the white
wall leaving a pink slime behind.

He eats from the pot of food the housekeeper Mrs. Watson has simmering on the stove. He locks himself in the study going through the mountain of bills. There are phone calls to return, letters to attend to. He calls Raul who has been running the funeral home these last two months as he cannot dress another dead body, cannot touch another empty vessel that has no light teeming inside it.

He has spent so much of his life – he has spent his whole entire life – burying his sister, bringing her back to life again and again and then burying her again, that ragged red stew he saw in a bag up at the morgue, the only identifiable thing her green slippers with the plastic roses bunched on the toes. He'd picked them out for her in the store, and he remembered the velvet ribbons in her hair, soaked with so much blood, they'd turned black. How many memorials has he built? Then came Rosa, his half sister, his father's outside child. There was Althea come back to life, and he couldn't even see Rosa, so frozen was he. So what now? Here is his son whom he doesn't know at all; here are his wife's daughters he wanted only to discipline and shout orders to. Here are his children buzzing with life, laughing and playing and singing and jumping, and he has left early each morning until late at night, he has spent so much of his life absorbed with absolutely nothing but dead bodies. Repairing something it is too damn late to fix. What kind of life is that? And now his wife has slipped with the Chinese man. Slipped.

He sees it in his mind's eye, plays it over and over again in his head, the way the whole thing happened.

How they meet at a hotel, eat dinner at a little corner table and afterwards go upstairs, overcome by desire. Robbie Chen takes off her pumps, removes her stockings and massages her feet. He takes her toes and, one by one, dips them slowly in his mouth. She is nailed by the heat between her thighs. In the bed in the hotel room, she lies with her head on his chest; he scratches her scalp. There is the tap tap of his beating heart, the low grunt as he listens with a cocked head. Under his gaze, she is a little girl again, soft, full of giggles. Then she remembers her marriage, she remembers Septimus.

Can't you put that away? she says, annoyed at the cock swollen again – even though an hour ago when the undertow was madly dragging her away, it did not annoy her. They are on the couch near a window that looks over the pool. A dog lifts its leg to piss in a thicket of chrysanthemums. Robbie Chen laughs. He catches Fiona in his big arms, and roars with laughter.

The entire afternoon is chewed up in his study going over bills for the funeral home and when he steps out onto the verandah that overlooks the valley below and the green hills beyond, he spots his son out there with a soccer ball going at it by himself. The boy is not so bad he thinks, his girlish son is not a good-for-nothing, he has the ball on his chest now, on his forehead, back again on his thigh, on the tip of his shoe, on the tip again, on the tip.

In the bedroom, he hauls on sneakers, takes off the robe he's been drudging in all day and puts on sweats. He steps out into the garden where Hanif is still busy with the ball.

Come, he calls to his son.

In no time, he is panting and wet with sweat. He's laughing and yelling at the boy, fighting him for the ball, tackling and letting go and tackling again. The boy is quick on his feet. The boy has his hair pulled away from his face with an elastic band. The boy looks so much like his mother, the nose like a trumpet shooting out of his face. The boy has a voice like cream, smooth and effeminate, even when he's excited, even when he's rushing at his father and screaming in defeat and stalking away, throwing up his hands. The boy falls first, and he falls in a tumble over the boy, the pile of limbs struggling still for the ball, the laughter, his face washed with sweat, his heart hammering, gasping for air. Okay, okay, he cries to the boy. The boy is tireless.

You all right, the boy says.

He is laughing and coughing, he is holding his waist and gasping. His face has turned from blue to purple.

Yeah, man, yeah, man, he hisses, holding onto the waist of a cassia tree, the long brown slats dangling above his head. He crumbles to the roots, his legs splayed ahead of him. Tears are leaking out of his eyes.

You all right? the boy says again, sitting next to him on the gnarled stump, holding his father's thigh. There are wasps everywhere, circling the nearby mauve blossoms.

I'm not as fit, Septimus says, and he is weeping and weeping. I'm not so fit at all.

And the boy is next to him looking on, one hand on the thigh while his father weeps. The boy is still, his face strangely calm and happy.

They do this now every evening, even when it rains and the grass is slick. He can't wait for the boy to come home from school. The boy is all he has now, for his wife has slipped with the Chinese man, and he wants to keep the boy. He is desperate to keep something. All morning he's up to his neck with bills in the study. All afternoon, his eye is on his watch until he hears the car groaning over the hill, halting at the gate, the boy's soft shrill voice saying goodbye to his friends. The door slams; there is the clang clang of the metal rods on the gate. His beautiful son is home. He should be picking him up from school, but for weeks now he can't leave the house. He greets his son at the door. He is so shameless now with his affection. He musses up the boy's hair, wiry like April's, his first love. You learn anything at school, he says to the boy, laughing and taking his backpack from his shoulders and following the boy to his room, with the bed neatly made and all his books put away on shelves and nothing at all on the rug. A pair of trousers is folded over the back of a chair. A pair of shoes is underneath the chair. There is the new stereo he went out and bought his son for his birthday.

The boy ducks, he tries to slip away from his father, his face aflame, his face like a saucer with a big wide grin stretching it out. The boy doesn't know what to do with his father or with his father's affection. The boy has waited and waited his whole life for this. The boy sucks up his father's attention, he sucks it up until he's completely satiated, and then he opens his mouth again to suck for more.

1 1 .

His father comes to him in a dream virtually every night now. Sometimes his father is walking down the road on the way to the bank, and Septimus hails out to him, picking up his step, glad again to see his father, who is brand new and without the diabetes and the cancer and the stroke that devastated him at the end. He is walking tall and straight again, the bones high and pointed on his cheeks, but when they are just about to pass, the eyes meeting directly, the eyes grinning a proud hello, when his father is just about to pass him, brush against his yellow shirt, he sees that it's not his father at all, in fact, nothing about this person resembles his father, and to think all along, all this time, he thought the person shambling down the road, the old man limping along the roadway with his mouth ringed with white from hunger was his father.

12.

He doesn't know how to look at Fiona, what tone of voice to use to talk with her, and in bed now, he doesn't know if he should fuck her or turn his back on her. He doesn't know if he should stop talking to her completely, if he should just take his things and move out. Every time he looks at her now, he sees Robbie Chen swallowing her up with his big arms. He wants to beat her, he wants to take off his belt and destroy her with blows, and yet he knows if he so much as loses his guard, that would be the absolute end of everything altogether. A part of him loves her still but the rest is completely devastated. It would've been better he thinks, if he did not know, living day after day blighted in ignorance. He sees her daughters now with new eyes. Did they know about Fiona and their father? He feels his son's eyes on him, now, and he knows that the whole world is watching to see what he will do, to see if he's a man and exactly what quality of a man.

They are all the same, this is what he is thinking, these women he has loved, April and Fiona and even his mother. His mother did not even wait for his father's body to turn properly to dust. Every time he goes over there to his home, there is Anglin pressing his ass into the pillows of the chair on the verandah and cocking up his feet on the ledge, there is Anglin under the almond tree eating dinner that the helper is serving him, there is Anglin driving up in the new blue Vauxhall to pick up his mother so they can travel to the mineral bath at Milk River.

13.

Do you want me and Hanif to move out? he says to Fiona one night. You want us to go? He doesn't want to go, but how is he to live feeling like this, with the rage beating at him like this?

I don't want you to go, she says. I love you.

The two of us, he says, me and the Chinese man.

There is the light from the moon peering in through the curtains and it falls on her face. He used to believe her. He used to believe every word; it used to be a face that comforted him.

You can't love two people, he says. You're married to me, he says, tapping his heart. You want a divorce, is that it? His voice is rising.

She has been lying on her back, her eyes staring straight ahead. Now she turns to her side, now she holds him. And he wants to lean in, he wants to be there, comforted, but he cannot trust.

What is wrong with me? he says. Because something must be wrong, how else to explain; he has been a good man to Fiona; he's never cheated nor raised his hand to her, never come home drunk or raised his voice at her children.

There isn't anything wrong with you. She holds him. Her head is on his chest. He feels cold on the inside. He feels hard and cold. You're a good, good man, Septimus.

Then maybe that is the problem, he's too good a man. But when he's good they leave, and when he misbehaves, they leave.

I had to see him, Fiona says, It's been three years. We had to talk, to close up things. I couldn't go back to a man like that, Septimus. But I had to see him and close the chapter.

His chest is heaving up and down. It's as if there's some huge load he's carrying and he wants it off. Off!

I want to believe you, he says.

I understand, she says.

No, he says, you don't fucking understand.

Three hundred people had been invited to the first ceremony with April. Three hundred saw his shame a year later when she ran away from him. Twenty-five at most came to his second wedding with Fiona. He didn't want a big show. Only people close to him. Maybe he married Fiona too quickly; maybe he should've waited, waited until she was really and truly done with the Chinese man.

Winston invited me up there, he tells her. Maybe I should go. And Hanif can go to his mother. And you can figure out things. Figure out if you love me or if you love the Chinese man. Figure out which man you want. He has never wanted to go to America so badly as at that moment.

She pauses as if to digest this piece of news. I don't have anything to figure out, she says. You are the one. She holds him. It's you. You! She kisses his face. Her own face is wet.

I'll go for two weeks or so, he says, and that will give you time.

I don't need time, she says, I've figured it out. But you should go anyway, go and spend time with your brother. See his life.

He is quiet. Suddenly he doesn't want to go any more. He is afraid to spend all this time with his brother whom he doesn't know any more, his brother who disappeared for twenty-five years and then showed up a few months ago to shove his father into a coma and then to help bury him. He's afraid that when he returns he'll have no home. He's afraid, but he cannot say that now.

14.

They are on the verandah with their backs leaning against the wall, watching the rain tear against the banana leaves, watching the swiftly moving black clouds, watching the rain beat down the hibiscus flowers, watching it lay gutters in the dirt.

You miss your mother, he asks his son, you miss April?

He feels the boy's eyes resting on his jaw, searching his face, considering how to answer.

The boy lets out a tremendous sigh. Sometimes, he says. But I see her often enough.

The boy sees her every other weekend; his uncle picks him up at school on Friday afternoons, drops him off again Monday mornings.

You'd prefer if we got back together? he says to the boy and then he regrets asking such a stupid thing. It's been so long now, how to patch up something so broken. Why even to stir up feelings, put out words that can't amount to anything. Though he would give anything just to see her, just a glimpse. After all these years.

A streak of lightning tears at the sky; they wait for the crack of thunder to follow. He is glad for the downpour that will cool down the afternoon. The air had been too heavy, too oppressive.

I like it here, the boy says carefully.

Septimus feels an opening in his chest. It's the first time he's been able to talk to the boy like this. He knows the boy doesn't yet relax with Fiona, he knows the boy is saying this just for him.

I know you don't care for Fiona much, he says. You don't love her as you love your mother.

You love her, the boy says.

Yes, he says, his belly swelling up. We're going through a tough time.

It will pass, the boy says. First there is the storm, and then the storm passes.

He looks at the boy next to him, the boy whose face is straight ahead staring at the rain pouring down in silver sheets. He looks at his son who is growing up into a man and understanding things.

I loved your mother, he says. Even after she took you and left. I was young, he says, and stupid. You can't just raise your hand and strike a woman, he says. And then he looks at his pretty son whose effeminacy he's struck out against so many times.

You can't just knock a woman, he says again slowly, remembering how she said she was leaving him, how she said she wasn't in love with him any more, and wasn't sure as a matter of fact if she'd ever been in love with him.

She hadn't wanted to sleep with him in months. Everything had fallen to pieces around them. All the expectations, all the plans, the future lay ahead in shambles. Then, as if with a mind of its own, his hand had struck out. Bam! Bam! Her face darkened at once, and her eyes filled.

At first she said nothing. Perhaps she was stunned. Perhaps she was calculating what to do next. It was the middle of the night. He was tired, he had just come in from a wake, and the fire was hot in him. His hand at his side was tingling, and he hated himself at that moment; he hated her. Then she pushed him and ran wordless out of the house and into the night, taking the boy with her. He went after in his tight suit – he had gained all this weight – in the shoes killing his corns. At one point he saw the white nightie shimmering in the distance. He couldn't catch them. That was the last time he laid eyes on her. A car approached, the car slowed down, he heard the door slam, and he heard the car reverse and turn. There was no closure at all, all these years. Every one of his dealings with her has been through her brother who treats him with such scorn, who treats him to this day as if he is nothing at all, just pure steaming shit.

You can't beat down your children either, he says, and his voice breaks up completely.

Beside him, the boy is still.

Beating solves nothing at all, he moans. Absolutely nothing. You need to set limits, yes, you need boundaries, but not with lashes. I sorry for the lashes, he says to the boy who has his mother's face with the mole and the trembling lashes, and the thin narrow lips. I didn't know better. He stops to draw in a huge breath. And he hopes the housekeeper doesn't find them, he hopes no one is listening.

Fiona needs to figure out things. Maybe I not a good husband to her. Maybe I don't know how to be a good husband. I don't know if she wants to still be with me. I need to go away on a trip.

I'm coming with you, the boy says.

He is a little taken aback by the boy. He had not thought the boy would want to come of his own volition. He thought the boy would want to be with his mother. He had never travelled with his son, all these years. It is almost unimaginable, walking the city streets of a foreign country with his son. He was so busy with his father; he was so obsessed with his father.

Okay, he says, okay. I don't know anything yet for sure. He doesn't want to disappoint the boy. But we'll go somewhere. Just you and me, we'll go.

15.

Late one morning, he and Fiona set out for Treasure Beach, the southern coastline of the island where the sand is the colour of molasses. There are few tourists on this part of the coast, and the guesthouses and hotels don't all belong to the foreigners. Along here the undertow is much more dangerous, the waves towering, the coral reefs much more plentiful as they jut out black and startling. It is Fiona's idea that they take a few days just for themselves. Her new girl, Hazel, is running the haberdashery and they've arranged for a driver to take the children back and forth to school. Since his father's death, he himself has hardly been going in, once, twice a week at most, and not even the whole day. They're driving via Mandeville so they can lunch with Fiona's uncle who is a dentist at the public hospital. The hotel sits on the bluff of a hill and it looks out to the sea only a few feet below. It is scorching hot even after the heavy rains that followed them from the capital and flooded out some roads, put houses under water. Some kind of a depression the meteorologist said on the news.

In the hotel at Treasure Beach they make love, as this is the only language he knows, but when they are done, the chasm between them is even wider than before and he doesn't know what to do with his wife, with his marriage, with his own damn self, with the disgust battling away in his chest. There is no peace whatsoever in his head. At night no sleep comes, and in the day with the oppressive heat overhead, it is almost impossible for him to move; everywhere there is a terrible, terrible weight. He drinks a shot of Appleton on the rocks; it numbs him a little, relaxes him, puts him to sleep, but the truth is the moment he's awake, the whole damn thing rears up in him again.

Fiona is in the sea and he's alone in the hotel room, and suddenly all the walls are stretching closer, suddenly the miniature palms with their long slim spikes seem about to assault him, and the lizards are watching him too, nodding and sticking out their yellow tongues, and there are the bloody ants carting away pieces of bread, carting away what looks to be his shoes.

We should divorce, he says finally when she has returned from wading in the sea. There is nothing satisfying in their relationship now. Nothing whatsoever.

No, she says, sitting next to him on the verandah that looks out along the coastline. She is sipping on his glass of Appleton. She seems calm and content. She seems as if she's done the very right thing with her life, even if that is to fuck up their marriage.

But why not, you already mash up things between us with your actions, he says, I mean how I going to believe you now when you say a thing?

He understands that she needed to see Robbie, to resolve things with him and that perhaps in resolving one thing, other feelings got stirred. He understands it completely, for he recognizes these same feelings for his ex-wife, his billboard love. But you can't allow these feelings to get out of hand; this is how he sees it. This is how he sees life. You have to practice restraint. She did not restrain herself with the Chinese man.

He sees the two of them again, sees them over and over, cannot get them out of his blinking head, sees them there somewhere on the coast on a boat that bobs softly on the water. He sees that there is a soft warm rain that falls slowly on them. He sees him handing her a box, squeezing Fiona's legs underneath the table.

If it's jewellery, she says, you might as well save it for the girls. She peeks in anyway. It's a bracelet.

It's over, Robbie.

She watches as his face crumbles. Something in her throat crumbles as well.

Despite herself she goes with him to a nearby hotel after their meal. He quickly undresses, he slips into the sheets. His body is still sinewy with muscles, but his breasts now are like those of a woman, the skin around his belly no longer taut. She's undone the clasps of her bra so her breasts can breathe. She's kicked off her heels and removed her stockings; she's taken off the heavy earrings and dropped them in her purse. On the side table near the couch sits a glass of scotch, and a pack of Matterhorn. It's the rage that has overtaken her all of a sudden that has left her there silently watching him and seething.

He knows every inch of her body, he has kissed and massaged it, oiled and bathed it, he has adorned it with gifts. He knows the history of every scar, every dimple, every mole. He has sat with her during two births, during morning sickness and breakwater, his hand has been on her stomach since conception, during the first kicks. He has been steady with his love, he has been profuse with his feelings; still he is a coward.

Fee, he calls, his voice wet with lust. And she thinks they are all the same, for in the end, this is what it boils down to. If she curses him now, if she calls him all the nasty names piling up on her tongue, if she abuses him now, he would come over, he would apologize, he would beg forgiveness, and in the end it would come back to this.

It is not because of Septimus, she tells herself, as she drives back across town tossed between rage and desire. It's because the same course would simply repeat itself, nothing would've changed. And where would that leave her?

It is too warm inside the hotel room and near the sea is the only place where there is a breeze. There is great moon, but the moon is partly covered by clouds, and so the night comes across as if there's nothing but fog. Sometimes a sliver of light manages to escape and it shimmers on the water. And the whole damn thing has a romantic glow to it, except that he doesn't feel romantic at all, he feels lost, as if every important thing has been taken away.

He stops to look at her, though he can't really make out her face in the night that has the look of fog. Not far from them, he sees the glow of a cigarette, lighting then dulling. A gust of wind sweeps across the beach then stops.

The truth is: here is his big strong wife next to him and he's so destroyed inside.

She holds him around the waist. Her head is on his chest without a shirt. He feels cold on the inside. He feels hard and cold. He pushes her away, and she lets go of him and walks off down the beach in the direction of the glowing cigarette and the hotel.

He lies down on the sand, flat on his back; he watches her disappear into the night and then, what must be hours later, he watches her appear again bringing with her the smell of kelp.

I know we've hashed this and hashed this and come to no grand conclusion, he says when she is back again near where he is sitting on the sand and she has folded herself up next to him. But I made my decision now, he says. Have your affair with Robbie Chen. Have it and get it out of your system, he says with no anger at all in his voice. I will go away, he says, and give you time. I will work on my resentment, he says. I don't want to feel resentful. I just want to be free, he says. And he sighs heavily. And if you decide you still want the marriage, he says, then I will be here.

He is not sure how he's going to do this, how he's going to separate for some time and not feel anger, not want to punish her, but he wants to do it, for his chest feels wide and at the same time it feels light. He feels as if at the end of the day he's going to have much more room inside his chest, he feels as if there'll be more width and he likes the idea of all this space. He feels a great calm settle over him, a calm that seems to come from the wide-open mouth of the sea. There is Fiona sitting beside him on the sand, silent as a stone, and there is the moon that hardly looks like a moon for it has that white sheet covering it, and there is the sound of the sea, the slap, slap of the waves, the spray of the salt on his face and his bare chest, the faint smell of oil and exhaust from boats.

Come, he says, and he rises and gives her his hand. She rises with him and they walk out into the sea, not far, not far, for she probably doesn't want the water to mess with her hair, which has just been straightened, but it is way too hot to go back inside the hotel room and he cannot bear to sleep with the air conditioner breathing on him, but then maybe they could camp out on the beach; he hasn't done that since he was a boy, but then maybe Fiona would be afraid of the crabs nipping away at her bottom.

Oh, well, he thinks, oh, well. But he could put it to her, anyway, he could ask her and see, maybe she'd be in the mind for an adventure.

THE FAMILY

1 .

The plane had barely left the ground, had barely settled itself more firmly in the sky and levelled off, her ears had only just stopped popping when their father appeared wearing the same light blue bush-jacket with red embroidery on the pockets he used to wear on Sundays for the afternoon meal.

So you going to America with Winston, he said.

She looked across at Winston who was sitting in the aisle seat fast asleep, his chair pressed all the way back, his mouth wide open. And then she looked again at her father, who'd once been her grandfather, sick unto death, but who was sitting in the empty middle seat now. Then she looked out the tiny window at the blanket of white cumulous clouds covering the vast, immeasurable sky. She pinched her leg.

I thought you dead, she said.

I am, he said, but you have the gift.

I saw them lock you down in the box, she said, I saw them throw the dirt.

He flicked his wrist as if brushing away something nasty. That just the body sick and tired and diseased, he said; this is the real me now; all that drop off, he said, sickness and such; all that gone.

She didn't know if she was glad to see him or not now that he had become her father. What was she to do with the person who was her grandfather, the person she'd loved so much? Furthermore, he did not look like the old woman who glowed with the purple light and sometimes the white light, the old woman who was her sister and her great grandmother and her best friend and her daughter and her mother all rolled into one. He did not have the old woman's spirit, he did not talk the same way the old woman talked; the light pouring off him was dim, she had to strain to see his form. Still, he smelled the same, of Old Spice and Dettol and Canadian healing oil and Bayrum. And he looked younger too, more lean, but his eyes were shiny and hot; she couldn't bear to meet them for long.

You coming to America with us? she asked him, looking at Winston turning in his seat.

I'll come when I can, he said. Busy times these – Septimus to care for and your mother and Nora and all those people I wronged, and you know how many children I have. He sighed wearily. I'll come when I can. But they have me busy at this place, so many meetings and councils, so many people to fix up things with.

You with the old woman then, she asked him, you with Althea? In Sunday school they say people die and go to heaven. You in heaven, then, she asked him, you with Althea and the old woman and the others?

Heaven, my foot, he cried angrily. Then after a long while he said, this place alright, I suppose, not rosy, but alright. He grinned and blue light beamed out more fiercely around him. Althea and the old woman not here, everyone else is here; to see Althea, they say I have to wait a long time. Don't know how long, he said.

After studying him for some time, she concluded that she didn't mind him sitting down beside her in his bush-jacket and blue light. She wasn't done with him though, she had big things to ask him, bones to pick with him, her grandfather who was now her father, but this wasn't the time. You look better now, she said, reaching out to touch his legs that had once been so rigid, and her hand went right through and into the fabric of the plane seat.

She cried out in dismay and Winston stirred in his sleep.

I know, he said, in a voice that seemed used to this kind of reaction, everybody say I feel different now.

You remember Harold, he said, changing the subject. It was Harold who came for me at the end. Then he laughed. All this time I thought he in Panama, but he's a big man now in the council. He grew sober again. I know you thinking about me and your mother, he said, shaking his head. I had all these plans, all these things I intended to do, but I don't know, he said, I messed them up, every blasted thing. I didn't plan carefully enough, and this blasted place down here can be tough as hell. So much accounting I have to do now, he said hissing, so much repair.

She remembered her mother down there at the shop, her mother in her little yellow dress, her mother who Winston took her to meet and who carried the smell of roasted peanuts and dried molasses and shame.

Look, he said, I'll come again; the air-hostess about to come now with food, and Winston about to wake up and I've to go now to council. I'll see you, he said.

And just as suddenly as he'd arrived he was gone. She put her hand on the still warm seat and Winston now was rubbing his eyes and yawning and stretching and leaning across to look out the window on her side. I had the weirdest dream, he says, kissing her on the top of her head and sighing. Are we almost there, Rosa, are we almost home? The sky now was grey and impenetrable. Yes, indeed, he said, nodding and grinning, yes indeed.

She turned to look with him at the vast unending stretch of silver, and tried not to think of all that awaited her there – which was what the old woman had said: no need to look at the past or at the future my dear, just stay in the moment.

She relaxed, though, knowing her grandfather would come, and the old woman, too, and that she would never be alone again, and true to his word, he was already at the house waiting, sitting on her bed upstairs on the third floor when Winston showed her to her room and she sat next to him for a long time, her grandfather, warmed in the blue glow that glinted off him, until a whole host of other people started coming in.

Who them? she cried, disturbed by the noise and the quarrelling and the cold in the house that had no end.

People from before who used to live here, her grandfather said.

A tow-headed little boy pushed her in the chest. Who are you?

She shoved him back. Get out, she barked; this my room now.

The boy fell on his bottom and knocked his head against the door. He started to wail.

Winston looked at her, his eyes shining. You like your room, Rosa? We can paint it another colour if you like. Welcome home, he said, turning the knobs on a box near the window rattling out heat.

Suddenly the boy's mother was slamming up the stairs and into the room, and at the same time she saw the candle turning over on the rag rug in the living room, and the great raging fire that sprang up all at once and she could hear their shrieks echoing through the house as the boy and his mother tried to beat back flames, only to be swallowed in the blaze.

Sometimes this is what would wake her in the night, the screams from the fire, the blazing heat crowding up around her, and the smell of burnt hair that fastened to her teeth. She'd be unable to sleep, and the next day she would doze in class and the teacher would glare at her and send Winston a note and then he would get cross.

After two solid months of putting up with the goings and comings of the boy and his mother and the everlasting fire, she decides finally she has to tell Winston so they can do something about it.

She chooses one of those evenings he's actually cooking dinner, not the usual sandwich, or pizza or Thai food he takes out from the place down the road, Tantawan, and this she takes to mean he's in a good mood, and there is a little more time to spare, not the constant hurry. Still he's doing everything at once, defrosting the meat, stacking the dishwasher, putting away the groceries, sweeping the kitchen floor and sorting his mail. This and the people racing back and forth in the house and quarrelling give her a headache

Help me chop these, please, Rosa. He lays out a red onion and cloves of garlic, half a red bell pepper, two stalks of scallion, a thumb of ginger, a cutting board and the small paring knife. There's olive oil heating in a pan on the stove.

When *All Things Considered* comes on, he opens a bottle of Sam Adams, pours half a glass and offers her a sip, which she loves. Her grandfather, when she sat in his lap, used to let her sip his stout and his glass of rum, but all that happened a long time ago, all that seems far away. The chicken is finally in the pot and browning. He pours in the chopped items, sprinkling in the yellow curry, the massala powder, a taste of salt and too much red pepper flakes as usual and as he's going to forget the vinegar, she reminds him.

Winston don't forget the vinegar.

He looks at her sitting at the counter in the middle of the kitchen and smiles. Forgot about it completely, he says.

It's the first smile she's seen on him today and now she's afraid that what she's about to tell him will ruin his face completely. He's been sad over Marie Jose – he thinks everything is all because of Marie Jose, but she can see her grandfather over there, weighing heavy on his throat.

Winston, she says, there's people in the house.

He looks out at her from underneath his eyebrows, black and thick like her grandfather's used to be.

People? he says in that tone that tells her right away where his mind is going; he thinks he has to find a doctor now for her head.

I can see them, she says, and there was a fire that burned them up, but they're still here.

He's nodding now. Returning to his beer, he takes a long swig, and she watches the staggering Adam's apple. Okay, he says, and she can see he's biting his tongue, trying not to scream at her.

Maybe you could get Marie Jose to clear the house, she says, grateful to her grandfather who is quick on his feet today with suggestions.

Marie Jose? he says, as if he has no idea who this is.

Yes, she says, maybe Marie Jose could come over and douse the house, or open a coning and ask the deva of the house to clear them out. Where these words are coming from, filling up her mouth, she has no idea, except her grandfather is over there by the door nodding.

He finishes the beer in one gulp and wipes his mouth with the back of his hand. He burps noisily. Okay, he says.

She can see that he, too, is wondering where the hell she gets all that from, but he says nothing.

He's slicing into a hunk of that dry, leathery, salty manchego. He's gained fifteen pounds since he's been back, which makes his face look swollen, so he's started wearing a goatee. He used to be worried about his belly, his spreading thighs, but he's done with that diet; he reaches for the bread he's been hiding in the freezer and drops a slice in the toaster. Want some, he says.

She shakes her head; she has no appetite at all. She watches him bite into the toast.

Who else is in the house, he asks quietly, dangerously, his mouth full of food. He does not look at her, but at some place in the middle distance near her ears.

Winston, she says, near tears now, she does not like the look on his face whatsoever, and there's her grandfather standing in the doorway looking pleased with himself. She's beginning to think her grandfather is not a good person, not even in death.

Who else is in the house, Rosa?

Grandpa, she whispers.

Jesus Christ, he cries, throwing down the toast, I knew it, I fucking knew it. You brought him here didn't you, you brought him here.

He followed me on the plane.

No wonder I can find no peace at all in this damn place, no wonder I feel like shit every day. Jesus Christ! Tell him to go, he says, talking to her now through his teeth, his hands trembling, his face washed clean of any trace of blood, and the veins standing big in his neck. I can't believe this shit, he says, and he's grabbing his coat and his hat, he's grabbing his keys from the hook, and he slams out the house into the cold, grey afternoon, trembling the windows behind him. Moments later his car screeches away.

An eerie silence settles into the house after that.

Maybe you should go, she says to her grandfather who has his head in his hands. You're only causing trouble. You're not a good person.

He'll come round, the grandfather says softly. Winston will come around.

She turns off the radio that has the blasted NPR people begging for money again, and she turns off the stove.

Maybe you should go, she says again in a stern voice and from the corner of her eyes she notices someone else leaning up in the doorway, the old woman, whom she's not seen in some time and immediately the old woman fills up the entire room with her glow and this sends a gladness all over the house. She is covered in white, the old woman, and the white descends on the kitchen and Rosa finds herself starting to breathe evenly again, from the bottom of her spleen, and this brings her to tears. She cries for a long time on the floor surrounded by the gladness and the glow and the white.

What if he doesn't come back? she asks the house.

A half-hour later she hears his car pulling up in the drive.

She runs to the door.

He's gone, she says. I told him to go. He's not going to come back, ever again. I told the old woman too. And the little boy and his mother that burned in the fire. I told all of them to clear the hell out.

She can tell he doesn't believe her.

It's alright he says, taking off his coat and hat. In his hand he has a paper bag. I bought some stuff that might work, he says, some smudge sticks. Over at the stove he lights a bundle which immediately perfumes the house with a cedar tree smell. Here, he says, handing her one of the bundles pillowing with smoke. This is supposed to be good for clearing. She follows behind him through the rooms, waving the smudge sticks like a magician and from the couch, the mother and her son watch them suspiciously. Maybe her grandfather left after all – she doesn't sense him anywhere in the house. But the old woman is there sitting on her bed upstairs and knitting, a bundle of yarn lying at her feet. She peers closer to see what the old woman is making and she sees it's a pretty red scarf with a diamond chain stitch that runs down the middle. She thinks she's seen this scarf before, but she can't quite place it. She must remember to ask Winston on another day, not this one, she thinks, sitting beside the old woman and leaning into the white pouring off her shoulders and smiling as it envelopes her entire face and chest.

2.

Two in the morning and he calls his mother on the phone. He has talked to his mother twice since his return. Mostly he hands the phone to Rosa when she calls and later he takes it to close, the exchange between them cool and lacklustre. But tonight he wants to be with his mother again, he wants to be in her soft laugh, in her pauses and sighs, tonight he wants to be in her moans. He imagines the shrill ring of the telephone dragging her from the depths of sleep and back into the big empty dark room and he imagines her trying to find the blasted phone, her hands scrambling around on the night table trying to stop the awful jangling, and knocking her glass of water to the floor with a crash.

Things all right there, she cries, when she hears his voice.

Yes, he says, shambling over to the window in the kitchen and staring out at the impenetrable dark.

Winston, you there? How's everybody? How's Rosa? You all right?

Yes, he says, not quite able to put his sentences together yet. He can't say exactly why he's called. He doesn't sleep any more, he cannot sleep through the night, there is the picture of his father, there is his father on top of him, there is his father's breath screaming in his ears, his father who has taken up residence now in his house.

I know it's late, he says, but I just wanted some comfort. I just wanted to hear your voice. I miss you, he says.

You miss me? She sounds surprised. But that is nice, Winston.

Yes, he says. All these years I've missed you and tonight it just feels awful.

You have to come home again, you and Rosa. Come more often.

Yes, he says, opening the cabinet and pouring himself a tiny glass of anisette.

Come in the summertime when school is over. Lots of changes to the house.

She doesn't mention Anglin and he doesn't ask either, he figures she'll tell when she's ready.

It'd be nice to see you again, Winston.

He sees her in a rumpled blue house dress at the bottom of the garden near the willow trees, her uncombed hair pinned up with bright yellow clips, and she is laughing at something Anglin has just said. He cannot imagine her now with Anglin, cannot imagine her in Anglin's arms. How long had she and Anglin been courting? Had they just been waiting and waiting, counting down the days? He used to think he knew his mother, but now he's not so sure. He sees her again as he'd seen her at the funeral, tall and slim and austere in a black hat that tilted saucily at an angle. The mantilla covered her entire face.

You think I killed him, Mother? He takes the glass of anisette to his mouth and drinks it down slow and deliberate.

He hears the sharp intake of her breath. Then she rushes to fill the silence.

Who? Mass Sam? Then she lets out a sigh that sounds like a wail. Oh, don't bother with that now, Winston. Don't bother with that. Is that the story you spin for yourself up there in the cold? Don't bother with that now at all. Mass Sam was on his way out, you hear me. Plus, you know Mass Sam and his temper. You know your father and his temper. Same way he lives, same way he dies.

She pauses to inhale sharply and to swallow saliva. And he sees in the night that there are a thousand different shapes out there and that the tall trees standing at the side of the house seem strikingly alert.

All the time I feel him in the house like he's hounding me.

Yes, his mother says, you may have to hire somebody to clear the house.

That's what Rosa says.

Yes, his mother says, Rosa would know these things. She has the gift.

He does not want to know exactly what this gift is. He doesn't want to open up that box now. I've been seeing a healer, he tells his mother.

What's that now?

Touch healing, he says. And when she does not respond, I'm trying to deal with my anger, he says, trying to put Papa to rest; I trying to deal with my heart.

Oh, that, she says in a vague quiet way, as if nothing he says can ever be out of the ordinary and he smiles, for that is precisely the way his mother has always been. Outside now, there are the stars glittering in the heavens and the moon which casts a purple haze over the whole world.

So how the healing coming along, this touch business you doing, what exactly is that now? America has everything you can think of, his mother says. You name it and America has it there invented.

It's not American, he says testily, it's Japanese. He picks the broom from the closet; he leans it against the wall. Rosa's books are scattered all over the living room table; he stacks them in a neat pile.

Same difference. Anything to make money. So how it works now, Winston, this touch feeling.

He hears the laughter in her voice and he wants to hang up.

Well, whatever works, Winston, whatever works. Belief kills and belief cures. Down here we have all manner of remedies, we have baths and bush teas and oils and powders, you name it, we have it, the obeah man, the pocomania people, the shouters. Whatever you can find, son, it is good. You have the intention to look and that alone is fifty percent. You hear me. Fifty percent. Some people don't look at all. They walk into the same wall over and over again and they don't think to look right or to look left, they don't think to look up or to look down, they don't stop to think that there might be another opening altogether sitting there waiting for them. She pauses again and he wonders happily if this is indeed his mother and what, dear God, has overcome her. But maybe it's he, all these years, blinded and foolish, and keeping them at bay.

So you keep on with your touch feeling, his mother says; I

going to sleep now. God's willing. All right, Winston, you try and get some sleep too; put Mass Sam to rest, you hear me, put your father to rest.

And she hangs up.

He found Darcy online and it was her picture that drew him right away; she resembled his father's people who lived in the foothills of St. Elizabeth. She had the same box face, the same protruding forehead with the V-shaped Widow's peak meeting at the brow, the same sharpened cheekbones and hooded deep-set eyes, the nose like a brown rose, the lips large and soft.

His first session with her was on a Friday morning, a day he did not teach, and he figured he'd have all day to recover before he picked Rosa up from school. He told no one, not even Silas, he wanted to resolve this thing with his father once and for all. Her office was downtown, where parking was impossible, so he had to leave his car a good distance away and sprint back to her office way up on the sixteenth floor with views of the steepled church roofs and the narrow cobbled streets below where the old women walked their miniature poodles.

Darcy's door was wide open when he arrived, out of breath and sweaty. She was wiry, not much taller than five feet, with a patchwork of lines on her face and her hair streaked with gold. A wave of intensity flowed off her chest and this overwhelmed him greatly. But then she smiled a smile that was so big and warm and good, he felt washed in a balm, and was immediately stilled. His hands, grown damp in his dash through the streets, dried at once, his heart rate quieted; he felt calm, which he'd not been feeling in the days since he'd come home, what with settling Rosa into school and then dealing with her nightmares, the bed wetting, the stream of notes from the teachers – for a while there he was getting two a day – the dead people she claimed were walking through the house and then the theft, which left him stumped for a good two days before he broke down and told Silas, who immediately wanted to punish her.

You can't let this slide, Winston, it could worsen into habit. And this is America, they don't have any mercy on our children when they act out. You've to show her this can't go on.

175

She had stolen six bottles of nail polish from CVS; security found them in her bag. What was Rosa doing with nail polish, what was Rosa doing at CVS by herself? Had he overnight turned into the kind of person she couldn't ask for money? It was the manager who called him and he found her in his office, her back hard and rigid in the chair, her face a barred door. He tried to imagine why of all things nail polish, and not even a variety of colours, but all the same shade of moody maroon. Was it some boy she was dressing up to impress, had that time arrived already? Was it some kind of bet? They drove home in silence, the car full of his held-in disappointment and rage, the car full of the fear that was starting to set in his heart. Pretty soon her periods would start and the boys would begin to call. Already mounds were starting to grow underneath her blouse and on the streets already, heads were turning to stare at her brazenly. Soon he'd have to be the watch dog, searching through her drawers, and reading her mail, even the diary which he'd encouraged her to keep, soon he'd be foraging through that. And how the hell was he going to ensure that nobody would rape or molest her, or even steal her away? How was he going to ensure she wouldn't get mixed up with drugs or get into trouble with the law? Jesus Christ, he had no idea what he was getting into when he asked for the child, had no idea when he'd accepted her request.

Finally inside the house, he took out her suitcases from the closet and sat her down. You do that one more time, he cried, and I'll send you straight back to Jamaica, put you on the next flight, and let Septimus take care of you.

She said nothing to any of that, she stood before him hard and cold, her eyes like nails boring through his heart. He found that he was the one with the eyes big and bubbling and this weakness worried him no end, because what kind of discipline was this, what kind of way was this to scold her? He was beginning to think he was afraid of her when she drew into herself like this.

On top of Rosa, there was Marie Jose with whom you could say he had no relationship left at all, just the coming and going between them that had no heat left, just pure ceremony now, and how many times in his head has he replayed that scene with his father that morning in his mother's kitchen? What was it that had enraged his father so? Was it because he'd contacted Rosa's mother, was it that they were all naked now, everything exposed? Was it because he was taking Rosa and his father had nothing left? He did not know, he could find no solution that resolved his confusion. But at this moment in the presence of Darcy's smile, which crinkled her entire face, he felt centred – which was never a word he would use, but how else to explain the pull of gravity that was hovering underneath his navel and settling his feet so firmly into the ground, as if roots were growing at the bottom of them.

The room was washed in sunlight. Flute music played softly on a disk. At the back was an altar, and Qwan Yin was there, and the Buddha too and Jesus wearing his humblest look and Guru Mai whom he'd seen once on television, and some others he did not recognize. An electric fountain poured water over rocks. And everywhere there were the crystals he recognized from Marie Jose's cancer days, curved ones and double terminated ones, and bridges and gateways. The room hummed with their intense vibrations, his head too; he even felt his legs turning slowly to mush. He sat down in the chair across from Darcy. He looked at her face that resembled his father's tribe and he immediately felt safe and at ease, as if all would be well again. She was a psychotherapist and a healer but he was not interested in talking today; across the room near the window where the massage table lay was where he was drawn. He wanted her hands on him, he wanted to feel every one of her ten fingers probing inside his cells, soothing them, and the need pouring out of him was visceral.

You'd like a healing on the table? she asked, four minutes into the interview.

Yes, he whispered, breaking out at once into small patches of sweat.

Just take off your shoes, then; lie on your back, get comfortable, she said. I'll be back.

This was not exactly what he thought he'd come here to do, but there he was hoisting himself on the table, relieved that he'd remembered to wear decent socks. There he was settling himself comfortably on top of the soft white table.

She looked at him, but he had the feeling she was not looking at him at all, but through him, that in that moment her entire body had become this one giant sensate organ, listening and feeling and tasting and perceiving every pulse inside his body, and when that was done, as if she hadn't garnered enough, she went even further back, scanning his body for its history and his father's father's history, looking for wounds and defences and blocks and all other pieces of legacy he was carrying in his heart through time.

You all right? she asked, folding a blanket under his knees and covering him with another.

He nodded.

Just relax, she said; don't try to figure out everything. I can see you like to think about things. You're a teacher?

She was at his feet leaning up hot hands on the soles when the great falling began. He cannot even remember if he answered her or not. She belonged to his father's clan, of that he was sure, and so he allowed his entire body to fall down into the belly of the earth or wherever it was going. He did not resist. Immediately his dead sister Althea came. She met him at the foot of the garden near the blossoming lime trees and he fell into her arms full of pure beaming yellow refracted light. How long? Time fell away. The dogs came too, Blackie and Tiger. They died the summer he was ten. They barked and they played in the tall guinea grass and everywhere there were the nodding Spanish needles and the yellow clumps of rosemary and the waving willow trees. They sat on either side of him and, together with his sister, they washed him in the glimmer.

When he opened his eyes again, the hour had ended, and Darcy was at his side watching him. Oh, how she looked like his father's people from St. Andrews and from Troy and from Jericho Hill in Trelawney and from Mocco. Oh, how she looked like family.

Did you have a good visit with her, she asked.

He nodded slowly. He did not stop to wonder how she could've known he'd visited with his sister. The room reeked of Nad champa agarbatti and this brought water to his eyes.

It's okay, she said, laying hot hands on his shoulders and smiling. She loves you.

He was soothed by the sound of her voice and her eyes,

flushed with the love, by her hands on his skin, by the resemblance to his clan up there in the verdurous foothills and he loved her with a fierceness that was palpable.

He walked slowly back to his car, feeling slightly wobbly and drained of his strength. As if his skin had been peeled away, he felt both raw and papery; at the house, though it was only eleven in the morning, he closed the curtains and collapsed on the couch.

Who to call now and tell, who to explain it to, who would believe him now that his dead sister had come wrapped in a blanket of refracted light? He picked up the phone to call Silas but he was so tired, and then what exactly was he going to say to Silas, that made good common sense. He had no idea, so he put back down the phone, patted Ernest's head, which felt like a stone, fed him again, even though he was on a diet and had already eaten for the day, but something in the meow spoke out fiercely and Winston filled his bowl again and again. He boiled milk in a pan, ate bread slathered with butter, and when he finally fell asleep, the alarm set to wake him again in a few hours, it was a sleep that was like death, long and deep and still and completely devoid of dreams.

The next week he saw Darcy again. Again they did not speak. He could not say what was drawing him to the table, but there he was bending down to take off his shoes, emptying the loose change from his pocket, hoisting himself up and stretching out his spine. By the time her hands fell on his feet, he was already weeping. His sister did not come again. This time it felt as if ten pairs of hands were at work opening up his chest, pulling out old cords, cleaning them, repairing them, laying down new ones and then sewing him up again and charging him with colour and with light.

3.

It was a neighbourhood that had once been prosperous, but after The Flight it had lain heavily in ruins until the yuppies grew tired of the suburbs and moved in again to gentrify and to rebuild. Lots that once housed the poor were remodelled into cafes and restaurants and used CD stores and hairdressing salons and boutiques with beautifully dressed mannequins in the window. There was an entire block devoted to high-end design furniture, which, admittedly, was where he had bought the new white couch that Ernest had already put holes in. The only relic remaining from the old days was the nursing home across the street near the bank.

Impossible to find parking anywhere near her house, he leaves the car under a tree near the nursing home and watches as an ambulance with its lights flashing takes an old woman on a gurney into its maw . He walks quickly, the entire seven blocks, under-neath the cloudy, cold sky; March already, but spring nowhere in sight. He arrives at her door slightly warm and sweaty.

He rings the bell until finally there is movement, steps falling on the floor, the porch washed in a tableau of light. Somewhere inside the hollows of the building a dog howls.

Winston!

She sounds happy to see him, she sounds surprised. It's been almost a month.

Were you at the movies? They peck quickly on the lips.

No, he says, following her inside the cool dim house. She's dressed for bed, in blue silk pajamas he gave her one Christmas, the thick red glasses. I just wanted to see you, if that's okay. He grins. He no longer knows what's appropriate and what's not. It used to be he could drop by whenever, let himself in; now he has to call ahead, or if he's lucky like tonight, he'll catch her home. She's suddenly busy these days, taken up with singing, she says, some kind of women's *a cappella* and there's rehearsal two, three times a week.

In the kitchen she makes tea and he starts a fire in the grate. He can tell by the stilted movements of her tail that the dog is not sure what to make of his visit. Me neither, he says to the dog, stooping to scratch behind the long, floppy ears. On the mantelpiece their pictures still sit out in gilded frames which, depending on how you look at it, could be a good sign. A hibiscus he gave her last summer thrives in the window.

He sits on the lime-green chair across from her, holding the mug of tea sweetened with the creamed honey she also likes on her toast. They try to make small talk, but the small talk soon crumbles to dust, leaving only a long unbearable silence. She asks about Rosa and he explains the after-school programs he's got her in. But they always talk about Rosa; it's easy to talk about Rosa. This evening, he wants to talk about them.

Let's open a coning, he says to her, finally.

She looks at him suddenly, her eyes trying not to smile.

Why hadn't he thought of this before? Meet her on her own turf. He pulls a blanket from the hallway closet and begins taking off his shoes. Let's do it here on the floor, he says. The moon looks in at the window and he goes over to pull the curtains. Outside, somewhere in the neighbourhood, on the roadway, a motorbike roars by. Then the street is empty again and quiet.

Enid watches him warily, starts to growl and then thinks better of it. She yawns, closes her eyes and goes back to sleep.

Marie Jose slurps her tea noisily, her face tightened now into some kind of knot. She does not look at him, lying there on the floor on the rug in front of the fire underneath the blanket, she looks instead at the blossoming jasmine plant sitting in a pot on the floor near the lime-green chair and he feels himself growing annoyed, growing embarrassed. He should go home now, he thinks, he should take his coat and his hat and go home, relieve the sitter, go through the stack of students' papers sitting on his

181

desk so he can turn in their grades. School will be over soon and he needs a rest before his brother comes.

What's wrong, he says.

You think you're clever.

He smiles privately.

I don't want to do a coning with you, she says.

He digests this piece of news slowly. You said you'd give it six months, he says; we're in month number four.

It's not working.

Not working? We haven't even been trying. You avoid me like the plague. You're always busy with this meeting, that meeting. We make a plan, at the last minute you cancel. That's not trying, he says.

You've chosen, she had said sadly when he came back into the country with Rosa and saw her again. And it's a fine choice, she'd said, a wonderful choice, but I don't want to raise more children.

He did not argue with her, he was not even mad, but he was sad. Hadn't he nursed her back to health after the two cancer surgeries, week after week at her bedside? And now that he has made a choice for himself, she cannot meet him. He saw her selfishness for the first time, and he saw, too, his need, his constant giving and caretaking. Still he could not blame her, he'd been seeing what child-rearing took, he'd been seeing it was no easy business. But he loved her; he wanted to keep walking with her, though now he was beginning to see she might never be ready.

I used to think you were brave, he'd said to her in the restaurant where they had at last met for lunch, when I saw how you beat back the cancer with your self-love and your diligence and your community. I wanted to be like you. I wanted your strength. But in many ways you're a coward like me, he'd said. You've refused to face life again after your divorce, and all this time you've just been using me to hide behind. And I thought you were beautiful, but I see you now, he said; the screen is gone, and it's a cruel awakening to finally see the thing that's right in front of you.

He was crushing her, and he could see he was crushing her. Her face suddenly turned ashen and she got up and walked out of the restaurant. He did not follow after her, he finished his meal, some kind of seafood stew which, come to think of it, was not even tasty, and the entire bottle of white wine they'd ordered, even though he had a class to teach that afternoon. He paid, he walked out slow and measured; he could feel every eye staring at him. He did not call her again for three weeks. It was after that that the holding pattern began. They'd see each other, they'd go through the motions of love, but at the centre everything was a frozen sea. He's been here with women before and he's never been able to leap forward.

He walks over to the couch where she sits tucked in a corner. He takes her hands in his, rubs the slim gold band on her thumb, rubs the soft fleshy palms. She does not pull away, but she is not forthcoming either. He tries to meet her eyes, but she turns them away. Her long slim neck in the fire's glow carries the smell of lilac, and he remembers again the early days of their love, how just the smell of her, just the brush of her arms against his, just her low voice calling out his name would set him off. How for hours their bodies, long and muscular and glinting, thrashed like eels.

He leans over and kisses her hard. This catches her off guard. He kisses her again and again until she finally opens. He removes the red glasses, pulls her down on the floor on top of him, peels off the bottom of her pajamas, pulls down his trousers. Behind them Enid starts to bark – wow, wow, wow, she goes, moving towards them and backing up and coming towards them again. Wow, wow, wow. He wants to reach Marie Jose's heart, the very centre of it; he wants her to let him in. But she is a noisy lover, and he's always worried about the old Indian woman who lives by herself upstairs, who claps at the television, and avoids him on the stairs, even though she always has a smile ready for Marie Jose.

After their breath has steadied again, and the heart has ceased its great rattling, he gathers her up in his arms in an effort to stave off breakage, but it's inevitable.

Can you spend the night? Marie Jose asks.

This is a trap. She knows he cannot, that he has a child at home. But how to say it now without a fight, without her pulling away, freezing up on him again. He'd told Rosa he'd be gone only a few hours and he knows she's waiting for him to come and tuck her in.

Why don't you come home with me instead? he says, in the gentlest voice he can muster. She's not slept there since Rosa arrived. At first she'd said maybe he needed to bond with Rosa first, and he'd thought maybe she was right, but he's come to see now that it was only an excuse.

I can't, she says.

Rosa would love it, he says, the three of us, breakfast tomorrow; I'll make your favourite. He is pressing and at the same time he is holding her and at the same time he's letting go.

The three of us nothing, she cries, swinging away from him, and stepping into her pajamas again, pressing down her hair which has gone wild.

I feel like you're doing everything in your power to push me away, he says wearily.

Look, she says, in that metallic tone she uses with him so often now, I'm tired, okay. I've a meeting early tomorrow, and I've to go to bed.

Okay, he says, pushing himself up off the floor, careful not to step on her glasses, and tucking himself back into his trousers. He knows his cue and he has no life left in him for a fight. A man must cut his losses. Wasn't that what Silas said a few nights ago when he was over for a drink and smoke, and isn't that what's being asked of him now, to walk away like a man, not beg, not grovel, just acknowledge all the work he's put in, and all he's gotten back, and accept that they can't walk further together, accept that once and for all? It's a clear realization, clear as water and it comes to him as he hauls on his shoes and his coat, sets his hat back firmly on his head and stretches his fingers through the thin black gloves. Goodnight, he says to no one in particular, as he lets himself quietly out of her house.

Across town, in a completely different neighbourhood altogether, sleepy and suburban and full of close-together Victorians that all have the same triangular patch of crab grass out front, and grand old maples at the side, and an abundance of small Armenian dry goods and pastry and produce stores and rug shops bunched together in the square, he calls a cab for the sitter and goes upstairs to Rosa who is wide-awake, reading.

How can she concentrate with all this racket?

One by one, he turns off the lamp by her door, the one on the desk near the window and the harsh overhead light. On the television, a woman laments the war, and he turns that off – and the radio where a soprano sax blurts out a sad song. He switches off the music box that Silas gave her in mid tune.

He needs to buy tapes that have the sound of waves, something soothing that will take her down in the evenings, relax her. He can't bring himself to ask, but he wonders if the dead people are still in the house. He must remember to ask Darcy what to do.

How is Marie Jose? she says.

He shrugs, feeling weary, now, feeling the weight of the whole unhappy evening.

Outside a taxi honks. Hold on, he says and he darts downstairs to walk the sitter to the cab and to pay her.

He sits for a while on the couch going through the channels on television, looking for something to hook him. On the splintery hardwood floors there's the kilim he's had since graduate school.

Rosa pads down the stairs wrapped in her blanket. She's never warm enough, no matter what she wears, or how high the heat. He's beginning to think it's psychological. She plops herself next to him. Your face looks bad, she says.

He touches his face, the overgrown moustache he's taken to wearing now and the goatee; then he looks at Rosa and at that moment he wants to be alone with his misery. He never gets to be alone any more. Tires crunch against the crushed stone driveway next door. A car door slams.

She'll come around.

He turns to her. Tonight more than ever, he wants to believe her. She jams the thumb in her mouth.

Hey, aren't you supposed to stop with that thumb.

She takes it out. She eases herself closer to him. He's suddenly conscious of how much he smells like sex. She leans her head on his chest. Her hair smells of castor oil.

He must wash it tomorrow and buy pomade and some new clips. He must make an appointment for her to get a straightening or a curl or a nice twist. There's a woman in the English

Department who does Caribbean Literature and who wears her hair in twists. He must ask her where to take Rosa. He must remember Mortite too for the leaks in the window frames, bird food for the parrot. He strokes her temples with his fingers.

Winston, I want to write Beverly a letter. Can we write Beverly a letter?

Beverly, he cries. He'd completely forgotten about Beverly. He sits up in the couch. What would you like to tell her?

I don't know, she says.

What's that, he says wearily.

You think she loved me?

It's late, way past her bedtime and she has to go to school in the morning. Ernest pads into the room and pushes his face into his leg and curls his tail around it.

Of course she loved you, Rosa. But we'll write her, he says, we'll write Beverly and we'll ask her all these questions, just not tonight, okay, another time. You should go to bed now, he says.

There is Ernest now clawing at the leg of the brand new white couch he bought. Rosa has already leaked ink on it. He bats at the cat with his sock.

Shouldn't we go up to bed, Rosa?

He is standing up now, yawning and stretching out his legs and arms, running his hand over his head and yawning again and scratching himself. He must remember to buy detergent and milk and to send the check to the telephone company.

Can I sleep with you, Winston? Just tonight, please. I having nightmares again.

He looks at her. She used to look like Althea, she used to have the spirit of Althea, but now she looks exactly like Beverly. Sometimes he thinks he's brought an absolute stranger into his house.

Okay, he says, switching off the television and turning off lights and pulling down the old rice-paper shades he brought over from his tiny condominium in the city, that don't quite fit here. He should just wait, he thinks, and get velvet curtains or maybe some sheer ones with embroidery he saw in a catalogue. Something elegant, like those in the home-decorating magazines. All these things he planned with Marie Jose, all these things he

186

planned. Go on up, he says. I'll be there soon. I just need to take out the garbage, do a few things.

She goes back up the stairs, wrapped in her blanket, and he hears her switching on and off lights, opening and closing the closet doors, pulling out sheets and pillows, climbing into bed, getting out again to get water from the tap in the bathroom, climbing in again.

Goodnight, Winston, she calls, her voice wet with an emotion he can't quite recognize.

Goodnight, he says, yawning.

He sits back down on the couch, the room in utter darkness. He tries to think what film he can show his students tomorrow morning at eight thirty; he has no lecture prepared. From the time he wakes to the time he falls into bed again, the entire day is chewed up with Rosa and teaching and dinner and playtime and homework and papers and lectures. He turns on the television, searching for something that will hook his attention. Something about humanity, something to help him understand relationships, anything about forgiveness, some kind of affirmation, something, anything. He bats again at the cat who is destroying the leg of couch and then he picks him up, all twenty-five pounds, and begins to stroke the belly and the head and the paws one by one, stretching him out, and back again to the belly full of so much meat, and just running his hand along the ridge of his back until he falls asleep on the couch.

4.

Saturday afternoon Rosa calls Marie Jose from the phone in her room.

What's going on, Marie Jose cries.

Nothing, Rosa says, nothing.

Is Winston there, something's happened with Winston?

No, Rosa says, it's just me, me calling. Winston and Silas are at a function. Can you bring over the dog? Can you bring over Enid?

Now, she cries.

Well, sometime today, if you've time. It's Saturday and it's warm finally. We can walk her at the river near the house.

There is a long pause on the phone.

He didn't put me up to it, Rosa says, he went with Silas from early, just me and the sitter here, just me and Dorothy. She's always on the phone with her boyfriend. It would be nice to see the dog though. I ask Winston to get me a dog. I don't know. I don't think he has any money left.

Okay, Marie Jose says, sighing through her mouth. I will come.

Rosa dances all the way to the bathroom, sings at the top of her voice in the shower, and in the bedroom she puts on a green sun dress with spaghetti straps and sandals. Downstairs she puts her head in the doorway of the living room. The sitter, who is a physics major, has her face plunged into a big fat book, and the television is turned on though there is no sound, and for a while Rosa watches the pictures moving across the screen until the sitter looks up.

Are you hungry? She is the cousin of one of Winston's students. Would you like me to make you some eggs?

No, she says.

It's almost noon, the girl says, glaring over her glasses.

She doesn't like the girl's tone, has never liked her attitude. She is tall and has a face full of freckles and red curly hair like Miss Burdicks, her mathematics teacher at school.

You should eat more, the girl mutters more kindly, you're growing.

She steps away from the living room where the girls has all her books spread out. Pretty soon the boyfriend will call, and for the remainder of the afternoon, she'll be glued to the phone making disgusting noises and talking in low tones and filling up the house with electricity. She likes the other girl better – Carolyn, who is brown like she is, and sometimes she braids her hair and puts in beads and Winston pays her extra and she talks about Mississippi where her family comes from, her family who used to chop cotton on the flat sandy Delta and who worked as sharecroppers and lived in shotgun houses. The girl speaks with a long narrow winding and drawn-out accent she likes.

She opens the fridge and in the door there's yogurt and organic milk and eggs from a dairy farm in Vermont; on the shelves, there are green apples from Portland, Costa Rican bananas turning brown, lamb from New Zealand wrapped up in brown paper and defrosting for dinner, bright yellow cheeses from France and Vermont, a half open bottle of white South African wine which she uncorks and sips and puts back, olives stuffed with almonds from Italy, olives stuffed with anchovies from Spain, a pineapple from Belize which is threatening to spoil if they don't eat it soon, a piece of cake left over from Silas's birthday party made by Rosie's Bakery. She eats that, the entire hunk of chocolate with white frosting, wipes the crumbs from her face and closes the door of the fridge.

She waters all the plants in the house which is her task on Saturdays and remakes her bed, the sheets folded at the top just the way Mrs. Gladison, the old housekeeper, showed her.

What? she says to her grandfather, who is standing in the corner with his hands folded across his chest. He's wearing all grey today and a black bow-tie. His face doesn't look so good; it looks battered. Must be the judgment.

You playing with fire, he says.

I lonely, she mutters.

You interfering with what doesn't concern you.

Who I should play with then?

I just saying, he says; you have the gift. Don't mean you should abuse it.

I'm not abusing anything, she says. Furthermore, I don't like you any more, she says; you neither my father nor my grandfather, and on top of that, you dead.

I just saying, he says, his voice and his light dropping to merely a whimper.

She hears the howling long before the door bell even rings and then the dog is at the door, and the sitter too, and Marie Jose, her face both flushed and harried, as the dog bolts past the sitter's legs and dashes up the stairs, which is close to impossible with her little legs so short, she leaps on Rosa, the tongue, warm and wet, all over her face.

Down, down, she cries finally, in her big strong voice, and the dog squats down at the floor by her feet moving her tail from left to right and grinning, and obediently follows her down the stairs.

This is Marie Jose, she tells the sitter whose face has irritation marked all over it. And this is Enid. I'm going with them to the park.

No way you're not, cries the sitter barring the door. She has big strong shoulders and she towers over Marie Jose. What if something goes wrong? Who'd be responsible then? She'd be responsible. She'd be the one they cart off to jail.

In the end, she relented, but only after a call was put through to Winston's cell, which only went to voice mail.

One hour, she says, tapping her watch and glaring at Marie Jose who is slightly amused – and the old woman too, who Rosa sees is sitting on the couch looking at the images on television.

They wait for the light at the crosswalk; they edge across the street between cars, brushing up against bumpers and the overheated grills. As usual, Enid lingers and lingers, pushing her face into thickets of flowers, the edges of buildings, the base of a hydrant, tires of parked cars. Finally they arrive at the river and they take the narrow winding footpath. There are men sitting along the banks reading and smoking and talking in soft voices and throwing out their rods. She sees fish jumping in the tall white plastic pails. There are runners and dog-walkers and strollers and roller-bladers and waddling ducks vying for space on the tiny path. Enid grins at everyone. Finally Marie Jose sets her loose in a large field full of mallards which she chases for a while until they grow tired of her antics and ignore her altogether. She returns to quietly sniffing the low bushes and pissing at the roots of trees.

Winston is afraid I might get pregnant.

What! Marie Jose whips around. Christ, how old are you, even?

Almost ten. They are sitting on a bench facing the field and, at the far end of it, the glittering water. He says he has to talk to me about the birds.

Oh God, Marie Jose groans.

I don't even like boys.

Well, that's good. No need to rush that. I was twenty-three, she says, when I started to raise kids. Three of them, she says, and that's no joke.

A grey cloud is starting to form near Marie Jose's head. She shakes it away but it's either stubborn or attached.

I tell you a secret; don't rush into love, it can make you crazy.

Out in the middle of the river there's an island populated by a gnarled old tree with large spreading roots surrounded by sand. Around the tree root an assortment of waterfowls romp and peck each other and waddle and laugh.

At school they say love is the most beautiful thing.

Marie Jose turns to look at Rosa. The cloud attached to her head shifts briefly. It is the most beautiful thing, she says; your teachers are absolutely right, the problem is how to keep it beautiful all the time, especially when life steps in, distorting and mashing up everything.

I was twenty three, she says and I climbed into a relationship with my whole self and just handed it over. I gave up school, I gave up career, I gave up everything – and I had just come too, just come from Spain, and the first thing I did was jump into love with a man and his dead wife and their three children, she says, and when I came out of that relationship I was sick with cancer, almost as if I'd taken everything inside my own body, all his grief and his rage and his terror. I love Winston, she says, I love him, but how to love now and not take cancer into my body again, how to love now and not kill myself. I don't have regrets, she says, I don't have them any more. I just don't know how to move forward. Excuse me, she says, after a pause, getting up to put the leash back on Enid who is too near the water's edge.

I don't even know why I'm telling you these things, she says frowning, once she's returned. Look at you, with your beautiful future ahead and I'm sitting here running my mouth. Just forget everything I'm saying to you, she says, trying to laugh now, just forget it all.

The grey cloud bobs around her head like a balloon. A jay walks up to them, scoops up a green caterpillar crawling near their feet and flies off with it squirming in its beak.

I'm not looking for another mother, Rosa says, finally. I just want a friend.

What, Marie Jose says, swinging around to look at her again, her face covered in a scowl. Then she is quiet, for a long time she is quiet, and the cloud on her head breaks up into pieces and comes together again, and her eyes – big and soft and round and black – are quiet.

I like the dog, Rosa says, and I like to walk and I can dance, she says, hopping off the bench. At school we learn hip hop and jazz and swing and ballroom, she says, slightly out of breath as she shows Marie Jose some of the steps she has learned, her skinny legs whipping in the dirt and the dust swirling around her feet, and Enid starting to bark.

Come here, Marie Jose says, taking her hands and drawing her close and looking in her face and watching her eyes which are dark brown, almost black, and without a centre it seems like. I know Winston put you up to this, she says, and he's a manipulating brute for doing it, but I like you, I like you very much. So it's a deal, okay, this friendship thing, it's a deal.

5.

Did her mother love her? All week, everyday, this has been her new obsession, to write this letter to her mother, to find out if indeed her mother loved her and just how much. All Winston can think of is the utter confusion that must've overtaken the poor mother's spirit. The man she took to be her Godfather had turned into something else, had pushed his way into her. And even if she could force her mind to forget, here was the appendage on her belly. He can only imagine the shame, her belly pushing through the school uniform, her classmates watching and pointing. He can only imagine the rage that had no outlet at all, that had to be swallowed, the love that was in utter turmoil, and oh, what a disappointment. Who was there then to sit her down, hold her hand, who was there to ask her, how you feel, Little Miss? He can only imagine the loneliness, and everything stuffed down inside her belly, her rage, the breach of trust, the violence, all to be released at some later date on the person with whom she grows intimate.

What else do you want to say to her? Winston asks, draining his mug for the third time. He wants a refill but the line is almost to the door and they are nestled so far back into the corner of the cafe, it's impossible now to get up and cry excuse and wade his way through all those bodies. What else you want to tell her, Rosa?

She has been studying the same few lines, over and over. Dear Mother, I am fine here with Winston in America. I have some new friends, Chris and Marcus and Uncle Silas. We have a nice blue house with red doors and a cat name Ernest and a bird named Alphonso and maybe I will get a dog but Winston might have to build a fence first so the dog doesn't stay cooped up in the house all the time.

Why she left me out there on the verandah?

He looks at her quickly, at the dark wall her face has become and the tone he does not recognize.

Dogs, mosquitoes, rats. Anything could have eaten me up out there. Anything could have happened. You do that to someone you love? She stares him down, daring him to cross her.

Rosa, he says, and he feels his face grow hot, his ears too, and he puts his arms around her little shoulders.

She shrugs him off, the eyes small and hard and bright.

A woman turns to look at Rosa and then to look briefly at Winston and then to return to her coffee and newspaper and he can tell by the cock of her head, she is listening into his business.

When Grandpa used to carve up your back, you call that love?

He didn't know any better, he says softly, a little stunned that he's been put in a position to defend his father.

Liar.

Rosa.

If he loved you, he wouldn't treat you like a dog.

Rosa, okay, enough. He tries to find iron for his voice.

You tell me over and over, oh, Rosa, your mother loves you, oh, Rosa, this and that, but she left me on the veranda. She left me out there like rubbish.

The woman is staring directly at him now; he can feel her boring into his neck and he turns to look at her, and he doesn't know what to make of her eyes or the expression inside them. He turns back to Rosa.

He's never seen her like this, monstrous like this, the veins like ropes in her forehead and neck, teeth bared, the air around her jagged and electric.

Stop this, he says, hissing now; it feels as if the entire café is watching them, and the last thing he wants now is to be seen.

She hates me like Papa hates you, she cries.

Stop this, Rosa. Please stop this. He is near tears and he knows she is too. He holds one of her little fists in his big hand. Please stop this. He doesn't know her like this; he's never seen her like this. It's as if he's opened something awful inside her, something bitter and he wants to put a lid on it quick.

He never loved you, she says in a voice like razor. They never wanted us, she says, folding her arms over her chest and glaring at him and he knows he must do something, he must do something; his stomach is roaring under his shirt, and he can only imagine what is shooting through hers.

When she came to the counter and hugged you, he says, when she said she would be your Godmother, when she just held you and held you, didn't that mean anything?

She looks at his face, trying to read beyond it.

But what about the veranda and what about after that, all those years?

She thought of you every night. Every night she went to bed, she said a prayer for you and then she said one for herself.

I don't believe you she cries, slamming her fist on the table.

He thinks that's it, that's it, he thinks they must get up now and leave at once. But he can also see that she desperately wants to have something to believe, something to hold on to.

I see how you might believe she didn't love you, he says softly, quietly bringing her down, bringing her down. But remember this, she didn't give you away to an orphanage; she gave you to Papa who she knew had the means to take care of you. She didn't have anything, Rosa, she was young, she was thirteen, fourteen at most, not much older than you. I mean imagine yourself with a baby? But she knew that Papa would love you, and that Aunty Nora would love you. And somewhere in that puzzle, I am there too, he says, trying to smile. She gave you to Papa so that I could come later on and take you and care for you and love you. Sometimes, he says, life doesn't always work out the way we would like it, but it's working out pretty well. Think about this, he says; if she had kept you, different people would have had to take care of you while she went to school everyday or if she wanted to go out dancing or be with her friends. Everyday you would be there at the bar waving away the smoke from all those men drinking and talking. She had nobody, he says, no mother, no father, she only had her grandmother, and she was an old woman. So how was she going to take care of you and her aging grandmother? She put you on the verandah right near the bedroom door so Aunty Nora or Papa would hear you as you cry. She was no fool. She talked to the dogs and she talked to the rats and she talked to the mosquitoes and the red ants and she told them to leave you alone. She called on all her angel friends – you know those – she told them to watch over you, he says, watch over you until someone came to the door to take you. You weren't there more than five minutes before Aunty Nora came. She heard you crying and she came and took you in and you were so beautiful lying there covered up from head to toe in a red scarf so mosquitoes or ants wouldn't touch you. Right away she loved you, he says, something about your face, how sweet and kind it was, something about your essence, how gentle it was – and she just loved you.

She has grown quiet and her fist in his hand has relaxed and she's reading and reading his face and his head and the field around his head, listening and drinking and interpreting.

Does that sound like somebody who doesn't love you? he whispers.

She doesn't say a word. She is considering. She picks up her scone, she breaks off a piece, she begins to nibble. She slurps at her mug of chocolate tea, and the foam builds a moustache on her face. The woman is watching him again; he doesn't meet her eyes, but his stomach no longer hurts, and the line has dwindled some. Here is his chance. He gets up slowly. He grabs his mug. Did all these people overhear them? He makes no eye contact at all. He is thinking of his father, his father driving home that night after he's violated the girl and dropped her off, his father sombre in the car, knowing full well he has broken her, as he had once been broken over and over again, back when he was a boy, and just the sheer weight of that reminder has him beating and beating the wheel with his fist until blood comes.

6.

In the middle of one of the most fervent downpours in years, which levelled levees and pushed rivers over their banks, felled trees, stalled cars and abandoned them haphazardly on the highway, put entire communities underwater, and locked down several major airports for hours, his brother arrives with his son. They were due in at two in the afternoon but it's now three the following morning; the streets are empty and black, the roads dangerously slick, and Winston drives quickly through the tunnel, wary always that this might be the time that an errant beam dislodges itself and comes hurling out of the tunnel ceiling and crushes him and Rosa who is sleeping in the back of the car. For days he's been cooking and baking and cleaning and fixing the house; he'd had a small welcoming dinner planned, nothing fancy, just Silas and Marie Jose, but all that had to be postponed with the delays that kept them sitting in Miami for hours.

At the airport his brother and nephew are already at the curve waiting. They are the only ones left, the place deserted and windswept; the plane must've come in early after all; the airport arrival recordings he'd been calling all night – no good whatsoever. They look tired and haggard standing there, his brother and his nephew; they look like country people in suits styled from earlier decades and way too big for them – the trousers sag at the knees and droop down over their shoes. He stops the car abruptly at their feet, rushes out to sweep them up, and they're so tired, so catatonic, they fall down wearily into his arms and he stuffs them and their bags into the car. He drives away at once, back through the tunnel with the fear hounding him again that this will be it, finally, and down the highway, empty except for the eighteen wheelers flying past him and rattling the windows of the car, and at the exit he turns down the black narrow streets of his little town, the eyes of windows shrouded in darkness, and his brother asleep, in fact the entire car soundly asleep around him.

At the house he directs them to their rooms; the nephew he puts to sleep in the study he shares with Rosa, Septimus in the room he uses as a gym and for storage. Tomorrow he says, tucking them in, sleep well, he cries, patting the snoring forms and downstairs in the kitchen, he puts away in the fridge sandwiches he'd prepared, the soup he had reheated, just in case they were hungry for something light, and he turns out the lights in the house before settling down into bed with Ernest.

It's strange to wake every morning and see his brother downstairs in the kitchen frying eggs for Rosa and Hanif, to see him outside sitting on the steps of the porch, the smoke from his cigarette coiling and diffusing in the yellow light. When his brother laughs he hears his father's great uproar. When his brother walks on the wood floor in his leather shoes, it's his father he hears coming down the hall, clack, clack, clack. His brother pisses in the toilet, he forgets to flush, he finds himself flushing after his brother, picking up socks his brother left on the couch, putting his shoes in the closets, wiping down the counter after his brother has cooked. His brother takes his coffee black and with three tablespoons of sugar. He likes his rum on ice only. In the shower he sings at the top of his voice and hawks up an extraordinary amount of phlegm. He looks out of the bedroom window one morning and there is his brother at the hedge talking to his neighbour George Lithotomos, the Greek from Lesbos, with whom he's not exchanged two words in the two years he's been living there, but his brother is there laughing and talking and inviting the man and his wife over for a grill. The boy, Hanif, adores his father. He knows how his father likes his coffee and he brings it out to him on the porch and brings him the paper too and his glasses which he's left upstairs on the night table. He leans against his father's legs as he talks to him; he hops on his father's back when they play ball in the yard. He notes his brother is no longer as standoffish with Rosa; he plays ball with the two of them on the patch of concrete in the back. He helps her with her reading, talking to her and bending his head to listen, laughing at her jokes and watching her with a question mark on his face when she is not looking, and patting her head and nodding. His brother seems softer somehow.

Those afternoons when they've walked all over the city and are too exhausted now to move, when even the birds meditating on power lines fall into ecstasy, they doze off on mats in the shade of the black cherry tree. Sometimes they talk stories, he and his brother, nothing that will disturb the delicate balance they've set up; sometimes they sit in utter stillness, listening to their breath heave up and down, and the cars rushing back and forth on the road a block away, watching black birds overhead fly in wild patterns as the world slowly sinks into night and the streets lights feebly colour the streets.

Yesterday they planted hollyhocks and day lilies and wild rhododendrons, white and purple hydrangeas, a weeping cherry tree. All morning they've been stripping the side of the house and sanding it, and now they are beat; lunch has put them out even further, and they sip rum in the shade to kill what's left of the day. Rosa and the nephew are hidden away in the cool house playing Parcheesi. Later Silas will come, and maybe he'll bring the new love, and they'll put meat on the grill.

Winston takes a sip of rum. He looks out into the afternoon, at the grey metallic sky; he sniffs at the breeze, which carries the smell of rain. He turns to his brother sitting beside him, looking like their father. I suppose you believe that I killed him, he says, his voice quiet and strong, no venom left, just questions now and a long stretch of emptiness. His brother has been here a week now, and in his head, the questions and perceptions have been building, and he wants clarity now; he's ready now for truth.

His brother does not look surprised, it's as if he too has been waiting; he too has been readying himself. He drains his glass, sucks noisily on cubes of ice, cracks them up and after he's swallowed, he begins.

When you left, he says, everything came to a full stop. We tried to pick up and carry on, but we had no heart left. We'd already lost

Althea, and now you. And the wound your absence left was always there, he says, open, searing, impossible to heal. Even as we went on, it never closed. And when you came back, everything, everything just burst out again, everything with Rosa and Althea, everything that had only been put up rough shod. We'd all been waiting for you to come back so we could carry on, he says growing quiet on the porch. Even Papa, he says, picking up the bottle and replenishing their glasses, and even if that means death, he says, even if that means Papa had to die to set us free, he says, even if that means the old way we used to do things can't work any more. His face is shiny with sweat.

Winston sighs a sigh so tremendous it comes out sounding like a wail. He slurps his drink noisily. What to do with his eyes that are nesting on his brother's face, trying to read it, trying to decipher? What to do?

Naively, I came down there thinking, we'd just bury him, you know, and that would be that, and I would just go home. Then all this anger, out of nowhere, as if it had been stored up inside me for years waiting now for release, and underneath that all this need. It was awful, Winston cries.

Sometimes I wonder what his childhood was like, you know, Sept. Sometimes I wonder if his father used to call him in a soft voice, hold him around his waist in a way that said, this is how a man holds a boy who is his son, and a son he loves more than life itself.

I mean, how can a man not love his son, not give two cents about his son or about the girl he's supposed to protect? I wanted him to see me, you know, really see me. I can't tell you what it was like everyday, everyday, that wall of silence he had round him, nobody could get in. Just you, he says to Septimus, just you and Althea, and after Althea, just you.

I may've been the favoured child, Septimus begins, but everything has a price. Just last month, I started seeing my son for the very first time. Just last month, I started to see Fiona and her two girls. I don't even know who mother is yet, he says. Life is funny. Yes, I was close to papa, but I couldn't cross him, I couldn't stand up to him. I couldn't stand up for you, or else he'd wall me out

200

too. I'd become the enemy too. I spent my whole life trapped underneath him, Septimus says. Everything has its price, even love.

At the end, Winston says, he leapt, he knocked me over, the two of us on the floor, in an embrace. Maybe he loved me after all, and that was his way. What you think, Sept? I know it sounds weird, because it wasn't kind, God knows, it wasn't gentle, but you think in there somewhere, in that rage and confusion, somewhere inside, there was love. I mean why couldn't he love me, Sept? I mean was I that intolerable to him, was I that unlovable?

It's like me and Hanif, Septimus says rushing in; I mean how you show those things, I mean it doesn't come easy for us, man. I mean, we know blows, that's what we know, we know blows and hard words, we know discipline. What do we know about heart matters, man? Heart's too soft. We know love tough as nails. Papa's generation, that's even worst; all they know is how to put down food on table, they know how to put a baby in a woman's belly, they know how to deal out blows, and sometimes they buy you a thing, give you some money, slap you on your back, that's the love right there, the things they give you.

Septimus is starting to cry.

How do you face up to fear? Winston is asking his brother now. They're out on new turf they've put down just hours earlier. It's cloudy and the moon is behind a screen and they're lathered in repellent for the air is noisy with whining mosquitoes. Now and again a hot wind lifts the lapels on their shirts and perfumes the air with lavender. Inside, the children sleep beneath the breath of air conditioners.

Intention, Septimus says to him. You say to yourself, I am going to do this thing, come what may.

You see somebody you love and they're suffering and you can't help them because it's their row to hoe, their bridge to cross, except that you're on the other side waiting.

You hold them in your heart, Septimus says, sounding to Winston like a preacher. You hold them in prayer. You remind them day after day how brave they are. And you back off; you don't add more pressure.

Septimus shakes his head. These things, I say them every day to the bereaved, but if I'd faced Althea's death, he says, and all those feelings it called up, if I'd faced your leaving, he says, and all those feelings it called up, instead of fucking all those women, and drinking all that white rum, maybe I wouldn't have spent my whole life attending to dead people. Maybe I would've come here sooner and tried to find you. Maybe I could've held on to my marriages.

I still feel like a boy, Septimus admits, the age Althea was when she died, and here I am stuck inside this forty year-old body. I have to hurry up now and grow, catch up with Hanif, catch up with Fiona's daughters, catch up with Fiona. And here he stops, for here he's flooded with feelings about his marriage and about his wife's affair and about all the things he wants to give his wife, but doesn't know how.

Winston holds his brother in his arms, he inhales the sadness that smells like corn falling off his brother. He wants to help, he wants to bring his brother relief, but what can he say about love, about relationships? He knows absolutely nothing. All his life, he has entered them and shat on them, and walked out. All except this one with Marie Jose, this one he's wanted so bad, this one he must watch crumble away like dust.

Take her on a vacation, his brother says to him suddenly.

What's that now? Winston pulls away from his brother.

Take her somewhere nice. Septimus is grinning. Just the two of you. I'll stay here with the kids, take her somewhere romantic and just talk, buy her some nice things, tell her some nice things. Look man, ain't this America, ain't this what you all do.

You think so.

Jesus Christ, Winston, that's what she wants, that's what every woman wants, that's what everybody wants, come to think of it. She wants romance, she wants alone time, she wants…

Winston starts to laugh. So why things with Fiona aren't working then?

Because you need distance to see these things. You need another man's suffering. That's what she has now with Robbie

Chen. He takes her here and there, he's romancing her; she's ready now to give up everything, ready now to run back to him, wreck what we have. I work too damn much, man. My son Hanif, that's what he wants too. Marie Jose can't be that different. Call her. I mean I know you trying to do this friendship thing with her now, but it doesn't matter, I bet she says yes. Old firewood can still light up in flames. Just need a little gas. I bet you a hundred dollars Jamaican she says yes.

But that's only two dollars, US. Winston is laughing.

Doesn't matter; a bet is a bet.

Okay, Winston says, okay.

And you don't mind taking care of the kids?

Look, man, if you can do, I can do it.

Okay, Winston, says, okay. And he grins a grin so big it covers his entire face.

Later that night, about three in the morning, he calls.

Christ, Winston, it's three a.m. It had better be fucking important.

I got us tickets to go away for the weekend, he says.

Come again.

Look, he says, it's a surprise, just meet me at the airport at noon.

You've lost your mind this time, I can tell.

I want us to talk, he says, and my brother will keep the kids and the dog. Septimus will take care of Enid, and just last week you were saying you had all these days at work and you needed to take some time.

Winston, it's really late and I have a meeting early tomorrow.

I know he says, but I bought the tickets already. They're non refundable. They were on sale. All meals included, he says.

Christ, Winston.

I know, he says, I know. Just give me a chance, he says, please give me a chance.

Septimus has not been inside a church of his own volition in ages, though he goes two, three times a week to bury the dead, but after dropping them off at camp one morning, he pulls up at the curb of a tall stone building with lions and gargoyles guarding the entrance, parks the car and steps in. It's dark inside, and cool, it takes a few seconds for his eyes to adjust, and someone inside is playing an organ softly. There're people kneeling at the altar praying. There're people with bowed heads singing in soft voices. They're people just sitting and thinking and looking and swallowing. He sits near the back. What does he want? He is not sure. He just wants to sit and be still. He doesn't want worry. He doesn't want thoughts. So he sits. He admires the stained-glass windows adorned with Madonnas and cross-eyed babies and the intricate moulding and woodcarvings, the marble statues. Then he closes his eyes. He lets his hands fall heavily into his lap. He says nothing at all, utters a word to no one. His father appears at once and yaw, yaw, yaw his father goes at his ears. Winston arrives too, and his mother and Robbie Chen and Hanif and his father again and Raul at the funeral home and Rosa and Fiona and April and April's Indian people and Fiona and Robbie Chen and Marie Jose as well, which is a surprise to him and there's his father again and Winston, yaw, yaw, yaw. All the dead people he has ever dressed, it seems to him, one by one by one, they parade up to him, laughing and nodding and pointing, and yaw, yaw, yaw. To them, he says nothing. He continues to sit. Rosa's mother comes too, but this time she's a young girl of ten and he sees her outside there playing hopscotch in the dirt and he sees his father over yonder in the playground watching her face bright with laughter, watching her teeth glistening in the sun, and he sees the words like a banner across his mind: a man must not yield to temptation, a man must walk upright in the world, a man must look at his issues, and at his shadow, and not succumb to them. Yaw, yaw, yaw. All around him, the people kneeling at the altar scrape themselves up and head out into the brilliant morning. Others trickle in and prostrate themselves and wail and murmur and leave again and the organ music continues its slow sad hymn.

That evening, as he's preparing the goat stew and the snapper that Rosa likes, he thinks to tell her about Althea.

I remember it clear as day, he says at the stove. We were playing marbles, Winston and me. She was outside somewhere playing with her friends and we heard the screeching brakes on the wheel of the vehicle and then nothing after that, just pure silence after that. You know after the brakes, you're expecting a crash, right, boom! But nothing. And then we heard this wail, piercing and loud and it came all the way up the hill and into the drawing room where we were playing marbles. It was Althea moaning, but as it turned out only I could hear that sound, nobody else heard it, probably cause she was my twin, you know, probably cause we were attached that way. The driver said he didn't see her, so the truck just smashed her – I mean everything, he says. And he sees it again, the whole scramble of blood and bones and flesh and fat smashed together, except this time he's looking at it and there's no pain attached to the scene. It's as if he's a bystander looking on at something strange, but he's not tied to it, he's not crushed by it, as he has been all his life for years and years. Then, even stranger, he sees it on the screen of his mind, sees it clear as day, enlarged and in colour, and then suddenly it's gone, and he rushes around in his mind trying to pull it back, trying to see it again, to relive it again, the crash, the body destroyed, the body in the bag at the morgue, but nothing.

She's in heaven, Rosa says, looking at him. Let her go.

He nods, somewhat stunned and he turns back to the stove and slowly he turns the fish over, one by one, so as not to burn them, even though he wants them crispy. His head feels lighter and his arms too and it's a strange sensation, and he doesn't know what to do with that space, he feels he needs to fill it up. He opens the fridge looking for a beer. Winston has any more liquor in this place, Rosa?

She shows him the entire chest.

Thank you, he cries, staring greedily at the selections and then he turns away momentarily confused; he notices his son staring at him.

You alright, Pa? Hanif asks.

He nods, he tries to grin, an awful scowl hovers over his face instead.

On the kitchen table there's the assorted pieces of the puzzle they've been working on in the evenings, and Rosa is at it again, fitting in the pieces.

I'll be back in a minute he cries, turning off the fire underneath the stew and the fish, and removing the pots to the unused burners so the heat won't dry them out. I'll be back, he cries again, hurrying to his room where he closes the door, crawls into his bed and howls with the pillow turned over his head.

8.

The phone rings and rings and when the machine picks up, he presses redial over and over, refusing to think. For all he knows she could be there with Robbie in her bed. But he can't face that thought right now. He faces the night through the window, the pinpricks of coloured light from the tall box-shaped office and apartment buildings, the moving headlamps on the cars far away.

When she answers finally, her voice groggy with sleep, he is so relieved, his eyes water.

Fiona, it's me, Septy.

Septy, she says, and he hears the great wonder in her voice that's coming slowly awake.

I miss you, he says. I just wanted to hear your voice.

She laughs softly.

He laughs too. Just to hear her soft laugh. You all right? he asks. The girls all right?

Of course she's all right. Her happiness did not depend on him. Her happiness used to depend on the Chinese man and then she learned that happiness should never depend on a man, should never depend on anybody at all. He left so he could learn, but here he is calling.

I miss you too, she says. I wish you were here.

Really, he says. He is giggling. He did not expect to hear that from her.

We've never travelled abroad. We should do that one day, she says.

And he takes that to mean she is not leaving him for Robbie Chen. She sees a future for them and this realization sends gladness up his spine.

Right before he left, he went home to see his mother and Anglin, for that is how it is now; then he went to his father's grave and sat on the cement covering and pulled up the weeds growing along the sides and he told his father he was going up to see Winston and Rosa, and he wasn't certain if he'd still have his home with his wife and her daughters when he returned, he wasn't sure he could still go back to the funeral home; everything around him was changing rapidly. He paused. It was late afternoon. The sun was starting its slow decline. Children were returning home from school, the women from market. They swayed slowly up the hill on the nearby road with the heavy baskets balanced on their heads. He saw the light slanting off their backs. He heard their rich laughter that rang into the hills. See you, Miss Gertie. Tomorrow, Angel.

He brushed the gravel from the knees of his trousers. An orange butterfly peppered with black dots circled his head and then it sat on the cement covering near him for some time, just resting it seems, and he felt a deep relaxation come over him and settle down into his feet as if his entire centre of gravity just shifted, as if all his parts went into a singular alignment, and he didn't feel overwhelmed any more; he felt that what would be would be; he would manage it, he would bear up, even if sometimes it felt to him like he couldn't take one more step.

He drove back to the capital with a feeling about him as if a great friend had come. He began to pack his things and his son's things. He whistled as he packed. He could open another business, he was thinking, and sell supplies to funeral homes; then he brushed that aside altogether for he did not want to have anything at all to do with the dead; he wanted life – the only problem was, he knew so much about the business of the dead, he would have to learn new things altogether.

The bed is empty, she is saying and she chuckles in that way he likes and he feels his cock rustling, and he smiles into the phone.

I thought maybe you had thrown me away, she continues.

No, he says. I wanted to give you time to work things out. The truth is he'd wanted to go the full month without calling her, but here it is only two weeks.

You still on with that, she says.

Trust takes a long time, he says.

I understand that very well, she says.

And he finds himself thinking how she too has had to learn trust-building herself after the hell she met with Robbie Chen. But then if she understands trust building, why'd she have to sleep with him again. Why?

Oh, Septimus. What is that, Winston had said to him. What is that in the largeness of everything? What is that?

It's big, he'd muttered into his shirt out there in the night where they'd been lying under the stars and drinking.

She went to test the waters again, she went to make sure she wouldn't drown.

But what if she couldn't swim? Septimus wanted to know, what if she couldn't blasted swim?

She wouldn't have gone in there, trust me, she wouldn't have put in not even a foot. Furthermore, Winston had said, next time it'll be you, you'll be the one slipping and you'll need her to forgive you. So drop it.

Septimus, are you there?

Yes, he says, I'm here. The smell of freshly mown lawn leans in at the window.

You're quiet, she says. You call me all the way from America and you're quiet.

I'm glad I married you, he says.

Really, she says. Boy, you must really be missing me.

You stretch me out, he says. Right and left, you stretch me out. Sometimes I don't even think I'm man enough to handle it.

But that can't be good, she says happily.

It's good, he says, it's good. Sometimes he thinks if he forgives Fiona, then April will forgive him. Sometimes he thinks people and things are connected like that, and wouldn't it be nice to have April back in his life, to have her as a friend. He'd like to see her again and apologize; a man can't just move through the world fucking and striking down things he don't understand, he would like to tell her, a man has to have reason, a man has to have compassion, a man has to learn care.

So much can happen in a day, she says.

Everything can happen in a day, he says.

Yes, she says. And she is quiet. Outside in the sky, there's a yellow broad-faced moon.

How is your heart? he says.

Oh, she says, and then she pauses. Oh, she says again.

As long as you don't close it down, he says, as long as you don't let it tighten around you.

Oh, she says again, unable to find words.

He wants to think of a story, something soothing to say to her, something that will help, but nothing comes to mind. He's glad she encouraged him to come. He knows that when they meet up again they'll be different people altogether, more complete in themselves somehow. He'll have more things to give her; he has learned so much these days here with his brother and his half sister and his son. It's like a thumb that finally starts to move again after many years and now he won't have to overcompensate with the other four fingers; every digit will have a place for itself.

I will call you again, he says.

You promise, she says.

I promise, he says.

Maybe we should marry all over again, she says, when you come back.

He chuckles. Okay, he says, we can do that. But only when your heart stops hurting. He pauses, missing her terribly.

I love you, he says, putting the phone gently back into the cradle and hugging himself. He puts his hands on his head and then turns to shut down the television with the bible-waving evangelists, the over-enthusiastic personal trainers, the advertisements for CD compilations from the fifties and sixties for $19.99 plus shipping and handling, only to make out Rosa sitting on the couch, her legs folded like the Buddah, her thumb in her mouth. The light from the street lamp filtering through the curtains hits the right side of her face, and for a minute she's almost unrecognizable.

You all right, Rosa? He's standing at the doorway, and he's irritable as hell. He came all the way downstairs; he turned on the television for background noise; he closed all the doors, and still no privacy to speak of. She probably heard every word.

She makes no move to follow him out, and he goes over to her on the couch. He sits down. He pulls a blue shawl over their laps. This is Winston's America, he is thinking, this is his brother's life. He came back looking for his childhood. He saw all this joy around Rosa. He thought: that is the childhood he would like, for it definitely wasn't the childhood he had. He had brought her back thinking happiness is something you find on the road wrapped in Christmas paper. And now look at this.

Can I come back with you? she says.

You're not happy here in Winston's America?

It's okay, she says. But I miss everybody. I miss my room near the tank, and Mrs. Gladison; I miss Grandpa. I miss Mama Nora. I miss the chickens and the cows.

He doesn't have the heart to tell her that his mother, in her need to quickly lose all traces of their father, tore down her room in her remodelling frenzy. A lot of things different down there now, he says. Even the house is different. Mother sold just about all the cows and the chickens. She says the upkeep is too much. Every week one of the cows escapes, or the bull, into somebody's property destroying the farmland.

She is quiet; she seems to be digesting all of this.

So this is my home now?

Winston loves you, he says.

Nobody wants me down there.

That's not true, he says weakly. He leans over to pull the chain on the lamp. A smoky light falls all over them.

Grandpa's dead and nobody wants me.

That's not true, he says. Everybody loves you. It's just that Winston thought you'd like it here. He thought you could go to good schools so you'd have an easier future, and because you're so young, it would be easier for you to adjust.

He looks at her and her eyes are like marbles. He touches her legs, skinny and hard under the shawl. He wonders about the mother, the barmaid Winston went to meet, the letter he mailed.

What about what I want?

The anger thunders in his ears. He presses the floor with his feet. Give it a chance, Rosa, give it one year, give it two. Every-thing takes getting used to at first. His poor brother, he is thinking, and then he stops. This is what Winston wanted, he

211

wanted a piece of his life back there, and so he brought it back with him. The problem is now the magic has worn off.

She looks towards the yawning black doorway as if thinking. He is studying her profile. He is trying to think what it is about her that used to make him think she looked like Althea. It's not in her features, not in her physical composition. It must be in her essence, he thinks. They have the same essence. It's curious to think she came back as his half-sister all these years later. As if she still has business in the family to attend to.

Grandma phones you? he asks. He is thinking of his mother with the blue light swirling around her head, standing in the doorway of his father's house, her face leaning into the afternoon.

Not often, she says. She's travelling now. I don't understand. What's all this travel?

He thinks better than to tell her about Anglin. Mama doesn't want to feel too lonely, he says, so she fills up her time.

And at night when she goes to bed, when the day is over, when she's no longer travelling?

I don't know, he says; she watches television; the television numbs her out.

That can't be good, she says, shaking her head and knitting up her brows. That can't be good.

He switches off the television with the remote. I will send a ticket for you to come at Christmas, he says.

And I can see my mother again?

Yes, he says stiffly, his voice suddenly gone from him. He clears his throat. You can see your mother again.

And my father? she says quietly.

Look, he cries, sweat breaking out on his forehead, you should probably ask Winston about that.

Winston's on his honeymoon, she says.

Look, he says again, we love you, all of us, we love you; no need to stir up the past now, he says.

Is Grandpa, she says; Grandpa is my father. Grandpa and my mother.

Look, he says, cross now, and raising his voice. Why you stirring up problems now. Winston give you a nice home. Look at your closets, full of pretty things; look at the expensive school

212

he's sending you to. Don't be ungrateful, he cries. He was just beginning to like her, but look at this, all these wild and compli- cated feelings now, all this rancour now.

He looks at her and outside, in the early dawn, a car purrs down the road.

Rosa, he says, trying to find softness again. He leans over to look at her. Rosa. He pulls her into his arms. She's all bones and muscles and her eyes, her eyes are like a hound's.

She allows him to hold her. She rests there in his arms against his chest. And he sighs loudly, holding her there, thinking of this place that his brother has turned into his home. Just three months out of the whole, entire year, they get a good dose of heat and light. Three months. And to see someone who resembles you, some- one with your same complexion, someone who when they open their mouth sounds like you, Oh God, you have to walk and walk before you can find that. That must be the loneliest thing in the world, his brother alone in this place, without family, only friends; he at least has good friends. He takes his hat off to his brother. The cold alone would kill him, that's all he knows. Her breathing is long and smooth as if asleep. And under the skin, by her temples, there's the slow moving sound of blood. A gust of wind sweeps across the window that's clothed in French lace, and then stops.

You miss Papa, he says. Out of nowhere there is suddenly this bursting wail of a thing. Out of nowhere. He thinks of his father; he remembers the two of them slogging in a field one afternoon; he remembers the soft warm rain on his face and his father beside him singing a song about Babylon.

All the time, she whispers. All the time.

Oh, God, me too, he says, me too, and I can't tell that to Winston, he says, I can only tell that to you; you understand it, he says, you know. Why he's even saying these things to her, he has no idea. She sighs heavily in his ears and he feels somehow that she has manipulated these feelings out of him, but here they are, and in that moment he misses his father so badly, it's terrible.

Come, he says after the wave of bad feelings has finally passed, let's see if we can get you back into bed. She allows him to scoop her up, with her legs dangling over his arms and her hair piled up in a nest on her head. She allows him to believe that she's a baby, maybe even his own baby. His son he never had the chance to baby at all, except now, and now his son is fourteen, it's not so easy to baby a teenager. We'll get through this, he says, breathing loudly up the staircase with its polished wooded handrail. She's heavy as hell, heavier than he thought.

Things okay with Fiona? she is asking as he moves towards the semi-darkened room filled with all her books and toys and an abundance of shoulder-high tropical plants that seem to be watching him. There is a green parrot in a cage asleep on one leg, and a goldfish in a bowl on her desk. There is the turtle, a big brown slimy, fossilized thing he tripped over yesterday in the kitchen, and a foul-smelling gerbil named Dermot. There is Ernest the overgrown cat purring at his feet, and soon there'll be a dog. Poor Winston, he's thinking, poor Winston.

You want me to read to you? he says. He feels bad; he wants to give her something. She is only a child after all, a child with a whole slew of questions. She didn't ask for any of this nonsense she was born into. Want me to read you a book, he cries, help you to sleep. He did not do any of this with his son, he left it to the housekeeper, and now the son is too old. But next week he and his son are going shopping. Winston will drop them off, they'll wander into shops, they'll take a meal at a restaurant, just the two of them in a sea of white people, and the boy will take a sip of his cocktail and screw up his face, and he'll start to tell the boy a story, only to hear him let out with a groan – he has heard that one already. He'll buy the boy everything he wants and together they'll get gifts for Fiona and for Fiona's girls, Morgan and Reba; they'll get gifts for the boy's mother, April, and for his own mother. Maybe even something for Anglin. Maybe while they're waiting for Winston to pick them up, they'll take an ice cream cone on a bench outside with the sun laying crossways against them. He'll make a joke and the boy will laugh with a face just as beautiful as his mother's.

Just lie here with me until I fall asleep, Rosa says. Maybe you can tell me a story. Grandpa used to tell me about the trickster spider, but it doesn't have to be about Anancy; just tell me one of your own choosing.

Okay, he says, tucking her in, and turning off the light and

214

stretching out near her legs at the foot of the bed and thinking of the best thing to tell her, the thing that would delight her most, but soothe her at the same time so she has the sweetest of dreams, the thing that would bring on the wildest happiness.

Sometimes, he says, we do the most cruelest things to the people we love the most. Where that impulse comes from in us, I couldn't tell you, he says, but you'll do it too, one day, if you're not careful. I have done it to a woman I used to love; Winston has done it too, he says, and it doesn't make it right, he says. It's as if there is goodness in us and love and kindness, and Papa had all those things in himself as well, but he had the evil too; he says and it was the evil he brought to your mother, he says, for there was no reason, he says, there was no earthly reason why he did what he did, but here you are, he says. Out of that most vile act, here you are, beautiful and smart, and look at your lovely smile, look at your face he says, just singing, he says, yawning himself and closing his eyes at the foot of her bed, uncomfortable as hell cramped there, but dozing off nonetheless.

In his dream, she goes to see Robbie Chen again. He's rented a house in the hills of St. Andrew and he sends down a car to fetch her every morning. They take walks in the hills surrounded by plantations of coffee owned now by Japanese investors. He draws her baths filled with medicinal leaves. He makes broths and spoon-feeds her. He washes her hair, he oils her skin, and he reads out loud from a book of poems until she falls asleep. And when he dozes off beside her, she opens her eyes and studies him. Mr. Robbie Chen. She'd given him fifteen good years of her life and now she's destroying her marriage.

The worst part is when the car comes at six o' clock to take her away and bring her back to her life. She wants to howl down the house.

Fee, Robbie Chen says, holding her. Fee.

You all right back there, Miss? the driver asks her every evening. Every evening she tells him, yes, fine thank you, never better.

At the house, her eyes red and swollen, she sits with the girls as they play with their dinner and she sits with them in the study

215

while they dawdle over multiplication tables and long divisions. If they've said anything to her, she could not have said what. She is there. She is not there. Once upon a time, she blurts out, a woman fell in love with a man. And every day he disappointed her for he was a coward. Still she loved him, for she knew that in life there was suffering, and it was rare in that place for a woman not to suffer over a man. Then one day, after ten years passed, she packed up her things and left. Even martyrs get exhausted. Later, when she was stronger, she went back to see what had attracted her so. Life is like that, it sends us the same things over and over for us to look at, until we finally master them. By all standards he had been a good man. He did not beat her. You could tell by the way he looked at her, by the voice he used to speak to her, the gifts he brought her and their children that he loved her. But he was married. It was a wife chosen for him by his family and she bore him five sons. And for whatever reason, he would not leave the wife, though he did not love her in the same way he loved Fiona. He loved them both. This is what he said. So every night he went home to his wife. And every night, whether he wanted to or not, he disappointed her; he destroyed things inside her.

She still loved him, but it wasn't with the same fervour as before – intense and intolerable and uncontrollable. Time had diluted it. Now she could see its subtle distinctions, what exactly it was made of. For what kind of love was this that hurt her so, disappointed her so? She had to stop and hold it up close to the light, smell it, feel the places where it was round and those places where it was smooth and soft and those places were it was full of potholes and prickles.

He was the same. His eyes still glowed when he looked at her. His voice still produced the same melody when he spoke to her. He was the same, he was not the same. He was older. He held his waist now as he walked and though he still ran five miles a day, he was more easily fatigued and prone to injury. His heart wasn't bad, but it wasn't good either, according to what his doctor had told him. He needed glasses now to read; there was a hump in his back; he had a dry cough that often left him wheezing and short of breath.

The car arrives the next day as usual and she rides up into the tree-covered hills, away from the noise and heat of the city. He is standing at the sink when she enters. He is peeling a fat yellow papaya. Outside on the terrace, a table is set for two. In the valley down below, through a pair of binoculars she sees the rotting zinc roofs, the collar of dirt that marks each yard, pillows of smoke billowing up from the outside kitchens, little brown bodies milling around. Out on the terrace there is a table set for two, and a bowl of cut fruit.

You are hardly a man, she begins to tell him, in this place where manhood means everything. You are just a shade. You have no spine at all. You are a coward. It was the wrongest thing to have loved you. It was the wrongest thing to dash away ten good years. I should never have stayed. I should've left you sooner. You are nothing. You are nothing whatsoever. Just a piece of a man. Just a poser.

She doesn't know what has over come her so. Where this rage has mushroomed from so suddenly. She wasn't feeling it this morning when she rode up. But now here it is, out in the open, as if it had been simmering and waiting all this time.

He turns, his face has gone slack. He looks old. He looks young again. Then he looks ancient. An old tired Chinese man. He lifts his hand. All of this happens quickly. She knows what's about to happen. And bam! He brings it down on her face.

She cannot speak a word. He cannot speak a word. What is there to say? The culprit is there trembling by his side. He doesn't know what to do with it. Whether to put it in his pocket, or to cut off the damn, offending thing.

Between them is a jagged silence. He's gone slightly pale; his back is stooped. Outside on the terrace, a table set for two and below that the valley full of brown bodies. A wind whips up for a moment and then settles. She's tall and she's young. Not as young as she once was when she met him at fifteen.

Now, like then, he's dressed in white trousers and a collarless white shirt with the sleeves rolled up to his elbows, his hair brushed back, still damp from his shower. Now like then, she can hear the crickets' wing-songs from way down deep in the valley. She steps away. Her eyes are cold; there is no light in them. Her body is now long and full and mature; she's borne him two children, and except for Septimus, he's been her only lover. Her long purple skirt with flowers embroidering the trim sweeps the floor. She reaches for the platter of fruit. The arrangement is stunning. In the centre is the deep velvet of passion fruit and around that slices of green kiwi and orange strawberries and yellow mango and brown naseberry and pink guineps and red melon. She wants to forget everything. She wants to erase the past. She wants to drop it on his head, but at the last minute she drops it on the floor far from his feet, and he crumples to the ground with a long sigh and blood spills from a gash on his forehead.

She is stunned. To think that for ten years, they'd never raised a hand to each other. And in just one week together, they've grown closer and yet farther apart than they've ever been. It's as if the cells inside her body, inside his body, are fighting against this closeness they've been trying to harbour.

The driver is outside in the yard hosing down the car. The yard swells with wild flowers. A night-blooming cereus leans against a post that holds up a barbed-wire fence. In the distance, there's nothing but lignum vitae trees and butterflies. The sky suddenly seems electric.

Come quick, she calls to the driver, whose name is Presley.

He comes running, wet and nervous. He finds a bottle of salts and waves it under Robbie's nose.

He opens his eyes. He stares uneasily at the scattered pieces of fruit, at the bowl cracked apart near his feet, at his open palms, at his spotless shirt, at the drops of blood sliding down his face. Then, as if he finally remembers, he looks wildly at Fiona, at the private island that her face has become, then he puts his hand to his wound; he begins to weep.

9.

Through the curtain of the guesthouse on the beach, a long quadrangle of light falls in on them and washes the sheets in ochre. Winston removes his clothes and snuggles in beside her; he holds her at the waist. He unbuttons the thin blue shirt. Is it okay, he says, holding the sole breast in his palm and feeling it tighten, the nipple growing taut against his thumb. He is at her long slim throat with his lips, the throat that has a trace of dewberry. A wave, long and vibrating blazes through her. He remembers how, after they took the left breast, for three months he could not get near her.

He guides her hand over his throat and his chest full of tight curly black hairs and over his belly that has a ring in the navel. He runs his tongue along the length of the scar on her chest, takes the breast like a small fist in his mouth, watches her close her eyes, feels her tighten, feels her let go, notices that her freckles have deepened as have the worry lines too across her forehead. She used to be good looking, now she is beautiful, softer, with thin lines fanning out from her eyes and from her lips when she laughs.

He catches her shoulders, his breath fast now. He has no urge to enter, he smothers her with kisses. Slowly she begins to drink them, slowly she begins to open as if some door inside her has finally unlocked. He boils with such gratefulness that songs he's forgotten from choir practice at his grandmother's church leap into his mouth: *What A Mighty Fortress Is Our Lord; What A Friend We Have In Jesus; All Things Bright And Beautiful.* He makes love to her differently now. For hours he simply anoints the body that has been hacked away, for hours he attends to her as if the whole wide world has shrunken away, the world with its wars and its suffering and its pyramids and its wild beauty, all those have sunken away, and the sea and the sand and the moon and the trees, everything gone, just the two of them left alone in the world.

He hunches over her tall, slim body; he traces the bones of her face with his finger. He watches her flutter and cry and moan, strong deep moans, and his fingers are everywhere, nimble and quick until finally, he finds her heart and he leans his mouth there, drinking and drinking until she ebbs. Then he watches her face grow rounder and softer with sleep.

1 O.

Her father doesn't come any more, just the old woman now and another young girl who must still be in training for she says nothing at all, speaks to no one, follows around the old woman as if she is blind, or unsure of her whereabouts. For a while she tried talking to her, but the girl seems mute. Either that or she has bad manners. She wears a green robe, this girl, and her face isn't exactly discernable. But everybody has somebody. She has the old woman. Septimus brought his own set of seven, little yellow people, no more than four inches tall, with big shaggy heads like sunflowers, who play pranks on each other all day and somersault throughout the house and laugh a laugh that sounds to her like bells. Hanif, too, has an old man who must be one hundred he is so wizened, his face like decayed lace, and so tall; he stretches beyond the house way above the trees and into the hills. She likes sitting next to him, she likes the tingles that run through her limbs. And his smell like sweet wet earth. Only Winston is alone. Nobody seems to want to go near him; everybody gives him a wide berth, which is weird. Even Marie Jose has her entourage; even Enid the dog – a strange backward-walking woman with a long gazelle neck named Tuba. One day she asked the old woman about Winston and the old woman studied his head for some time and then she made some symbols with her fingers. No worries, she says, I'm here for the two of you. Wasn't sure if she liked that. He should get his own as far as she could see. Everyman for himself. He has family round him though, has had all the bolstering he could ever need. Yet she gets the feeling that nothing might be enough for him. There will always be something else he needs.

Last week her mother sent pictures. Picture of when she was a young girl of ten standing in front of a stone church in a pleated white dress, frowning in the sun. She thinks she has her mother's eyes, long and wet and far seeing. There's one too of her mother's parents leaning against a gate and holding hands. The father she can see right away is a saga boy, he is handsome, he has a big smile on his face, and a big ring on his finger that glints in the picture and takes up centre stage. His shirt is open wide at the throat showing a ruffle of black hairs. You can tell that the mother in the picture has heartache coming swiftly down the road, but she doesn't see it yet; she is swept up in the glow and tremor of this man who has a wide gap in his front teeth. There is a picture of the old woman, her mother's grandmother, the old woman who is now her guardian. But the picture does her no justice at all; there is no light blowing across her face, no song singing, no joy unfolding, just an old woman with a sturdy black wig on her head, her face frozen in front of a camera.

11.

A week ago he told his brother to go. Go and fix up things with Marie Jose, he said. His brother did not look back. Now a week later, his brother wants a few more days. They meet in the square for lunch. His brother looks dishevelled, his hair, what little there is on his head, badly needs a trim, his face is smashed as if he hasn't slept in weeks and a thick patchy beard has grown making him look older and strange. They walk quickly to a noodles place that promises good, cheap food. It's packed with people and they elbow their way through the dense lines. They order at the counter and the steaming plates arrive in minutes.

As if he's not eaten in months, Winston attacks the food at once, shovelling it into his mouth without even tasting it. Anxiety, Septimus thinks as he watches the shaking hand lift the fork to his face. Either that or they must be fucking like kings.

How are things, he asks, grinning and yet bracing himself to be the burial man again, for one can never tell with women, the surprises they have waiting to catch you off guard.

Okay, Winston says, okay.

He takes that to mean so many wrinkles to iron out still.

Children okay? Winston asks finally, as if he's just now remembered all his other responsibilities.

Yeah, yeah, but you've got to get a new washer, though; that old dinosaur is dying.

His brother erupts into a joyful laughter and there're deep lines around his mouth, deep shadows under the eyes. There is the mall, his brother says, near the house on the left.

It will be my treat, he tells Winston. And his brother laughs even harder, and he looks like a mischievous boy to Septimus, his eyes squeezed tight, the milk teeth big and strong, one of them

223

slightly chipped from a fall. A horse had thrown him and he fell on his mouth, the whole of his face full of blood.

You remember that time with the horse, Septimus says. Parson's grey mare. Romeo, I think it was called. The one that threw you.

His brother shakes his head slowly.

That's how you chipped your tooth. You don't remember that! He doesn't understand how his brother doesn't remember anything of consequence; he doesn't remember Althea's death either, the closed casket funeral and the fog that hovered over the district for seven straight days and how the entire house waited for her laughter to shudder again all over the rooms and to soften the wall that was their father's face. How for months, her dresses and pantsuits still waited in closets, her shoes in neat rows on the floor; his mother couldn't bring herself to give them away. The green bicycle stayed leant up by the lime tree at the bottom of the garden for well over a year before someone finally rode off with it.

Since he came, three weeks now, he's been reminding Winston of things, but his brother has conveniently erased them. Even in his house, in the rooms, on the walls, there are no traces whatsoever of his life back there, of what he'd left, no photographs, not even a history book, a Caribbean novel – he's had time on his hands to scour the place from top to bottom. There are no traces of their father either. The bag of things Winston collected at his death is nowhere to be found. It's as if the house is this strange oasis with no past, just the present and the onward march towards a future. His brother has reinvented himself, through and through.

Marie Jose is working at home this week. We're trying to work out things, his brother says into his plate. In a couple days, bring the kids, get them off your hands, give yourself a little break. Then he's busy with the straw at his drink that is some kind of malt with little brown beans in it. He looks up, he smiles weakly. I'm sorry to drop them on you like this, ruin your vacation like this, he says.

It's nothing, Septimus says. I came to be with them, to be with you. I missed you, he says. Plus, I getting to know Rosa.

They study their plates for some time. Finally the bill comes and he pays. My treat, he says waving away Winston's wallet. It's the least I can do.

There's a place in the mall, his brother is saying again when they're out on the hot and crowded street; it's on the left when you enter. Don't spend too much money, he says, flagging down a cab. Bring the kids this weekend, he cries from the window of the cab already moving away. And then his brother is gone and he's forgotten to ask him about a barber so he can get a trim. He and his son badly need a trim.

On the way back to the car, he passes a fountain spouting water in the centre of a plaza paved with cobblestones. Nearby, a crowd gathers around a string quartet playing Brahms. He stands in the coppery haze of the afternoon and watches for a while. He'd like to smoke a cigarette, but in this place he feels like a bandit. He takes one from the crumpled pack, sticks it in his mouth, chews on it ruminatively and watches as the crowd backs away from him as if he's diseased. In the car, he winds his way down the narrow one-way streets, and at the light, he finds himself thinking about April. He reaches in his pocket for another cigarette but the pack is empty. Shit, he says, trying to remember now where he had seen a 7-11. He drives past the turn onto the house. He passes the cemetery and the row of tall thin houses fastened onto the next. He passes the CVS, the Hollywood video, people sitting outside underneath the green awning of the Starbucks. A boy leans his head out the window of a passing car and hurls out a cry. Ahead is the huge eye of the river, calm and clear today with the old men out with fishing poles and white plastic pails. He moves through the light and pulls up along the curve and cuts the engine. He winds down the window. There is hardly a breeze and the smell coming off the water is bathed in rot. Still he gets out, locks the door and starts to walk. Ducks are resting in the shade. A dog barks at him shyly from a window. A man is calling to him. The man is slouching up the road and calling to him and saying that it is illegal to park there, that they'll tow away the car. He doesn't hear the man. He hears the paddles breaking the dark silence of the water. He hears Althea calling to him on the edges of the wind. He hears her calling and calling and he does not call back. You in heaven now, he thinks; stay up there and look after us.

12.

That night, way into the middle of the night, Winston's father comes. He's wearing a suit of the silkiest green and a hat with a white feather in it. There are silver links at his cuff, a rose in his lapel, a watch chain looped across the bottom of his waistcoat. It looks like he's going to a wedding. He's grinning like a monkey, waving a gold walking stick and he's singing. But it's not a wedding at all, for suddenly the streets are flooded with people and it's impossible to hear Fudgie's horn in all that laughter, in all that noise, and at every corner there are white tents set up, tents as big as villages with houses and cars inside and outside markets with the higglers selling plastic combs for five dollars, and tubes of toothpaste for six. In the red dirt, the merry-go-round is swinging with children, and dancers in animal costumes are on the floats wafting down the streets; honey bees are busy at the heads of the snow cone vendors, circling and circling. A quarrel breaks out at the jerk-pork stand; a man swings a machete, a head rolls on the ground – but there's no blood at all, no blood though the dogs have gone slightly crazed from the pepper sauce, the dogs turn on each other savagely. There's his father coming toward him with a joyous face, there's his father whistling a tune and spinning the gold stick and laughing, his whole mouth speckled with gold. Come, his father, is saying, come.

He wakes in a sweat and beside him, flat on her back with a hand on her jaw, Marie Jose sleeps the sleep of the dead and on the floor near the bed, nestled in a blanket, Enid too is snoring. He gets up quietly and tiptoes downstairs and pours a glass of milk and takes it outside into the night that is damp now from the on and off drizzle of the last few days and the slightly cool outside air

226

marking the end of summer. He smells a flowering tree, honey-suckle, he thinks, but he's not sure. Isn't it late for honeysuckle? Dressed only in sweat pants, his chest bare, just his slippers on his feet, he follows the smell half way down the road and leans over into the neighbour's fence and breaks off a thin branch and brings it to his nose and inhales. It must be three or four, the night is still in the sky, and the sky is dappled with stars and the stars wink at him walking barefoot on the gravelled street, and he feels small, he feels insignificant and at the same time so large, so extended that with a great exhale he could touch the moon that's up there solemnly watching. He feels both great and small and deeply rooted to the earth and the moon all at the same time, the grinning stars and to the bodies of water lying quietly in the night and to his neighbour, Mr. Francois from Port au Prince, Haiti, who is fast asleep in his bed and dreaming of his dead wife, Sylvie. He feels safe in the world, perhaps for the first time, and he feels as if all would be well, and it is a good feeling that steadies his hips, steadies his spine and his calves and the top of his head into one grand alignment. Inside the house, he sticks the soiled glass in the dishwasher, locks the door behind him and carries the smell of honeysuckle crushed in his hands back to bed where he sleeps soundly for the rest of the night.

ABOUT THE AUTHOR

Patricia Powell was born in Jamaica and immigrated to the US in 1982. She holds a B.A. in English Literature from Wellesley College and an M.F.A. in Creative Writing from Brown University. Powell is the author of *Me Dying Trial*, *A Small Gathering of Bones* and *The Pagoda*. She currently teaches at Stanford University in California.

David Dabydeen
Our Lady of Demerara
ISBN: 9781845230692; pp. 288; August 2008; £9.99

The ritual murder of a mysterious Indian girl and the flight of seedy drama critic from his haunts in the back street of Coventry to the Guyana wilds to find out more about the fragmented journals of an Irish missionary in Demerara are brought together in a hugely imaginative exploration of spiritual malaise and redemption.

Brenda Flanagan
Allah in the Islands
ISBN: 9781845231064; pp. 216, August 2009; £8.99

When Beatrice Salandy, first met in Flanagan's novel, *You Alone are Dancing*, is acquitted in a trial that divides the sympathies of the people of Santabella between rulers and ruled, she attracts the attention of the Haji, the charismatic leader of a radical Muslim group. Against her judgement, Beatrice is drawn into his orbit.

Curdella Forbes
A Permanent Freedom
ISBN: 9781845230616; pp. 210; July 2008, £8.99

Crossing the space between the novel and short fiction, this collection weaves nine individual stories about love, sex, death and migration into a single compelling narrative that seizes the imagination with all the courage, integrity and folly of which the human spirit is capable.

Earl Long
Leaves in a River
ISBN: 9781845230081; pp. 208; November 2008; £8.99

What brings Charlo Pardie, a peasant farmer on an island not unlike St. Lucia, on the edge of old age, to leave his wife, family and land and take himself to the house of Ismene L'Aube, known to all as a prostitute? And what, three years later, takes him home again?

Anton Nimblett
Sections of an Orange
ISBN: 9781845230746; pp. 128; June 2009; £7.99

Writing with equal empathy about the lives of gay men and heterosexuals, young and old, Trinidadian country folk and New York urbanites, these stories, with their sharp ear for a range of distinctive narrators, announce a singularly attractive new voice in Trinidadian and Caribbean writing.

Geoffrey Philp
Who's Your Daddy? and Other Stories
ISBN: 9781845230777; pp. 160; April 2009; £7.99

Whether set in the Jamaican past or the Miami present, whether dealing with sexual errantry, skin-shade and culture wars, with manifestations of the uncanny, or with teenage homophobia, Geoffrey Philp's second collection confirms his status as a born storyteller.

Raymond Ramcharitar
The Island Quintet
ISBN: 9781845230753; pp. 232; June 2009; £8.99

In these sometimes seamy, often darkly comic and bracingly satirical stories, Ramcharitar reveals Trinidad as a globalised island with permeable borders, frequent birds of passage and outposts in New York and London. His characters scramble for survival, fame and fortune in an island struggling to come to terms with both its history and its present.

Ed. Courttia Newland & Monique Roffey
Tell-Tales Four: The Global Village
ISBN: 9781845230791; pp. 212; March 2009; £8.99

With contributions from Olive Senior, Matt Thorne, Sophie Woolley, Adam Thorpe, Catherine Smith and twenty others, this collection of stories from the UK-based Tell-Tales literary collective touches on love, sex, death, war, global warming, immigration and crime in sometimes dark and sometimes funny ways.

CARIBBEAN MODERN CLASSICS

Spring 2009 titles

Jan R. Carew
Black Midas
Introduction: Kwame Dawes
ISBN: 9781845230951; pp. 272; 23 May 2009; £8.99

This is the bawdy, Eldoradean epic of the legendary 'Ocean Shark' who makes and loses fortunes as a pork-knocker in the gold and diamond fields of Guyana, discovering that there are sharks with far sharper teeth in the city. *Black Midas* was first published in 1958.

Jan R. Carew
The Wild Coast
Introduction: Jeremy Poynting
ISBN: 9781845231101; pp. 240; 23 May 2009; £8.99

First published in 1958, this is the coming-of-age story of a sickly city child, sent away to the remote Berbice village of Tarlogie. Here he must find himself, make sense of Guyana's diverse cultural inheritances and come to terms with a wild nature disturbingly red in tooth and claw.

Neville Dawes
The Last Enchantment
Introduction: Kwame Dawes
ISBN: 9781845231170; pp. 332; 27 April 2009; £9.99

This penetrating and often satirical exploration of the search for self in a world divided by colour and class is set in the context of the radical hopes of Jamaican nationalist politics in the early 1950s. First published in 1960, the novel asks many pertinent questions about the Jamaica of today.

Wilson Harris
Heartland
Introduction: David Dabydeen
ISBN: 9781845230968; pp. 104; 23 May 2009; £7.99

First published in 1964, this visionary narrative tracks one man's psychic disintegration in the aloneness of the forests of the Guyanese interior, making a powerful ecological statement about man's place in the 'invisible chain of being', in which nature is a no less active presence.

Edgar Mittelholzer
Corentyne Thunder
Introduction: Juanita Cox
ISBN: 9781845231118; pp. 242; 27 April 2009; £8.99

This pioneering work of West Indian fiction, first published in 1941, is not merely an acute portrayal of the rural Indo-Guyanese world, but a work of literary ambition that creates a symphonic relationship between its characters and the vast openness of the Corentyne coast.

Andrew Salkey
Escape to an Autumn Pavement
Introduction: Thomas Glave
ISBN: 9781845230982; pp. 220; 23 May 2009; £8.99

This brave and remarkable novel, set in London at the end of the 1950s, and published in 1960, catches its 'brown' Jamaican narrator on the cusp between black and white, between exiled Jamaican and an incipent black Londoner, and between heterosexual and homosexual desires.

Denis Williams
Other Leopards
Introduction: Victor Ramraj
ISBN: 9781845230678; pp. 216; 23 May 2009; £8.99

Lionel Froad is a Guyanese working on an archeological survey in the mythical Jokhara in the horn of Africa. There he hopes to rediscover the self he calls 'Lobo', his alter ego from 'ancestral times', which he thinks slumbers behind his cultivated mask. First published in 1963, this is one of the most important Caribbean novels of the past fifty years.

Denis Williams
The Third Temptation
Introduction: Victor Ramraj
ISBN: 9781845231163; pp. 108; 23 May 2009; £7.99

A young man is killed in a traffic accident at a Welsh seaside resort. Around this incident, Williams, drawing inspiration from the *Nouveau Roman*, creates a reality that is both rich and problematic. Whilst he brings to the novel a Caribbean eye, Williams makes an important statement about refusing any restrictive boundaries for Caribbean fiction. The novel was first published in 1968.

All titles available online at www.peepaltreepress.com